**W9-CWD-416**

## BEYOND THE SEXUAL REVOLUTION

Nearly a decade has passed since the appearance of
Comfort's *The Joy of Sex*. It has been fifteen years
since publication of Masters and Johnson's *Human
Sexual Response*. The general reading public is in-
undated with descriptive and qualitative information
about sex. Yet there is still no popular book to satisfy the curiosity we all feel about sexual numbers.
This book will provide those numbers ... and attempt to satisfy those curiosities.

## About the Authors

Dr. Zev Wanderer earned his Ph.D. in Clinical Psychology from Columbia University. He is the co-author of the two best-selling books: *Letting Go* and *Making Love Work*. He is licensed as both a Psychologist and as a Marriage & Family Counselor, is a Clinical Fellow of the Behavior Therapy & Research Society, is a Certified Sex Educator and Therapist (ASECT), has served as the ethics chair of the Society for the Scientific Study of Sex, has been a Clinical Professor of Psychology at UCLA and currently lives in Malibu, California, where he maintains a private practice.

Dr. David R. Radell received his Ph.D. from the University of California at Berkeley in 1969 and was Administrative Director of the Center for Behavior Therapy in Beverly Hills, California, from 1971 to 1973. He is currently a Professor at California State University at Los Angeles while still acting as Technical Consultant to the Center for Behavior Therapy. During Dr. Radell's association with the Center, it has established a worldwide reputation for its pioneering work with phobias, sexual problems and assertion training. He has also authored the book *How To Meet Interesting Men*.

# HOW BIG IS BIG?

## The Book of Sexual Measurements

Dr. Zev Wanderer
and
Dr. David Radell

WARNER BOOKS

A Warner Communications Company

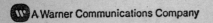

# ACKNOWLEDGMENT

We wish to thank Dr. William Masters and Virginia Johnson-Masters for personally giving us specific information and discussing with us the problems that they encountered in pioneering sex research; Dr. Alex Comfort for years of camaraderie in exploring the ideas that ultimately determined the frontiers of the sexual revolution; Dr. George Bach, our close friend, who in our many discussions has always insisted with great maturity that sex should be playful; Dr. Wardell Pomeroy, coauthor of the Kinsey Report, who took the time to share with us behind-the-scenes problems inherent in sexual measurement; Dr. Seymore Feshbach, for sharing with us the results of his quality systematic research on the reciprocal effects of sex and aggression; Dr. John Money of Johns Hopkins University, a tireless researcher who identified some of the latest sources that would enrich this book; Dr. Manuel Smith, author of *When I Say No I Feel Guilty* and *Kicking the Fear Habit,* for his collaboration on research and his ongoing discussions with us concerning the psychophysiology of sexual arousal; Dr. Albert Ellis for the earliest guidance on rational attitudes toward sex; Dr. Aaron Haas, author of *Teenage Sexuality,* for sharing with us insights concerning adolescent sexual behavior; Dr. Barbie Taylor, for her contribution of scholarly knowledge about various sexual subcultures; and our associate, Dr. Donald Cowan, for his advancement of clinical sexual techniques.

We are also grateful to Doris and Stanley Fleishman for their support and suggestions for improving this book; Maria Rivera Radell for her valuable suggestions, assistance, advice, and support; and Dr. Leonard and Ruth Gluckson for years of sensitive avant-garde discussions.

We wish especially to thank Robert McGarvey for taking on the tedious job of assuring the accuracy of the statistics throughout this book and for his invaluable research and editorial assistance; Dr. Neil Malamuth for his research, critical commentary and editing; and Kate Dickson for her painstaking editorial help.

For their suggestions in improving this book, we also wish to thank our editor Ed Breslin, Mark Greenburg, Jonathon Lazear, and Gene Light at Warner Books.

# PROLOGUE

How do I love thee? Let me count the ways.
I love thee to the depth and breadth and height
My soul can reach...

—*Elizabeth Barrett Browning*

# TABLE OF CONTENTS

is a man around the hips? How many American men have brown hair? How many American men have black hair? How many American men have blond hair? How many American men have red hair? How many men have straight hair? How many men have wavy hair? How many men have curly hair? How many men are balding? How many men wear glasses? What's the ratio of men to women?

3. **NO BODY IS PERFECT—FEMALE ANATOMY / 55**
How big are the average woman's breasts? Is there a way to make breasts larger? Can breasts be reduced in size? Are a woman's breasts identical? How large are the "lips" at the entrance to the vagina? How long is the vagina's entrance? How deep is the average woman's vagina? Is a mature woman's vagina ever too small for intercourse? Can a vagina be too big for sex? How long is the average clitoris? How thick is a virgin's hymen? Is penetration of a hymen painful for a virgin? Can virginity be restored? How large are the ovaries? How big is a human egg? How many ova does a woman have? How is a woman's anatomy determined? How tall is the average woman? How much does the average woman weigh? How large is the average woman's waist? How large are women's hips? How large are the average woman's thighs? How many American women have brown hair? How many American women have black hair? How many American women have blond hair? How many American women have red hair? How many American women have straight hair? How many American women have wavy hair? How many American women have curly hair? How many American women wear glasses?

4. **KEEPING UP WITH THE JONESES—MALE PHYSIOLOGY / 77**
How many erogenous zones does a man have? In how many ways can you touch a man to turn him on?

How many men blush when sexually aroused? How many men get erect nipples during sex? When does a boy get his first erection? How quickly does a man achieve an erection? At what angle does an erect penis stand? What is the average maximum duration for a man's erection? Can a man urinate when he has an erection? How common is circumcision? Do circumcised penises feel more than uncircumcised penises? How early can a man have his first orgasm? At what age do boys have their first ejaculation? How many men have had "wet dreams"? At what age do men have their first wet dream? How many men have multiple orgasms? How much semen is in a man's ejaculate? How far does ejaculate spurt? How fast does ejaculate travel? How many calories are in one ejaculation? How many sperm are in one ejaculate? How long do sperm live? How many sperm generally must one ejaculation provide to impregnate a woman? At what age is a boy typically capable of making a girl pregnant? Is ejaculation necessary in order to impregnate a woman? How many men are infertile? At what age do boys begin sex play with girls? At what age is a boy considered an adolescent? Is there a connection between hairiness and sex? At what age does a boy first caress a girl's breasts? At what age does a boy first fondle a girl's clitoris? How old is a boy when his penis is first stroked by a girl? How many teenage boys have made love? How often do teenage boys masturbate? How does a man learn to masturbate? How many first ejaculations come from masturbation? At what age does male masturbation result in orgasm? How many men have masturbated to orgasm? How long does it take to masturbate to orgasm? How long does premarital foreplay usually last? Who is a man's first sex partner? How many men enjoyed making love their first time? How many men have had sex with a prostitute? How many American men make love in the missionary position? When making love how

11

long do most men take to ejaculate? How many calories are expended while making love? How many men are impotent? How many types of impotence are there?How many men come too quickly? Are there men who fail to ejaculate during orgasm? Can a man die during orgasm? Is there sex after death? On how many teenage boys has oral sex been performed? On how many men has oral sex been performed? How many teenage boys have performed oral sex on girls? How many men have performed oral sex on a woman? How many men have participated in incest? How many men have performed heterosexual anal intercourse? How many men have tried sadomasochism? How many men have reached orgasm with an animal? At what age does a man marry for the first time? What is the largest number of marriages reported for one man? What is the duration of marital foreplay? How frequently does a married man make love? How many married men have had sex before they were married? What was the most children fathered by one man? How many married men have had extramarital sex? How long does the average marriage last? How many sex partners can a man look forward to after divorce? Are there aphrodisiacs for men? How many men find their sex life affected by alcohol? How many men say marijuana enhances their sex? How many males are gay? When does a gay male identify himself as a homosexual? How many men have been approached by a homosexual for sex? How prevalent are sexually transmittable diseases?

5. **I'VE COME A LONG WAY, BABY—FEMALE PHYSIOLOGY / 137**
How many erogenous zones does a woman have? When does a female grow aware of her sexuality? When is a woman's sexual peak? Can females be circumcised? At what age does a female have her first menstruation? What is the average length of the

menstrual cycle? How long does the menstrual period last? How much blood flows during a woman's period? How many women experience pain during their periods? At what age does menstruation end? After menopause how many married women have sex? Is sex healthy during a woman's period? At what age can a female have babies? Does the beginning of menstruation mean that a female is fertile? At what age is a female considered an adolescent? What is the pubic hair's main function? At what age do girls first pet? How old is a girl when a boy first caresses her breasts? How old is a girl when a boy first fondles her clitoris? How old is a girl when she first caresses a boy's penis? How many females blush when sexually aroused? How much do a females breasts expand when she is excited? How big do a female's nipples become when she is sexually excited? How many teenage girls have made love? How many sex partners does the average teenager have? How many non-virgin teenage girls have had an orgasm during sex? By what age will most women have had an orgasm? Do women really come during an orgasm? How many women have had "wet dreams"? How fast after stimulation does a receptive woman show signs of sexual arousal? How much does a woman lubricate? How many types of female orgasm are there? How many mature women have never been sexually aroused? How many women have never had an orgasm? Can physical conditions prevent a woman from reaching orgasm? How long does a woman's orgasm last? Does the anus respond during orgasm? How many women have had an orgasm when their breasts are caressed? How many women frequently have more than one orgasm during a single sex act? How many women masturbate? At what age does the average female first masturbate? How often do teenage girls masturbate? How does a female learn to masturbate? How many female masturbations result in orgasm? At what age do most women have

13

their first orgasm while masturbating? How long does it take a woman to masturbate to orgasm? How often do women masturbate to orgasm? In what manner do most females masturbate? Who is a woman's first sex partner? How many females bleed at their first lovemaking? How many women enjoy making love their first time? How many women enjoy making love? How many women have had a virgin man? How long does premarital foreplay usually last? How many women have never had an orgasm during sex? How many women have orgasms at the same time as their partners? While making love, how many men have an orgasm within 6 minutes as reported by women? While making love, how many women have an orgasm within 6 minutes? How many women prefer the missionary position for lovemaking? How many women prefer to be on top during sex? On how many teenage girls has oral sex been performed? On how many married women has oral sex been performed? How many teenage girls have performed oral sex on a male? How many married women have performed oral sex on a male? How many women have had incest? How many married women have tried anal intercourse? How many women have played the aggressor during sadomasochistic sex? How many women have played the victim during sadomasochistic sex? How many women have had sex with more than one partner at a time? How many women have had sexual contacts with animals? At what average age does a woman marry for the first time? How many American women are "virgin brides"? How many premarital sex partners does the average woman have? What is the largest number of marriages reported for one woman? How long does marital foreplay last? How often does the average married couple have sex? How many married women regularly experience orgasm when making love? Do married women have sex as often as women who live with male

14

partners? How many women have had extramarital sex? How many extramarital sex partners do women have? How many women regularly have an orgasm during extramarital sex? What is the largest number of children reported for one woman? How many young women have had abortions? How many fertile women practice birth control? Without using birth control, how many women would become pregnant during a year of sexual relations? How many couples are sterile? What are the odds a pregnancy will result in twins? How many sex partners can a woman expect after divorce? Are there aphrodisiacs for women? Does alcohol affect a woman's sexual pleasure? Does marijuana affect a woman's sexual experiences? How many women get turned on to other women? How many women have been raped? How many women have experienced a homosexual overture? How many women are lesbians? When does a women identify herself as a lesbian?

6. **WASN'T IT GOOD?—MALE PSYCHOLOGY 191**
How many men worry that their penises are too small? How many men think they are good lovers? How many men think sex is very important? How many men think sex is the most important pleasure in life? How many men think sex and love are linked? What is love? How often do men think "true love" comes? How many men think love comes by the fourth date? How many men are indifferent when a love affair ends? How many men approve of premarital sex? What is a boy's chief source of sex information? Who do men think *should* provide sex education? How many teenage boys tell their parents "almost everything" about their sex lives? How many teenage boys believe they need not be "romantically involved" with a female before having sex with her? How many teenage boys say they have been in love? What qualities do teenage boys most value in a girl?

How many teenage boys approve of premarital sex? How many teenage boys believe a man should be a virgin when he marries? How many teenage boys believe men should be sexually experienced before settling down with one person? How many teenage boys believe girls should be sexually experienced before settling down with one man? How many teenage boys believe a girl should be a virgin when she marries? Of the teenage boys who have fondled female breasts, how many enjoyed it? Of the teenage boys who have caressed a female's vagina how many enjoyed it? Of the teenage boys who have had their penis caressed by a female, how many enjoyed it? How many teenage boys fantasize while masturbating? How many boys approve of receiving oral sex from a girl? How many teenage boys approve of giving oral sex to a girl? How many teenage boys fantasize about sex? How many teenage boys approve of sex between a white man and a black woman? How many teenage boys approve of sex between a white woman and a black man? How many men approve of sex with older women? How many young men have ever been asked out on a date by a woman? How many young men enjoyed being asked out by a woman? How many college men insist on paying all expenses on dates? How many men believe their dates expect to have sex on the first date? How many men do *not* think masturbation is wrong? How many men disapprove of their son masturbating? How many men disapprove of their daughter masturbating? How many men fantasize while masturbating? What do most men fantasize about while masturbating? How many men sleep in the nude? How many men enjoy hugging and kissing if intercourse will not follow? What form of foreplay do men most enjoy? How many men prefer the lights on during sex? How many men think it should *always* be their job to make the first sexual move? How many men are turned on when a woman takes the sexual initiative? How many men communicate their true sexual desires during sex? How many men want sex more than once daily? How many men are satisfied with their sex lives? How many churchgoing men find sex pleasureful? How many men who don't attend church find sex pleasureful? How many men have changed their attitudes about sex during the past five years? How often do men think their sex partners have an orgasm? How many men deliberately try to delay their orgasms during sex? How many men think sex ends after both partners have orgasms? What is the most common reported feeling of men after climaxing? How many men would like to try different positions more often? How many men want their sex partners to be more active during sex? How many men enjoy giving oral sex to a woman? Do men become excited while giving oral sex to a woman? How many men think anal sex is acceptable? How many men have fantasies during sex? What do men fantasize most during sex? How many men fantasize about being raped while masturbating? How many men fantasize about rape while masturbating? How many men have *ever* fantasized about raping a woman? How many men can ejaculate by fantasy alone? How many men have voluntarily viewed erotic or pornographic materials? How many men are aroused by erotica? How many men are turned on by being bitten during sex? How many men are attracted by women's breasts? How many men are aroused by lacy lingerie? How many men are turned on by the natural fragrance of their sex partners? How many men are turned on by perfumes? How many men are turned on when a woman uses sexually explicit language? What most irritates men during sex? What is the most common turn-off for men? What quality in a woman makes a man feel most nervous? How many men are turned off by heavy makeup? How many men find hair on a woman's legs or underarms unattrac-

17

tive? How many men find women less attractive during menstruation? How many men say fear of pregnancy has prevented them from free sexual expression? How many men find a pregnant woman less sexy? How many men are aroused by watching animals have sex? How many men are happy with today's contemporary woman? What do men most look for in a potential wife? How many men believe their first sex partners were virgins? What besides love do men think is the main reason for getting married? How many men consider monogamy to be the ideal sex life? How many men say it does not matter what sexual experience a wife had before marriage? How many married men say their sex lives have improved since their honeymoons? How many children do men want to father? How many young men definitely do not want children? How many young men expect to become fathers by the age of 30? How many men believe women alone should shoulder the responsibility for birth control? How many college men say that, were a safe and effective birth control pill for men available, they would use it? How many men disapprove of homosexual activities? How many men approve of extramarital sex? How many men intend to cheat on their wives? What is the chief cause of extramarital sex? How many men would be tempted to cheat by a "beautiful woman"? How many men approve of unmarried couples living together? How many men favor group marriage?

7. **GREAT COMPARED TO WHAT?—FEMALE PSYCHOLOGY / 237**
How much is female sexual pleasure affected by penis size? How many times do women think they will fall in love? How often do women think "true love" comes? How many women think love comes by the fourth date? How many teenage girls tell their parents everything about their own sex lives? What is a

18

woman's chief source of sex information? What do women believe is the *ideal* source of sex information? How many women openly talk about intimate sexual matters with a person other than their lovers? How many teenage girls have ever been in love? What quality do teenage girls most value in a boy? How many teenage girls approve of having sex? How many teenage girls think a female should have sexual experience before settling down with one person? How many girls think a boy should have sexual experience before settling down with one girl? How many teenage girls believe they should be virgins when they wed? How many teenage girls want to marry boys who are virgins? Among the teenage girls who have had a male fondle their breasts, how many enjoyed it? Among the teenage girls who have fondled a boy's penis, how many enjoyed it? Among the teenagers who have had their vagina touched by a boy, how many enjoyed it? How many teenage girls fantasize while masturbating? How many teenage girls approve of giving oral sex? How many teenage girls approve of receiving oral sex? How many teenage girls fantasize about sex? How many teenage girls want to live with a man before marrying him? How many teenage girls approve of sex between a white woman and a black man? How many teenage girls approve of sex between a white man and a black woman? How many women prefer older lovers? How many college women have asked men out for dates? How many college women feel fine asking men for dates? How many college women always pay their own way on a date? How many college women resent paying for themselves on dates? How many men, according to young women, expect to have sex on the first date? How many women approve of masturbation? How many women enjoy masturbation? How many women have fantasies while masturbating? How many women use mechanical sex aids? How many women sleep in the nude?

19

How many women prefer sex with the lights on? What factor most influences a woman's desire for sex? When do most women become sexually excited? How many women think any time is appropriate for sex? How many women think there's a "most" appropriate place for sex? How many women ever initiate sex? What are the two most important factors women cite as facilitating their sexual response? How many women think they are very good at sex? How many women think they get enough sex? How many women want more sex than they are getting? How many women are satisfied with their sex lives? How many women think men are informed about female sexual desires and responses? How many churchgoing women find sex pleasurable? How many non-churchgoing women find sex pleasurable? Do women let their partners know when they are ready for sex? How many women think orgasms are important? Do women try to have orgasms quickly? How many women say their regular sex partner knows when they have had an orgasm? How many women feel frustrated if they are on the verge of orgasm and then it doesn't come? How many women fake orgasms during intercourse? If offered a choice of only clitoral or vaginal stimulation, how many women would choose clitoral? Of all the aspects of sex, how many women most prefer the feeling of closeness? How many most prefer orgasms? How many most prefer satisfying a partner? How many most prefer many most prefer oral sex? How many most prefer masturbation? How many most prefer anal sex? Do women play an active role in intercourse? How many women enjoy giving oral sex? Why do women give oral sex? How many women enjoy receiving oral sex? How many women like anal sex? How many young women fantasize during lovemaking? Why do women fantasize during lovemaking? What do women most frequently fantasize about during lovemaking? How many women have fantasized about raping men? How many women have fantasized about being raped? Are women less aggressive than men? How many women can have an orgasm through fantasy alone? How many women have seen sexually explicit materials? How many women are aroused by pornography or erotica? How many women have used erotica for sexual arousal or in foreplay? How many women enjoy being bitten during sex play? How many women like to dress in erotic clothing to add spice to sex? How many women enjoy being undressed by their lovers during sex? How many women like their natural fragrances? How many women sometimes switch settings to add flair to their sex? Which part of sex do women least like? How many women say guilt feelings have inhibited their sexual expression? How many women believe religious training interfered with their sex lives? How many women say fear of pregnancy has restrained their sexuality? How many women believe social pressures interfered with their sex lives? How many women's sex lives were affected by fear of VD? How many women are turned on by watching animals mate? How many women are married? How many college women definitely want to get married? How many women approve of extramarital sex? How many women believe they will have an extramarital affair in the future? How many women who have not had extramarital affairs want to have them? What's the most common reason for infidelity in a marriage? How many women who have tried extramarital sex say it is enjoyable? How many women approve of unmarried couples living together? How many women favor group marriages? How many women have tried mate swapping? How many women want to try mate swapping? How many college-aged women want to have children? How many of those college-age women expect their first child will be born before they turn 31? How many children do most women want? How many women cite birth control pills as their preferred contraceptive? How many say female sterilization? Vasectomy? Intrauterine devices? Condoms? Rhythm or withdrawal? Diaphragms? Foams? How many women approve of abortion? How many mothers approve of a son's premartial sex? How many mothers approve of a daughter's premarital sex? How many mothers object to a daughter's premarital sex? How many women think homosexuality is always wrong? How many women would have a lesbian friend?

# HOW BIG IS BIG?

## The Book of Sexual Measurements

# CHAPTER 1

## Introduction—Why You Need This Book

As late as 1970, 20 percent of medical students erroneously believed that "a woman must have an orgasm in order to conceive." Most of those sexually ignorant students are practicing medicine today.

Information about sexual realities has long been suppressed by censorship. Not only has censorship been common in both literature and the media but also in universities and medical schools. In a 1961 survey, 50 percent of the medical students and 20 percent of the faculty in five Philadelphia medical schools actually believed that masturbation caused mental illness. Our experience in lecturing at various universities and medical schools confirms the findings that physicians know little more than the general public about sexual measurements and usually have difficulty answering basic questions about sexual norms.

Most people who report sexual dysfunction also suffer from ignorance about sex. It has become clear that access to accurate information is important for healthy sexual development and that ignorance is at the root of most of the anxiety associated with "sexual problems."

Yet even Dr. William Masters, who pioneered the most important research into sexual dysfunction, believed that he was helping others by witholding certain sexual statistics that he had gathered. He states "When we published *Human Sexual Response*, we purposely did not include information about the average size of penises. To some degree, we hoped that by not doing so, we would neutralize the concept that penis size is crucial to sexual response."

However, we have found that when sexual norms remain unknown, anxiety generally results. This is because the unknown is frightening; for it is worse not to know than to know the worst.

A man or woman who constantly has to compare his or her sexual equipment, ideas, and practices to the unknown can only imagine a standard of incomparable and unimaginable proportions. Most of our patients have been happy and relieved to learn that the norms and extremes of sexual equipment and behavior are far more modest than they ever imagined. Many patients who have come to us for sex therapy have discovered that they had no sexual problem other than a sense that their sex lives were not in stride with the Herculean performances that the media have promoted and depicted as normal.

Most people have distorted self-images based on

erroneous information widely disseminated in sensational magazines, locker rooms and even at Tupperware parties. By providing access to accurate sexual measurements, the distortions can be corrected and self-images based on truth can emerge.

Where do most of us learn the truth about sex? Columnist Art Buchwald once described his early sex education: "I had no formal sex education where I was a student. . . . we got all our sex information at the local candy store after three o'clock. The information was dispensed by thirteen-year-olds who seemed to know everything there was to know on the subject, and we eleven- and twelve-year-olds believed every word they told us. . . . For example . . . the method of kissing a girl on the mouth determined whether she would become pregnant or not. Every time I kissed a girl after that, I sweated for the next nine months. . . . When I turned thirteen, I became an instructor myself and passed on my knowledge to eleven- and twelve-year-olds at the same candy store. . . . I was amazed with how much authority I was able to pass on the "facts" of sex as I knew them. . . . We were all emotional wrecks before we got to high school."

Nor are the young and unlearned the only ones who suffer emotional strain. In *A Moveable Feast*, Ernest Hemingway remembers his encounter with a frenzied F. Scott Fitzgerald. "Zelda said the way I was built I could never make any woman happy," Fitzgerald confided to Hemingway. "She said it was a matter of measurements. I have never felt the same since she said that and I have to know truly."

After taking a look at the other man's penis, Hemingway remarked: "You're perfectly fine. . . . It's not basically a question of the size in repose. . . . It is

the size it becomes. It is also a question of angle."
And, with that, Hemingway proceeded to give Fitzgerald a brief course in sexual techniques topped off by an inspection tour of penises on the Greek statues in the Louvre Museum. Did Hemingway's advice work? On that point he is mum—perhaps because the true answer could only be discerned in the bedroom shared by F. Scott and Zelda Fitzgerald.

Hemingway's useful but incomplete advice to Fitzgerald dates from the 1920s. Sixty years later we are in little better shape. Nearly a decade has passed since the appearance of Comfort's *The Joy of Sex*. It has been fifteen years since the publication of Masters and Johnson's *Human Sexual Response*. The general reading public is laden with descriptive and qualitative information about sex. Yet, there still is no popular book to satisfy the curiosity we all feel about sexual numbers. This book will provide those numbers and attempt to satisfy those curiosities.

In writing this book, we have been frustrated in our search for information by the fact that the comprehensiveness and quality of sexual research does not as yet compare to the quality of other scholarly research. Nonetheless, the commonly held belief that volunteer sexual questionnaires are unreliable because respondents are invariably an atypical, deviant group has been refuted by Barker and Perlman. In their study they found that sex volunteers were not an atypical group and were not different in any significant way from respondents in other volunteer surveys.

The fact that most sexual studies are still based on volunteer surveys despite past criticism is simply explained by the lack of any other feasible technique for assessing general sexual attitudes. Although many of the studies cited in How Big Is Big are of variable quality, especially in research design, this is the first attempt to collect in one volume everything about sex of interest to the popular reader, that has been measured.

Throughout How Big Is Big, we refer to the best available sources. Both scholarly and popular sources have been cited in order to provide the widest perspective. In most cases, facts we cite correlate closely with our clinical experience at the Center for Behavior Therapy in Beverly Hills, California. In many instances, too, several conflicting sources which have studied a single issue are mentioned and analyzed to provide an understanding of the entire scope of professional thinking about sex. Only numbers and percentages are derived from most of the cited sources to which are added our interpretations and discussions. In some cases the numbers exceed 100 percent because in those cases people provided more than one response per question.

The method of citation we employ is designed to be clear but not distracting. Below every question, to the right of the answer, the source of the data for the entire discussion of that issue appears in parenthesis—like this: (2). This number refers the reader to the numbered References at the back of the book. In this way, readers with a special interest in pursuing a topic can find a sizable number of sources that deal with specific issues in human sexuality.

We have purposely excluded data reported in the 1981 *Hite Report on Male Sexuality* (156), because

1. Some of the Hite Report statistics were not credible and conflicted with those of other

reliable sources as well as with findings from our own clinical and research experience.

2. The *Hite Report* relied on the vague and possibly romanticised reminiscences of adult males about their long past smorgasbord of first experiences.

3. The *Hite Report*'s opening apologies for the lack of scientific approach and the nonrepresentative nature of her sample attacks the credibility of all of her figures for men.

4. The naivety of the *Hite Report* research design suggests that the author was insufficiently schooled in social science methodology.

In short the *Hite Report on Male Sexuality* sheds no new light on the sexual behavior and attitudes of American men and in places is clearly in error.

Finally, although we believe that this book can be therapeutically important, it is written in a light style because we believe that sex should be fun and that it is often very funny.

# CHAPTER 2

## Do I Measure Up?—Male Anatomy

Almost every man, particularly in his teens and twenties, worries about his body, his physique or his penis size. Am I too short? Too tall? Too big? Too small?

It is amazing that most of us know so little about human sexual anatomy. The fact that clothing hides much of our anatomy from plain sight is in part responsible.

In this chapter, the present known anatomical norms for American males are presented and discussed. It must be realized that there has never been a constant, universally accepted standard for an attractive male body. The Greeks idealized a heavily muscled body, yet if we look at the statue of Hercules returning from a lion hunt, displayed at the Getty Museum in Malibu, his muscular legs support an ample paunch. At times during the Roman Empire, corpulent men were in vogue. During the nineteenth century also, well-padded, even obese men were the cocks of the walk. A well-rounded frame proved to all that a man was a gentleman of means, a fellow who could afford to enjoy the luxury of good food.

During the 1960s in the United States, the lean and hungry look became popular and very thin male bodies were in style. However, with the advent of the running craze that swept the U.S. in the mid 1970s, muscular athletic bodies regained popularity. Yet, a recent survey of women's tastes revealed that English women now prefer a man who has a slight paunch rather than one who has an athletic body.

It serves us well to remember there is no ideal male physique that does not fall victim to changing social tastes and to the unique individual preference and prejudices of any given woman in any society.

How big is the average relaxed penis?
*4.0 inches (10 cm.) in length.*      (Reference: 47)
The largest number of American white males (21.7 percent) report relaxed penises which measure 4.0 inches with more than 90 percent of men's flaccid (relaxed) penises ranging between 3 and 5 inches in length.

There is considerable variation in the size of a given individual's relaxed penis depending on prevailing environment and psychological conditions. Cooler weather tends to reduce the size of relaxed penises and in warmer weather relaxed penises tend to increase in size. In addition, the retracted penis of a man who has not had sex in a while tends to be smaller than it would be if he had been sexually active a short time before measurement. Nonetheless, all of these variations in the size of a particular individual's relaxed penis are only temporary. Were the cold man to warm up or the temporarily celibate man to have sex, their relaxed penises would respond accordingly.

**How big around is the average relaxed penis?**
*4 inches (10 cm.)* (Reference: 47)
The largest number of American white males (28.1 percent) report relaxed penises which measure 4 inches in circumference. More than 93 percent report penises that range from 3 to 5 inches in circumference.

**From the average size of a relaxed penis, can you tell how big an erect one will be?**
*No.* (References: 72, 85)
An erection, which results from blood flowing into the penis in response to sexual arousal, increases the length of that boneless and muscleless organ several inches in most men. Yet, there is no correlation between the size of a relaxed penis and one that is erect. Some current research suggests that the penis that is smaller when flaccid shows a greater proportional increase in length during an erection. We are not saying that the smallest retracted penis becomes the largest erect penis, merely that a small relaxed penis is likely to experience a greater percentage increase than a larger relaxed penis.

One knowledgeable researcher believes that the maximum size of a fully erect penis can be ascertained by pulling the head of the relaxed penis as far away from the body as possible and measuring its length. However, this technique does not give a measurement quite as long as a fully erect penis, falling anywhere from one quarter to one half inch short.

If the penis is thought of as having properties similar to those of a balloon, we quickly realize that just as the lengths of various uninflated balloons have little relationship to their lengths when inflated, so the lengths of flaccid penises have little relationship to their lengths when erect. This is because length in inflated balloons and erect penises is less related to their uninflated length and more related to the thickness and elasticity of their skins and to the volumes of air or blood that flow into each respectively.

It should be clear to all that a locker room full of relaxed penises is no place to make relative conclusions or generalizations about the size of "ready-to-use" sexual equipment.

**How big around is the average erect penis?**
*5.0 inches (13 cm.)* (Reference:47)
The largest number of American white males (24.1 percent) report erect penises which measure 5 inches in circumference. More than 93 percent of men fall within the range of 4 to 6 inches in circumference.

**How big is the average erect penis?**
*6.0 inches (15 cm.)* (Reference: 47)
The largest number of American white males (23.9 percent) report an erect penis which measures exactly 6.0 inches. Almost 90 percent of men fall within the range of 5 to 7 inches in length.

At one time or another, no man has escaped worry

about his penis size. Is it too small? Too large? A man may worry that his mate's previous lovers were "better hung," as the slang has it. Furtive glances in a locker room do not provide comparative answers because the penises on display under those circumstances are typically quite relaxed. These concerns continue because myths still stoke the fires of male insecurity.

Considering that 89.5 percent of American white males fall within the range of 5 to 7 inches in length, and 96.7 percent measure between 4.5 and 7.5 inches in length, there seems to be little for men to worry about.

It is interesting to note that the Kinsey study of penis size found that when men were asked to *estimate* their own penis size before self-measurement, their estimates were generally lower than their actual measurements.

Dr. Wardell Pomeroy, Kinsey's coauthor, discussed this issue with us and said that he believed the reason the estimates were smaller than the measurements was that a man's penis looks smaller to himself; in looking down he suffers an optical illusion caused by the angle of his erection, the angle of his vision and the presence of pubic hair. This allows him to see less of his own penis than he would see if his pubic area were clean shaven and his penis were horizontal to his line of vision.

Using self-measurements of erect penis size poses several other problems. First, most of the men who reported their measurements reported sizes exactly on the half inch and inch increments, with very few reporting the one quarter or three quarter inch increments which were listed. The reason for this is the difficulty of measuring one's own penis while holding a ruler in one hand and the penis in the other. Under these conditions, trying to read the measurements from above or trying to mark the ruler with the fingers of one of the already occupied hands is difficult. As a result, the respondents seem to have rounded off their measurements to the nearest half inch. We also have some suspicions that there may have been a fudge factor—a man faced with a rounded off choice of 5½ inches or 6 inches may have chosen to boost his size and ego with the measurement of 6 inches.

However, we will probably never know because as Dr. Pomeroy pointed out to us, were a researcher to be present to measure a man's erection, the man would probably lose at least part of it because of the researcher's presence.

**What was the biggest erect penis ever measured?**
*13 inches (33 cm.)*          (References: 62, 126)
Robert Latou Dickinson, one of this century's first science-oriented sex researchers, reported he had personally measured an erect penis that was a bit over 13 inches. Nonetheless, Dr. Dickinson would be the first to admit that this length is quite unusual. However, *High Society* magazine recently reported that comedian Milton Berle and actor Forrest Tucker (of "F-Troop" fame) both sport penises that rival the one measured by Dr. Dickinson. Although we have all heard tales of other incredibly long penises, these stories should be viewed with some skepticism. Gangster John Dillinger, it is said, sported a penis that stretched to 20 inches when erect. It has also been erroneously rumored that

Dillinger's organ is on display in the Smithsonian Institute—which claims no knowledge of this aberrational appendage.

Readers of men's magazines that feature numerous letters purportedly authored by readers soon become convinced that the *average* penis is "a trusty 9-inch tool." Nonsense! In the previously mentioned survey of white men, only 7.5 percent claimed erect penises of 7 inches or longer, with the survey's longest being 9.25 inches. The shortest was 3.75 inches. But reputable medical literature does cite several fully erect penises that measure no more than 0.5 inches.

So, good advice for readers seeking a *truly* long penis is to head to a nearby zoo or aquarium. Blue whales, for instance, feature 10-foot-long penises. Elephants, while not in that ocean league, often measure in at 6 feet. Any human might feel underendowed by comparison.

These numbers remind us of a former patient who came our way under a court order to seek help in curbing his habit of "flashing" (publicly displaying) his penis to passing woman. Asked why he enjoyed flashing, the man amiably responded that because he was well hung, he received pleasure from knowing he was exciting women by exposing them to exceptional equipment. For this patient's therapy, we suggested he visit a Los Angeles area nudist park where, flash as he might, there would be no formal complaints because he would be in the midst of dozens of unclad "manhoods," as playwright G. B. Shaw euphemized. From the patient's viewpoint, this opportunity to expose himself in a nudist environment would continue to satisfy his exhibitionist urges while freeing him from fears of arrest and prosecution. Nine months later while conducting a workshop at the same nudist park we spotted our former patient in the audience and, when the program concluded, engaged him in conversation. "Are you still having difficulty handling your problem?" we inquired. "What problem?" he answered. Pleased that he no longer found it necessary to "flash," we complimented the man by pointing out that indeed, we could see that he *was* well endowed. But he was not flattered, for he shrugged as he responded, "That's true, but since I have been coming here, I have discovered that so is everyone else."

**Are the penises of black men larger than the penises of white men?**

*No and yes.* (References: 47, 76, 126)

The largest number of white males (23.9 percent) as well as the largest number of black males (25.4 percent) reported their penis length as 6 inches. However, in the sample for blacks, no one listed a penis size of less than 5 inches compared to 3.2 percent of whites for these smaller sizes and 13.6 percent of blacks reported penis lengths in excess of 7 inches compared to only 7.5 percent of whites. In other words, the average white male and black male have the same length penises (6 inches) but proportionately fewer blacks seem to have short penises and proportionately more blacks seems to have long penises.

This is not the final word, however, because when we compare the circumferences of penises belonging to white and black males, a contradictory picture emerges. The largest number of white males (24.1 percent) report an erect penis circumference of 5 inches, whereas the largest number of black males (21.8 percent) report an erect penis of only 4¾ inches, with only 18.2 percent reporting a 5 inch circumference. In summary, it appears that average white males and average black males have penises that are the same in length but the average white man's penis is slightly larger in girth. Yet, proportionately fewer black males have short penises and proportionately more have longer penises than do white males.

If the statistics confuse you, don't be concerned. The bottom line is *that there is no significant difference in the size of penises between the average white male and the average black male.*

One less than adequate attempt to study the relationship between penis size and nationality or race was conducted by the British sexologist, Dr. Robert Chartham. His hunt was aimed at uncovering large penises and he reports the longest erect male penis he discovered was on an Englishman whose penis touched the tape at 10.5 inches. Arranging his results by the longest penis found within a given nationality, the rest of his data follows: West German—8.5 inches; Danish—8 inches; French, American and Swedish—7.75 inches; and Black—7.5 inches.

Chartham also listed the smallest penis he found within each national or racial group: Swedish and Danish—5 inches; Black—4 inches; French, West German and American—3.5 inches; and English—2.75 inches.

Two factors weigh against drawing any significant conclusions from this admittedly interesting information. For one, Chartham's sample was small. Each group ranged from as few as 9 to no more than 121 men. But, even granting any validity to Dr. Chartham's findings, a reader would be hard pressed to draw any conclusion whatsoever. The English, for instance, sport both the largest *and* the smallest penis. This is why at this time there is not acceptable evidence to indicate a racial or ethnic variation in the average size or range of sizes of penises. Nonetheless, the "black super-stud" myths persist. We are reminded of a black physician who, during therapy for overcoming the loss of love, admitted that he was reluctant to bed white women. Racial prejudices did not worry him. The problem, he confessed, was that he did not want to be the one to shatter whatever illusion might be harbored about the relative hugeness of black sexual equipment. Nor did he want disappointed lovers. That is why, he laughed, he restricted his affairs to black women, who would know his equipment was comfortably within the normal range.

**Does penis size determine sexual performance?**
*No.*                                (References: 16, 17, 85)
That "no" is emphatic. Certainly, extremely short or long penises, the sort found on less than 2 percent of men and rank as statistical anomalies, might prove difficult for some female to embrace, although there are almost no limits to the ability of vaginas to stretch to accommodate any human penis. Any deficiency in size can usually be overshadowed by the competent sexual techniques of an imaginative lover.

In some cases, a large penis may function as a potent *visual* turn-on, but that is a question not of anatomy but of psychology. Then too, about as many

40

women are fearful of unusually large penises as are aroused by the sight of such members. So, for the most part, penis size is irrelevant in sex.

What is far more important in making love is sensitivity and imagination. Many women report having thoroughly satisfying sex with men endowed with smaller sexual equipment but bountiful imaginations coupled with polished technique. In one instance, a married couple came to us for therapy because the man had a relatively small penis. His wife insisted that he was an outstanding lover and that he always satisfied her totally. It was the husband who worried. His penis size caused him to be insecure and to doubt that his wife's professed satisfaction was genuine. For a change of erotic pace one night, they checked into a motel which piped hardcore X-rated movies into its rooms. Watching this performance, the man was surprised to discover the lack of sexual imagination and artistry as well as an indifferent emotional attitude on the part of the overly endowed porno star. It was then that he realized for the first time that he was truly a far more competent and satisfying lover than the king of hardcore actors, whose claim to sexual fame rested only on his sizable anatomy.

**Is there a connection between penis size and the size of other body parts?**

*Probably not.* (References: 84, 85)

Study hands, noses or feet, and you will come no closer to guessing their owner's penis size, no matter how hard you examine those other body parts. In Masters and Johnson's surveys, for instance, the largest flaccid penis they measured belonged to a 5′ 7″ man who weighed 152 pounds. The smallest was on a man who stood 5′ 11″ and weighed 178 lbs.

Unfortunately, these findings are not widely known and the myths persist, partly because no one has adequately researched the subject. In one instance, a self-conscious and somewhat insecure patient came in and reported a strange experience. While having dinner one evening, his new date, whom he found attractive, volunteered that she was not likely to ever go to bed with him. Why? Because she could tell that his penis was too small. "How could she tell?" we asked. "She said she could tell by the size of my *feet*," he answered. "Well then, if you ever date this woman again, we suggest you wear larger shoes."

### Are there ways to artificially enlarge a penis?

*Yes, temporarily.*                    (References: 72, 140)

Arabs believe that handling, pulling and rubbing the penis can make it longer. The ancient sex manual *Kama Sutra* advises rubbing a penis with bristles followed by oil for ten nights, thereby causing swelling. The owner of the penis is advised to lie face-down and to allow it to hang through a hole cut in his cot to assure gravity's help in adding to its length. Although the authors know of no one who has tried that method, we know of no mechanical way to *permanently* increase the length of the penis. Nor will exercise, as some adolescents imagine in masturbatory fantasies, "build up" that organ. But sex shops sell an array of sex aids that provide the *semblance* of a longer and thicker penis. These de-

42

vices are penis replicas (prostheses) and they fit over the wearer's penis much like a glove envelops a hand. Made of plastic, the replicas come in a variety of lengths.

**When a man is fully clothed, where does his penis lie?**
*To the left of his pants' seam.* (References: 47, 78)
Odd as this finding may seem, more than 75 percent of all men say their penis hangs on the left side. About 17 percent express a liking for the right. The rest will go either way. The meaning, if any, of this habit is unknown.

**How big is the average testicle?**
*2 inches long; 1 inch in breadth; 1.25 inches wide.* (5 cm.x2.5 cm.x3.5cm.) (References: 72, 85, 92)
Even if your rulers are at stand-by, this is one measurement we doubt many (male) readers will attempt to duplicate. The sperm-producing testicles are extremely sensitive to touch.

As with all sexual measurements, there is great diversity among testicle sizes. Some sufferers from advanced cases of venereal disease have testicles that rival grapefruits in size. Males afflicted with elephantiasis, a chronic disease that often results in a grossly enlarged scrotum, sometimes have testicles the size of basketballs. Often the penis of these sufferers is also enlarged, occasionally to lengths approaching two feet.

For the record, blue whale testicles typically weigh about 100 lbs. each. Elephants, by contrast, are veritable midgets. Their testicles weigh but 5 lbs. apiece.

The animal kingdom aside, variations of a half inch or so are commonplace among humans. Interesting too is the fact that an individual's testicle size is not a constant. Temperature conditions also influence these organs, with colder temperatures producing temporary shrinkage and warmer temperatures yielding some expansion.

### When do the testicles descend?
*Before birth.*                          (Reference: 72)
In a male fetus, the testicles usually are comfortably lodged *within* the body until a few weeks before birth, when they descend to their normal position outside the body. The physiological significance of this descent is enormous. Sperm can thrive only in a temperature that is a degree or two below the typical body temperature, and this fractionally cooler climate is found in the lowered, external position. While the testicles on nearly all males (98 percent) do take this plunge before birth, in most of the remaining cases the drop occurs before puberty—which is when sperm production begins and testicle position takes on its biological importance. In a very few instances, the testicles never descend on their own and corrective surgery must be performed.

### Do testicles hang at the same level?
*No.*                          (References: 76, 85)
A few years back, a distressed adolescent came to us and insisted he was abnormal. One of his testicles, he sadly confessed, was lower than the other. It was with great relief that he learned the facts. Just as penises tend, inexplicably, to hang to the left, the

left testicle tends to hang a bit lower than the right on about 85 percent of all men.

Nor do testicles always stay in the same position. During heights of sexual arousal, the testicles frequently pull closer to the body and penis, and in some few individuals even enter the abdominal cavity during sex.

**Can a man who lacks a testicle perform normally in sex?**

*Yes.* (Reference: 58)

A testicle can be lost as an accident of birth, disease, injury, or semicastration. Semicastration (also known as hemicastration, monorchy) is the surgical removal of one testicle and is known to have been practiced by only four societies, two in the Micronesian Islands of the Pacific, one in Ethiopia and one in South Africa.

The practice among the Ponapeans in the Carolina Islands of Micronesia was best known. The surgery, which is no longer customary, generally was performed between the ages of 14 and 16. It was considered exceedingly brave to perform the surgery on one's own testicle. The second testicle might also be removed in one's later years as a sign of loyalty to the chief. (It is also reported that chiefs usually managed to avoid removal of even one of their own testicles.) Sex lives were not usually affected because one testicle suffices nicely in sex and, as long as the penis remains intact, a man so equipped will function with only a marginal difference from men with the normal pair. As with many other body parts, such as kidneys, the duplication is more a redundant safety backup than a matter of biological necessity.

A patient of ours, a young Marine who had lost a testicle in combat, still expressed the fear that during sex his loss would be discovered and perhaps ridiculed by his sex partner. His is not a rare worry but, as we explained to him, during an initial sexual encounter, such an anomaly is unlikely to be discovered because women are generally reluctant to handle a male's scrotum the first time they make love. Then, if a relationship blossomed and additional sex ensued, the woman would already *know* that his equipment worked quite satisfactorily. Therefore, ridicule is a highly improbable result.

**Can a man who lacks both testicles still have normal sex?**
*Yes.*                                    (References: 58, 72, 126)
Although no society has required castration of all of its males, castration has been commonplace for some members in many cultures.

Because the Roman Catholic church believed that the Bible prohibited women from making any sounds in church (I Corinthians 14:35), the *castrati*—castrated male sopranos—were required to sing female parts in the church choirs. The custom was abolished by Papal decree in 1878.

It is interesting that although most of us are aware of the use of eunuchs (castrated males) in the harems of Islamic societies, we may be unaware of the fact that castration was forbidden by the Koran and that the eunuchs used as harem guards were castrated slaves usually purchased from European Christians who had no religious reason not to supply a tailor-made product demanded by their Islamic customers.

Limit castration to severing the testicles, however, and a man's sexual abilities and desires may not be diminished at all. (Nonetheless, in many instances castration involved removing the penis too, effectively ending the ability to have sex.) Hundreds of stories exist of testicleless eunuchs who managed frequent flings with a sultan's wives. Better documented is the case of a man whose testicles were removed as part of a tuberculosis "cure" and his sex life was diminished not in the slightest. In fact, it increased. Before the operation he reported an intercourse frequency of about once monthly. Afterward, three times weekly was his norm!

All of this is possible only *if* sexual maturation is completed before removal of the testicles. Such a man then becomes sterile, but his system often continues to produce ample sex horomes to give him a sex drive and a fully erect penis when circumstances warrant.

### How big is a sperm?
*4 microns in length.*                    (Reference: 72)

Unless you have access to a powerful microscope, you have never viewed a sperm, the male ingredient that fertilizes a female's egg and leads to conception of a child. There are 1000 microns in a single millimeter which, in turn, is only about 1/25th of an inch.

In the absence of genetic deformities or castration in a normal male, sperm production continues from adulthood throughout a man's life. The process is an ongoing one and males can produce essentially an infinite number of sperm. Semen, the transporting fluid that combines with sperm in an ejaculation, is continuously produced also. Men have not always understood this principle. In Victorian England, for instance, males zealously warded off ejaculation whenever possible in the belief that an ejaculate's ingredients came in but limited quantities and wanton waste could be potentially fatal. "Waste" as much as you wish; the healthy body will always produce more.

### Are there super-males?

*No.*                                     (References: 72, 78, 90, 91)

There are males whose chromosomes, the microscopic building blocks that determine the characteristics of a specific individual and make him or her different from all others, differ markedly from the norm. The average male has two sex chromosomes, an X (from the mother) and a Y (from the father). But some males show *three* sex chromosomes in an XYY pattern. Although claims are *not* made regarding these individual's sexual stamina, some people allege that this genetic structure is linked to a tendency to commit violent criminal acts. In France and Australia the hunch is codified into law: in those nations a criminal who makes his chromosomes a defense and shows the XYY pattern often is acquitted or awarded a lighter sentence. Nonetheless, there is no convincing *demonstrated* link between the XYY abnormality and a disposition toward violence.

Critical as chromosomes are in determining anatomy and other human factors, our knowledge is still imperfect. We do know that genetic irregularities can yield significant anatomical abnormalities. Perhaps 60 individuals are cited in this century's medical literature as hermaphrodites, possessing both female ovaries (where eggs are produced) and male testicular tissue. As a rule, both the male and female organs in these individuals are immature; certainly no case is on record of a human producing an infant in a solo act.

Less dramatic departures from the norm occur with greater frequency. Some males have penises and mature female breasts. Others possess a penis and two ovaries but entirely lack testicles. The frequency of such anomalies, although greater than for hermaphroditism, is still quite low. Yet many cases of sexual anatomical abnormalities may go undetected. An otherwise normal female who has testicular tissue within her in lieu of ovaries could easily lead her life without ever discovering this abnormality, although she would be unable to bear children.

### How much is the average man's body worth?
$7.28                           (References: 4, 136)
That figure is merely for the scrap value of a man's body, particularly its naturally occurring minerals. That is why others peg the replacement value at closer to $6 million, a sum that takes in account the prices currently paid by some hospitals and medical research facilities for hemoglobin, bone marrow, insulin, genetic materials, and the like. Either way, however, we suspect most of us would prefer to avoid this sale even if it might turn each one of us into instant millionaires.

### How tall is the average man?
5'9" (1.77 meters)        (References: 27, 88, 136)
The height of American males creeps ever upward.

A generation ago, 5'8" was nearer the norm. But better nutrition, especially elevated protein intake, coupled with improved health care results in a steadily increasing average height. Most men are grouped in a narrow range of heights that measure from about 5'7" to 6'. But 10 percent are taller than 6' and a fraction of 1 percent measure in at under 5'. These deviations are minor, however, when compared to the tallest and shortest men in medical history. Robert Pershing Wadlow (of Aton, Illinois) reached a peak height shortly before his death in 1940 of 8'11". And on the short side, Charles Sherwood Stratton (known as Tom Thumb) measured a tiny 40" at his death in 1883. Yet, Tom Thumb is not the shortest man in medical annals. That title goes to Calvin Phillips (of Bridgewater, Massachusetts) who measured just 26.5" (a trace over two feet) at his death in 1812.

The Greek philosopher Aristotle, in scanning the range of heights in his land, offered this comment; "Personal beauty requires that one should be tall; little people may have charm and elegance, but beauty—no." But that is only one man's opinion. A different predilection arose in Victorian England when dwarfs, adults who measured around 45", were much prized as erotic playthings. Women, much more than men, found the "little people" enchanting in bed.

**How much does the average man weigh?**
*172 lbs.*                     (References: 27, 88, 136)
At 5'9" and 172 lbs., the average American man presents a relatively trim figure. But, as with height,

50

males come in an array of weights. Edward C. Hagner (alias Eddie Masher) weighed in at 48 lbs. and stood 5'7", and Robert Earl Hughes measured 6' and tipped the scales at 1,069 pounds.

Medical authorities estimate that 25 percent of America's adult men are obese, when obesity is defined as being 30 pounds over one's desirable body weight. And very few adult males, no more than 10 percent, qualify as underweight.

**How large is the average man's chest?**
*37–39" (98–102 cm.)* (Reference: 27)
Much depends on when the measurement is taken. Males at or very close to their physical peak, which commonly is 18 years of age, tend to be closer to 37". Older men, one with perhaps a few extra pounds on their frames, are apt to sport larger measurements.

**How big is the average man's waist?**
*31–34" (80–87 cm.)* (Reference: 27)
Age, again is a factor. As we grow older, there is a pronounced tendency to gain poundage which often clings to the middle of the body. That is why younger men tend to come in with smaller waist sizes than older men. The range of waists commonly found on American males is from 29" to 42".

**How big is a man's thigh?**
*21" (54 cm.)* (Reference: 27)
The usual caveat about age applies here, and this number is the one for younger men. Thighs of 18"–24" are common.

**How large is a man around the hips?**
*36" (92 cm.)*                    (Reference: 27)
Anywhere between 34" and 42" is comfortably within the normal range.

**How many American men have brown hair?**
*70 percent.*

**How many American men have black hair?**
*10 percent.*

**How many American men have blond hair?**
*15 percent.*

**How many American men have red hair?**
*6 percent.*                    (Reference: 136)
Brown is far and away the most common color on the heads of American white men (70 percent) and on their pubic areas as well, since pubic hair usually is the same color as the hair on one's head, although there are often shade variations. Blond hair—*natural* blond that is—accounts for 15 percent of men's manes; black hair accounts for 10 percent; and the other 6 percent are redheads. These percentages are for the *predominant* hair color. Many men's heads feature a few stray hairs of a different color. These numbers also apply only to Caucasians.

**How many men have straight hair?**
*25 percent.*

**How many men have wavy hair?**
*65 percent.*

**How many men have curly hair?**
*10 percent.*                    (Reference: 136)
A bit of natural wave is found on the heads of two
out of every three American white males. Perfectly
straight hair, by contrast, is found on only 10 percent
of the U.S. men, although 15 percent have hair that
is best characterized as essentially straight with
minor waves. Only 10 percent have hair that is curly.
These figures, again, are for Caucasians only.

**How many men are balding?**
*60 percent.*                    (Reference: 136)
No wonder makers of miracle hair-growth formulas
make fortunes! Baldness is not restricted to older
men; one third of the males between ages 30 and 40
already claim a bald spot. And, sadly for those who
wish for hairy heads, to our knowledge no hair-
renewal formula is reliable. Baldness is generally
hereditary in origin, and there is as yet no demonstrated way to tamper with hair-loss genes. It is true
enough, however, that some baldness is caused by
diet and nutritional deficiencies and that is a process
that can be halted, if not reversed, by specialists.

**How many men wear glasses?**
*44 percent.*                    (Reference: 136)
This is the number of men who wear spectacles
or contact lenses. Many eye specialists suspect that
at least another 10 percent would find their vision
markedly improved by glasses.

**What's the ratio of men to women?**
*The answer varies with age.*         (Reference: 78)

Here is the male to female ratio by age.

At birth—105 males to 100 females
At 18 years of age—100 males to 100 females
At 50 years of age—95 males to 100 females
At 57 years of age—90 males to 100 females
At 67 years of age—70 males to 100 females
At 87 years of age—50 males to 100 females
100 or more years of age—21 males to 100 females.

# CHAPTER 3

## No Body is Perfect—Female Anatomy

Women as well as men, have a desire to know the anatomical norms. Indeed, for women in our society, anatomy has always been of greater concern than it has been to men.

One of the motivations for writing this book comes from our experience in treating teenage girls who suffer from anorexia nervosa, the fear of eating. Afflicted with an intense and morbid fear of being fat, these young women diet until they are emaciated —and if left untreated, death from hunger often results. These anorexics are victims of a culturally imposed obsession. "Think thin" is their motto, and their self-perceptions are so distorted that, even after dieting until only skeletal frames remain, many still insist that at least one body measurement (often the hips, waist or thighs) is "hideously fat." Our experience is that *most* American women share the anorexic's distorted perception although the degree, fortunately, is far less extreme.

Worrying about being "too fat" is purely cultural in origin. Many societies highly prize full-figured females and scorn thin ones. No matter, however; the American concern endures. The fact that it rarely affects a male teenager indicates how much more important thin is to women than it is to men. Only hard information can put matters in perspective, and that is one of the reasons we believed it necessary to make the basic facts, *How Big Is Big?*, available.

### How big are the average woman's breasts?
*The average bust line is 35.9 inches (91 cm.).*

(References: 70, 136)

This average bust-line figure (35.9 inches) for American women includes backs as well as breasts proper. More pointedly, the typical U.S. woman wears a "B" cup and she buys a 36B bra. The proportion of women's cup sizes follows: "A"—15 percent; "B"—44 percent; "C"—28 percent; "D"—10 percent; others (such as AA or DD)—3 percent.

Intriguingly, manufacturers of women's clothing agree that the average American woman's bust size has expanded in recent decades, if only by fractions of an inch. Most authorities attribute this to improved diet and the widespread use of birth control pills which generally trigger breast enlargements in many women, lasting as long as the contraceptive pills are used.

As in the case of a man's penis, the size of a woman's breasts is in no way correlated with the size of any other body parts. Large women often have tiny breasts, and petite women often have breasts that are disproportionately large. The budding of youthful breasts often provides the first visible signals of an adult woman. Perhaps because American men are inordinately fascinated with this particular region of a woman's anatomy, many women become overly concerned about the size and shape of their breasts. Men's magazines, without exception, focus their photographic attention on breasts. Women's magazines also focus undue attention on breasts, with frequent and lengthy featured articles on the proper care of breasts, and with pages of advertisements that promise a bigger, more shapely bust line.

Search the anthropological and sociological literature, however, and you will discover that no culture, with the possible exception of the British, puts as much emphasis as Americans do on breasts.

Yet, paradoxically, in the United States, men's concepts and feelings about breasts are as varied as breasts themselves. Many men are turned on by small breasts, perhaps because they stoke fantasies of pubescent sex partners. Others are aroused by extremely large breasts; such responses possibly are related to the search for a nurturing woman. Still other men find breasts, large or small, less attractive than other parts of the female anatomy.

But why, in the first place, is there this obsession with breasts? Desmond Morris, author of *The Naked Ape*, speculates that because humans are the only mammals that have face-to-face intercourse, the breasts serve as the seat of passion for most primates. Because of their strategic placement, this theory continues, the breasts become a visual force in attracting a male for sex. This theory is certainly untrue for humans as a group, although possibly true for Americans and Europeans. Face-to-face sex in the missionary position is not the most common sexual position for Asians, and to further dispute Morris' theory, very few societies have the fixation on breasts that he claims.

The perception of one's breast size is so personal that sometimes it can be distorted by a woman's own poor self-image. One interesting case was related to us by a 36-year-old divorced architect who dated a small-busted woman in her late twenties, for several months. The man found the woman's lean body very attractive and he told her so. Then one day in his apartment, she happened to stumble across a picture of the man's large-breasted ex-wife. The woman became furious and accused him of deceit for saying that he loved her body when the architect obviously was attracted only to big-busted women like the one he had married. She was so offended by his apparent duplicity that she left the apartment and never returned, even though the bewildered man had been sincere in his admiration for the woman's petite, small-busted body. It was ironic, he explained to us, that he did not even particularly care for large breasts; they just happened to be attached to the first woman he married.

**Is there a way to make breasts larger**
*Yes.*                                    (Reference: 72)
Birth control pills or weight gain often yield breast enlargement. But the most common way that women undertake breast enlargement is plastic surgery. By

implanting layers of silicone within the breasts, a surgeon can augment breast size. The result is a pair of breasts that look and allegedly feel "natural," with minor scarring. Most physicians consider this surgical procedure to be relatively simple. Nonetheless in the past unsuccessful breast-augmentation procedures have fueled controversy. For the most part, those unhappy failures involved obsolete operations in which liquid silicone was injected into the breasts. On occasion, this silicone would literally roam around a breast, causing it to become "lumpy." Reputable surgeons no longer employ the injection technique; instead, through implantation of silicone into inert sacs within the breasts, the positioning is now usually stable. In addition, there is now no contact between the silicone and the breast tissue.

Some entrepreneurs prey on women's fears that their breasts are small, in order to sell mechanical devices that guarantee bigger and shapelier breasts. None of these devices has ever been shown to work. Some exercises might expand the bust line, but that is because the back or pectoral muscles underlying the breasts have been enlarged. The breasts themselves, which are not muscles but mostly fatty tissues, are not affected by exercise and cannot be expanded this way.

**Can breasts be reduced in size?**
*Yes.*                              (References: 72, 126)
The first recorded breast reduction surgery occurred in 1731. Given our breast-obsessive culture, it might sound strange that a woman would want

59

this operation. But many do because women possessing large breasts often feel as insecure as women who have a small bust line.

Breasts, as we've said, vary greatly in size, and the heaviest breasts documented weighed 26 pounds apiece, compared to just a few pounds for an average woman's breast. Nonetheless, breast reduction remains a relatively rare operation that is neither so simple nor so safe as augmentation, because it involves the removal of tissues that play a role in the physiological functions of breasts. In most cases the problem requiring surgery is not breast size, but the woman's perception of her breast size.

On one occasion, an attractive red-haired female patient in her early twenties who was feeling generally depressed expressed dissatisfaction with her figure and particularly with her small breasts, which she claimed failed to gain men's attention. She indicated that she longed to have large, shapely breasts like those of our 28-year-old receptionist. Less than three months later, our receptionist came to see us one morning and asked if we could recommend a good surgeon who could perform a breast-reduction operation. She complained that her breasts had been leered at by men since she was twelve and that she longed to fade into the crowd where men's fixation on large breasts would not get in the way of a meaningful relationship. Ironically, both women expressed displeasure with the way clothes fit them.

In another instance, a female patient admitted that her ex-husband had significantly shaken her self-confidence with his insistence that her breasts were "too small." But, in entering a dating relationship with another man soon after her divorce, her luck took another turn: this fellow began telling her he disliked her breasts because they were too large! In time, this woman realized the facts: her breasts were just fine. As she herself said so insightfully, "I am well rid of both of those insensitive bastards." Besides, she smilingly observed, her husband had been too thin and the second man too fat.

Add up these differing opinions and only one conclusion is possible: a woman is wise to reject all criticism of her breast size. Besides, as our last story demonstrates, the woman who accepts all male criticism of her shape can only become confused.

### Are a woman's breasts identical?

*No.*                              (References: 6, 72)

Just as no man has matching testicles, no woman has breasts that are exactly the same size although the differences are usually imperceptible to others. The two halves of a body never are perfectly symmetrical. There are minor and sometimes major differences between the two sides, a difference that is reflected throughout the body, including the right and left breasts. Unless extreme, this asymmetry is generally not perceptible to men, even if a woman is nude. But the differences may seem immense to a woman who has compared in detail the two breasts before a mirror throughout her life. Such differences, even when extreme, usually have no biological consequences. In the more extreme instances, plastic surgery is available for women who wish to make their breasts more uniform in appearance.

**How large are the "lips" at the entrance to the vagina?**
*Too variable to quantify* (Reference: 85)
At the entrance to the vagina, generally there are four skin-folds commonly called "lips." These folds of skin are the two *labia majora* (outer lips), which are outside the vaginal cavity and run along its side, and the *labia minora* (inner lips), which are two hairless skin-folds within the labia majora. The labia minora serve to enclose the introitus. The exact appearance and size of both pairs of lips differ a good deal from woman to woman. In some instances, the labia majora are clearly visible; in others, they are obscured by pubic hair.

During sexual arousal, the labia majora often show marked increases in size; the labia minora nearly always do, sometimes increasing two to three times in diameter.

**How long is the vagina's entrance?**
*2 inches (5 cm.)* (Reference: 72)
The introitus (or vestibule) is the vagina's external orifice. Constructed much like a funnel, it is readily visible only when the inner lips of the vagina are parted. The introitus's appearance varies greatly from woman to woman and depends also on whether or not the hymen is intact.

**How deep is the average woman's vagina**
*3 inches (8 cm.)* (References: 85, 126)
Tubelike in appearance, in its unexcited state the vagina—the female organ that embraces the penis during intercourse—measures about 3 inches in length and is about 1 inch in diameter. But the

vagina is *potential* space. When excited, it expands not unlike the way an aroused penis does. The vagina is similar to a balloon: it can encompass the largest of penises. When excited, the typical vagina expands to perhaps 5 inches in depth and can expand to 4 inches in diameter if necessary. During child-birth, a full-term infant usually can pass through the vagina without harm to the child or to the mother.

A medical oddity, albeit an extraordinarily rare one, is that some women are equipped with two vaginas. Typically, there is but one external opening that connects to two internal vagina tracts. In most instances, this condition does not become known until a woman becomes pregnant. It usually is surgically correctable.

Finally, to complete our catalogue of oddities, the vagina is capable of amazing feats. In some Parisian nightclubs, for instance, a featured woman performer will employ her vagina and only her vagina to "swallow" and then powerfully eject Ping-Pong balls and similar round objects. Other women have learned to play tunes on harmonicas with their vaginas. Amusing as these anecdotes may be, they also demonstrate a point: the vagina is a superbly versatile female organ.

### Is a mature woman's vagina ever too small for intercourse?

*No.*                    (References: 72, 84, 85)

An enduring myth of sexuality is that some vaginas are "too tight" or "too small" to accommodate certain unusually large penises. Yet no penis is as large as an infant, and a structurally normal vagina should be capable of stretching enough to hold any penis.

But the vagina's external opening, the introitus, in some women may sometimes pose a problem. The introitus is the gateway to the vagina and a condition known as *vaginismus* can so constrict the vaginal opening as to block insertion of even a tampon. Usually psychological in origin, vaginismus often is a consequence of overall tenseness, triggered by anxiety, fear or physical pain. If an attempt is made to force entry of a penis into an introitus blocked by vaginismus, the woman may suffer muscle spasms and acute physical pain. For the occasional sufferer, no therapy may be called for but for the chronic sufferers, treatment is available.

Typical of the techniques we have used is the treatment we prescribed for one married woman. We had her purchase a set of plastic centrifuge test tubes in graduated sizes (they are available at surgical supply houses). She was then instructed to coat with lubricant the smallest tube (about the diameter of a cigarette) and to insert it and hold it within her vagina for one hour a day. Every three days she was instructed to increase the diameter of the tube and in three weeks she was comfortably accepting a 2-inch diameter test tube. At that point she was permitted to have her first sex in 18 months. When, on a follow-up, we asked if she was now large enough to pleasurefully accept her husband, the woman happily replied, "Definitely yes. But, doctor, can you now do anything to make his penis as large as that last test tube?"

**Can a vagina be too big for sex?**
*Usually not.*                                    (Reference: 123)
However, in many societies the tight vagina is

prized. There are several ways to make a vagina tighter.

The mucous membrane of the vaginal walls can be constricted by the use of astringents. The Marquesan Islanders, who highly prize tight, odor-free and somewhat dry vaginas, apply several different astringents to female infants. These applications are continued until the onset of menstruation. The plant medications so used by the Marquesans include the leaves of the tu'ei'au plant, the unripened nut of the coconut, and fermented breadfruit paste.

In brothels catering to special tastes, prostitutes have often used alum for the purpose of shrinking the vaginal walls, thereby faking virginity for customers who are willing to pay a premium for the privilege of deflowering a virgin.

In our practice we have encountered several women who confided that they feared their vaginas were "too big." Most women with this complaint have mothered several children, and although it is true that during childbirth the vagina stretches and a few rips in the walls may occur, that does not usually prevent the vagina from returning to its former condition. Not too many years past, obstetricians concluded their work on a new mother by sewing a tiny tightening stitch, "a husband's knot," as it was popularly known, to speed return of the vagina to tautness. But this technique has been largely supplanted by exercise programs and the process works for all women who fear their vaginas are exceptionally loose, regardless of whether they have given birth or not.

The first step in the muscle-strengthening process is to identify the muscles needing exercise. Most women can easily identify these muscles by pinching off urination in midstream. Once she can feel these muscles that need strengthening, she can begin consciously contracting and then relaxing them, much as we can tighten stomach muscles by tightly pulling them in and then letting go. On the first day of exercise, the woman performs one set of ten contractions in the morning and one set in the afternoon. The next day, 20; then, 30 on the following day; and so forth. Within only a seven-day time period, her muscles and vagina should become quite as strong and tight as any woman or man could wish. Incidentally, a vagina that may seem "too big" may really be "too wet." In this case, the simple solution is to take a towel to bed with you and to use it to remove excess vaginal lubrication.

Different shapes and sizes of female sexual equipment are admired by different societies. Among the Marquesans, a flat pubic area is admired. Among the Mangaians, men are very interested in the shape, size and consistency of the pubic area and the sharpness or bluntness of the clitoris. The Marquesans and the Siriono find a flat vulva extremely attractive. Eastern Islanders prefer a large clitoris. Dahomeans, Kusaians, Marquesans, Nama, Ponapeans, Thongas, Truckese, and Venda admire an elongated labia majora and attempt to elongate them by stretching. The extremely long labia of Nama women have been called the "Hottentot apron."

The Kgatla prefer a long labia minora. One Kgatla woman explained the importance of a long labia. "If a woman hasn't got a long *labia*, we don't call her a woman at all, but a child. When you hear husband and wife quarrel at home, this is the main cause of their quarrel because this is the place where the husband plays every day and if his wife has not got them, there is no peace at home, for then he has nowhere to play, while other men boast to him about how they play with their wives."

Kgatla women begin pulling their labia at the beginning of puberty and even get help from their girl friends. They also mix a little potion to help. The potion, consisting of burned bats' wings ground up with fat, is applied to small cuts around the labia to encourage the labia to grow to the size of bats' wings.

### How long is the average clitoris?

*1 inch (2.5 cm.)*　　　　(References: 72, 85, 126)

The female counterpart to a man's penis, the clitoris, is laden with sensitive nerve endings and, like the penis, becomes engorged with blood when sexually stimulated. Unlike the penis, however, the clitoris is an exclusively sexual organ; it serves no urinary tract functions. Its size, shape and function led one sexologist to describe it as "a veritable electrical bell button which being pressed, rings up the whole nervous system."

Because the bulk of the clitoris is contained within the body, it does not expand significantly when aroused. Although the overall length of the clitoris is about one inch, the clitoral glans, the rounded tip that visibly protudes, is about one fifth of an inch. As with penis size, however, there is significant variation in the lengths of clitoral glans. The normal range is from 0.04 inches (1/25th of an inch) upward to a half inch. But far longer clitoral glans reach 2 to 3 inches, and some are so small they are never discovered. This should have no impact on sexual response: the clitoris will react whether or not it can be seen and size has rarely been shown to be correlated with responsiveness.

### How thick is a virgin's hymen?
*.05–.10 inches (.125–.25 cm.)* ( References: 72, 141 )

Hymens, which block the way through the introitus into the vagina, vary in shape, texture and size. Most have a small opening through which menstrual blood can pass. This thin membrane is physiologically functionless but it has been imbued with monumental significance and has inspired countless myths. Female virgins, so old husbands' tales go, had to have their hymens intact, and "the maidenhead" was expected to bleed on the wedding night. Otherwise a groom *knew* his wife had previously had sex. Wayward or simply cautious brides often took to procuring capsules of sheep's blood to crush on the honeymoon sheets to preserve the illusion of virginity. In some cases, the deflowering rituals became elaborate and, in some cultures, bloodied wedding sheets went on public display as evidence of the bride's prior chastity. All were based on misinformation and misunderstanding of female anatomy. Certainly, initial intercourse can tear the hymen, cause bleeding and leave a woman "deflowered." But the absence of an intact hymen is no proof of sexual experience. Because the membrane is so thin and delicate, it can tear with strenuous physical activity and often does so long before the first sexual encounter. Conversely, an intact hymen need not bleed with the first sexual penetration and some women who have especially elastic hymens have completed normal intercourse without the membrane tearing.

**Is penetration of a hymen painful for a virgin?**
*Yes*.                                                 (Reference: 72)
At least, it is with some women. In our clinical research, most women report that their defloration resulted in pain, although rarely was the pain intense. But with most of these women, their first sexual experience was a hurried one. Other women whose first sex was with an experienced and gentle lover, one who ensured proper arousal and lubrication of the vagina before penetration, generally report little or no pain.

Reports of pain also vary with the consistency of hymens. Where the membrane is thicker and sturdier than normal, the pain and bleeding are generally greater as well. In a very few instances, a thick hymen must be surgically removed. In some cases, pain and bleeding occur because the hymen is torn from the vaginal wall instead of merely rupturing.

**Can virginity be restored?**
*Yes*.                                                 (Reference: 72)
Our culture has largely progressed beyond the point where much importance attaches to the hymen. Other cultures have not, however. Surgeons in some nations, including Japan, do a brisk business in hymen replacement and repair, although the operations for obvious reasons tend to be cloaked in secrecy. A relatively simple operation, this procedure involves introduction of membranous tissue in the appropriate place.

**How large are the ovaries?**
*1.5 inches long; .75 inch in breadth; and 1 inch
thick. (3.75 x 2 x 2.5 cm.)*          (Reference: 72)
A woman's two ovaries house and nurture the eggs
that, throughout her procreative life, may be fertilized by sperm and result in the conception of a
baby. Intriguingly, although most women have two
ovaries, a few do not. Some perfectly healthy and
normal women have only one, a condition that should
not affect sexual response and rarely affects the
ability to procreate. Other women have three, even
four ovaries and, again, all responses generally are
wholly normal.

**How big is a human egg?**
*1/175th of an inch (0.14 mm.)*      (Reference: 72)
Unlike sperm, an egg (ovum) is visible to the un-
aided eye. However, because these tiny spherical
cells generally remain within a woman's body, few
of us will ever see one.

**How many ova does a woman have?**
*400,000.*                         (Reference: 72)
An important difference between eggs and sperm
is that, although a male continually replenishes his
supply of sperm, each woman has a limited number
of ova from birth. They exist as minute follicles in
the ovary throughout a woman's life and most females begin life with several hundred thousand of
these immature eggs. At puberty, the follicles begin
to mature and each month the menstrual cycle sees
one follicle bursting and releasing the egg it houses.
If not fertilized by sperm, that egg—one of perhaps
400 a woman releases during her lifetime—will be

discharged in the menstrual flow. Even though the typical woman always has many thousands of these ova within her, many researchers suspect that their quality deteriorates over time. That is why most physicians advise women above the age of 40 to avoid conception.

**How is a woman's anatomy determined?**
*Primarily by chromosomes.* (References: 72, 78)
Female anatomy is largely a product of chromosomes. Although in most cases males exhibit an XY chromosome pattern, females receive an X from each parent to produce an XX pattern. But there are departures from this norm. Some females have an XXX structure and are referred to as "super-females." But they are not demonstrably more feminine than XX females; nor are they more masculine.

A "single X" female who has but a single sex chromosome is another matter. Women with this genetic pattern, known as Turner's syndrome, forever remain in a physically prepubescent state with little or no breast development; and because their ovaries are immature, or in many cases not present at all, they are sterile.

**How tall is the average woman?**
*5 feet 3½ inches (165 cm.)*
(References: 47, 88, 126)
Adult females come in a wide range of heights but less than one percent grow upwards of 6 feet and 19 percent (about 1 woman in 5) are under 5 feet. If you tip the tape at more than 5'6", you are among the tallest 13 percent of all women. But matters change when just younger females are measured; 19

percent of women 18–24 are taller than 5'6". And successive generations, researchers believe, will be even a bit taller.

Intriguingly, at about 40 years of age, most people discover that they have shrunk a fraction of an inch or so after reaching their maximum height. Most people begin to experience a shrinking process as they age and their skeletons and joints settle into place.

As much as you shrink, however, you are not likely to match Pauline ("Princess Pauline") Muster's low mark. At full maturity, she stretched to 23.2" (not quite two feet). Nor, even if you grow furiously, are you apt to rival Jane Bunford who measured 7'7", a height taller than that of *any* player in the loftily exclusive National Basketball Association.

**How much does the average woman weigh?**
*143 lbs.*                    (References: 27, 88, 101, 136)
Pauline Musters again sets the low record. At maturity she weighed 7.5 pounds. Flora Mae Jackson, who stood 5'9", holds the record for being the heaviest documented female; she weighed in at 840 pounds. But many women nonetheless worry about being overweight. In our clinical practice, overly thin women often come in seeking diets. The average man, by contrast, is far more likely than a woman to be overweight. Yet he worries about it far less because our society does not demand that he be bone-thin to be attractive. Nor has the concept of thinness always been associated with beauty. The Flemish Baroque painter Peter Paul Reubens, for instance, reflected a seventeenth-century appreciation for full-bodied round females.

**How large is the average woman's waist?**
*29 inches (72 cm.)*                    (Reference: 101)
Younger women, those under 30 years of age, tend
to come in with an average waist that is an inch or
so smaller. More mature women (over 50) have an
average that is a bit bigger than this number, which
is for the mid-range in ages of women (roughly 30–
49).

**How large are a woman's hips?**
*39 inches (100 cm.)*                   (Reference: 101)
Again, the same comments about age apply here
as pertain to waist size. Given her 36"–29"–39"
figure, the average woman buys size 14 dresses.

**How large are the average woman's thighs?**
*22–24 inches around (56–61 cm.)*
                        (References: 27, 58, 101, 136)
That is measured at the thickest spot on the leg,
and younger women have on the average slightly
smaller thighs than do older ones.

In the great majority of societies for which there
is adequate information, a broad pelvis and wide hips
are desirable in women. Only a few societies prefer
slim women, among which are the Dabuans, the
Tongans, the Japanese, and modern Western societies. In a detailed anthropological survey of numerous societies, researchers found that 13 groups preferred their females to be full bodied; just 5 appreciated slim women and many listed slim hips and
narrow pelvises among the *least* desirable attributes.

Among the Mangaian men, sexual interest is
focused on women who have a plump behind with
big hips that can be rotated during dancing and sex.

A big woman is admired as a "bed with a mattress"; whereas a thin woman is referred to disapprovingly as "a bed without a mattress." Other societies which prefer very broad hips are the Chukchee, Hopi, Kwakiutl, Maricopa, Siriono, and Wogeo. The beauties of the Arabian Nights were often of great girth with wide pelvises and large hips.

The Marquesans highly prize women who are *tau tau* (corpulent). Women with heavy hips, buttocks, legs, and shoulders are prized for their endurance during sex.

Polynesians generally prefer heavy women. Among the African Hottentots, women have succeeded in developing fat in the buttocks, called steatopygia, that makes the buttocks enormous by Western standards and attractive by the standards of the men in their own culture. A Hottentot woman, once seated, may have extreme difficulty in lifting her behind from the ground.

How many American women have brown hair?
*70 percent.*

How many American women have black hair?
*10 percent.*

How many American women have blond hair?
*15 percent.*

How many American women have red hair?
*6 percent.*                         (References: 58, 136)
Women share precisely the same natural hair with men. More than half are brunettes; 15 percent

are natural blonds; 10 percent have black hair, and redheads fill in the remaining 6 percent. These numbers apply only to Caucasians.

Pubic hair tends to be the same basic color as a woman's head hair, but frequently there are differences in shades within that basic color.

In the Middle East, removal (depilation) of female body hair including pubic hair has always been common. Various methods have been used and some are still in use today. The common techniques include plucking, shaving, application of removal creams, waxing, and the use of a caramelized mixture of sugar and lemon juice. Men from those areas remove body hair only from their armpits.

In contrast, Western societies usually consider female pubic hair an erotic additive. However, it is also interesting that, in art, idealized bodies of both men and women have nearly always been lacking in body hair, probably because Greco–Roman tastes set the early standards in Western art. Among the Trobriand Islanders, even eyebrows are removed from both men and women.

When baldness occurred in some women of eighteenth-century Europe, they often used a pubic wig, known as a "merkin." Even today some prostitutes have been reported to wear blond pubic wigs to suit the tastes of their customers.

How many American women have straight hair?
*25 percent.*

How many American women have wavy hair?
*65 percent.*

**How many American women have curly hair?**
*10 percent.*                    (Reference: 136)

A natural wave is the predominant hair texture; and another 15 percent of women have straight hair that nonetheless shows a slight wave. Just 10 percent have perfectly straight locks, and 10 percent have naturally curly hair. Again, these numbers apply only to Caucasians.

**How many women wear glasses?**
*54 percent.*                    (Reference: 136)

# CHAPTER 4

## Keeping Up With The Joneses—Male Physiology

Physiology, in this chapter, is how and when males put their sexual anatomy to use. In this chapter we generally omit male attitudes about sex and other psychological matters—they will get their share of attention in Chapter 6. Nor will we use this section to cast doubts on men's statements about their own sexual performance by citing what *women* say about their men. There are excellent reasons for this (not the least of which is that women have their turn in the next chapter), but the best is that, strange as it may sound, there is no significant disagreement between the reports of the two sexes.

**How many erogenous zones does a man have?**
*8 major zones and a number of minor ones.*

(Reference: 72)

An erogenous zone is a part of the body that is unusually sensitive to sexual stimulation—a "touch me *there*, please" place. Although almost any chunk of a man's physical turf can be an erogenous zone, most of the chief erogenous zones are densely laden with responsive nerve endings that rapidly react to touch. The primary male erogenous zones are the mouth, the ears, the nipples, the inner thighs, the anus, the skin between the anus and the scrotum, the testicles, and the penis.

Other than these eight major zones there are a number of minor erogenous zones which include the eyelids, the tongue, the neck, the underarms, the inside crook of the elbow, the palms of the hands, the fingertips, the buttocks, the toes, and the area between the toes. Many men are uniquely sensitive in other areas as well. State of mind and receptiveness to sexual caresses are also factors affecting the responsiveness of erogenous zones. A caress close to a forbidden place is arousing to most men if they are in an amorous mood, and it is possible for the entire human skin to react as an erogenous zone when touched by the right person.

In how many ways can you touch a man to turn him on?
4.
There are four principal types of tactile caresses which produce sexual stimulation: dry touching; wet touching; breath touching; and hair touching. The intensity of the stimulus can vary from a barely perceptible breath to a good hard slap. Some men are rapidly aroused by simply blowing in their ears, others may require some forceful persuasion. The

Golden Rule in touching, as elsewhere, is: Do unto others as you would have them do unto you. This rule may not provide the exact caresses that stimulate your man most, but it is a good beginning for further exploration.

### How many men blush when sexually aroused?
*25 percent.*                                    (Reference: 85)
Sexual stimulation unleashes complicated processes throughout the bloodstream and in one man out of four the result is a "sex flush." This blushing can cover some or all of the body.

### How many men get erect nipples during sex?
*60 percent.*                                    (Reference: 85)
A common result of sexual stimulation—seen in 6 out of 10 men—is nipple erection, where the normally flat and soft breast nipples become hard and protrude from the chest. This is simply a sign of sexual arousal; but it vividly underscores the similarity to female breasts, which respond in precisely the same way when stimulated.

We mention this point because it is one that our culture often seems determined to ignore. In a not well publicized Los Angeles court case, for instance, the City sought to enforce an ordinance that required sex organs to be covered on public beaches—a law that saw women who went topless arrested. Attorney Stanley Fleishman, a nationally respected civil liberties specialist, defended the arrested females by arguing that they were denied their Fourteenth Amendment "Equal Protection" rights by this city ordinance. When Stanley called us to ask whether men's nipples and breasts were also considered sex organs, we pointed out that the nipples and breasts of both men and women are indeed sex organs. On some men, the breasts grow relatively large, and on others they even lactate. The point is that if men are allowed to enjoy the comfort of displaying their bare breasts on public beaches, from a scientific and clinical point of view there is no reason at all for denying women the identical right. Not even Stanley Fleishman can win them all, however. In this instance, a sexually ignorant judge claimed that anyone can plainly see a difference between the breasts and nipples of men and those of women. This is clearly untrue. For every utterly flatchested woman, there is a heavily busted man, and on the basis of chest photographs alone the judge would find it impossible to distinguish between a hairless man's chest and that of a woman. Good as such arguments are, they failed to convince this one judge and at least on the beaches of Los Angeles a man's nipples and breasts are still not officially considered sex organs, whereas a woman's are.

When does a boy get his first erection?

*Within minutes after birth.*    (References: 70, 76)

Newly born infants with fully erect penises are common. This is another instance of the early development of sexual response in children. After only a few days it is routine for male infants to achieve erection. When circumcision is performed, the infant's penis is almost always manually stimulated to erection without difficulty before surgery begins. Nor are these necessarily the earliest cases. Some researchers now believe that prebirth erections are also common.

**How quickly does a man achieve an erection?**
*3–8 seconds.* (Reference: 85)

Confront a normal, healthy male with erotic stimulation in a conducive environment and his penis responds nearly in a flash. Older men generally respond more slowly and some often require manual stimulation of the penis to gain a full erection. A man who has been drinking heavily, too, may find his responses delayed.

**At what angle does an erect penis stand?**
*Nearly horizontal.* (References: 47, 76, 111)

An erection generally projects in a nearly perpendicular line outward from the standing body. But there are enormous individual differences in the angle of erection. In some men (about 10 percent) an erection stands virtually flat against the body. In another 15–20 percent, the erection stands midway between horizontal and vertical, at a 45 degree angle pointing upward. Underlying musculature and bone structures come into play in determining the angle on a given man, and there are correlations as well between the angle and a male's age, with the angle typically increasing in step with the passing years.

Interesting too is that with almost 65 percent of males the erect penis is squarely centered against the body. But in nearly 29 percent of men, the penis inclines to the left; and in about 6 percent it tilts to the right. Among black men 53 percent of the penises are centered, 33 percent lean to the left and 14 percent lean to the right. Furthermore, about 52 percent of men's penises are straight, 28 percent curve upward, 27 percent curve downward, 2 percent curve to the right and 11 percent curve to the left. For a small sample of black men, it was found that only 35 percent had straight penises, 35 percent curved upward, 7 percent curved downward, 5 percent curved to the right and 13 percent curved to the left. However, no matter what the angle, tilt, or curvature of a penis, there should be no effect on sex play.

**What is the maximum duration for a man's erection?**

*It varies with age:*

| AGE | TIME |
|-----|------|
| 16–20 | 43 minutes |
| 21–25 | 54 minutes |
| 26–30 | 53 minutes |
| 31–35 | 47 minutes |
| 36–40 | 41 minutes |
| 41–45 | 31 minutes |
| 46–50 | 29 minutes |
| 51–55 | 22 minutes |
| 56–60 | 27 minutes |
| 61–65 | 19 minutes |
| 66–70 | 7 minutes |

(References: 17, 47, 76, 135)

We need not assume that a man is willfully attempting to delay ejaculation in order to reach his maximum, although many men do have their most prolonged erections by willfully delaying ejaculation. It must be observed that the average time-span varies considerably from age group to age group.

Among very young males, 12 minutes is the average maximum time one can expect. As a male ages, the average times first vault sharply upward but then begin to decline. For 16–20-year-olds, 43 minutes is in range; it is 54 minutes for males 21–25; 53 minutes when they are 26–30; and 47 minutes for men 31–35. Reach 66–70, and 7 minutes is about the average maximum. These are average maxima, however, and a man's performance may differ significantly from these averages. Reports of erections prolonged beyond two and one half hours are not uncommon, and it must be realized that ejaculation need not end an erection, although for most men it apparently does.

Why the considerable variation? Sexual inexperience and attendant excitement go far toward explaining the difficulties the very young have in holding erections just as the accumulation of sexual knowledge in later adolescence and the twenties help us understand the longer times such males evidence.

Why the drop in duration as a man ages? Overall physical fitness, muscle condition, and vigor of the blood circulatory system tend to decline as a male grows older. Some sources believe this decline in stamina may trigger the loss of ability to maintain an erection for lengthy periods. Dr. Alex Comfort, author of *Joy of Sex* and a geriatric specialist, once told us that he believed that the decline in sexual activity among the elderly is more likely attributable to two factors: first, cultural pressures that sex is "inappropriate" for the aged; and second, that physical illnesses of self or spouse lead to less frequent sexual activity. In turn, disuse leads to atrophy of function or as sex therapists put it: "If you don't use it, you lose it." Even so, with the past few decades, health care has revolutionized the overall vitality of people in their 60s, 70s and 80s.

Middle-aged or old, today's men aged 70 and over

83

are sexually active. Among those who are married, 70 percent still have regular sex, which they perform, on average, about once weekly.

Move up a bracket, to married men age 78 and above, and only 15 percent of them are still having sex on a frequent basis. A couple who are sexually vigorous when middle-aged will, barring debilitating illness, probably remain so long into old age. Certainly there is no physiological reason why they should curtail their sex lives as they age.

One artificial method of helping a man maintain an erection is the use of devices known as "penis rings" or "shaft rings." During an erection these rings can be clamped onto the penis shaft either in front of the scrotum or behind the scrotum, where they trap the blood and allow for a prolonged erection.

**Can a man urinate when he has an erection?**
*No.*                              (References: 47, 76, 85)

A fully erect penis is the surest way to prevent urination. Despite fears, or in a few instances desires, that some men have that they may urinate into their partner's vagina, it *cannot* happen. When the penis is fully erect, an internal urinary sphincter muscle reflexively and involuntarily shuts down and remains tightly clasped; otherwise, the semen's sperm would die when exposed to urine.

Because many men awaken in the morning with a loaded bladder and a urine-induced erection (the average man has three of these "piss hard-ons" weekly; one man in six has one daily), this inability to urinate when fully erect may seem baffling. It is easy to explain, however. The sphincter muscle comes into play only when the penis is at or very near its greatest size, and few things dispell an erection faster than thoughts of urination. The extremely selective coming into play of the sphincter also explains the ability of men to engage in sexual "water sports" and "golden showers" with their partners.

Many men routinely find that their stimulated and erect penises also pass a drop or two of a clear liquid other than semen. This is normal. The fluid's purpose is to lubricate the penis's tip and thereby permit somewhat easier passage into the vagina. Cowper's gland secretion is the substance's technical name and, on average, most men emit a few drops of it. But 21 percent emit none.

### How common is circumcision?

*Before World War II, about half the males in the U. S. were circumcised. Since then, more than 95 percent have been.* (References: 58, 69, 72, 85)

In circumcision, the foreskin (or sheath) that envelops the penis is surgically removed. Because it performs no biological function, the foreskin is routinely removed in most hospital births in the United States today—and about 95 percent of all U.S. births now take place in hospitals. But worldwide, the practice is far from universal.

About half of the world's male population have been circumcised. Egyptians performed circumcision before the year 2000 B.C. and some scholars believe that it may be of Stone Age origin because a stone knife, not a metal knife, is used among most primitive people in the areas where circumcision is practiced.

The Jewish religion requires the circumcision of all males, and although not required in the Koran, it is performed on most Moslem boys as well. Among black Africans the practice is common although *absent* among the Southern Bantu like the Zulu of South Africa, among the East African Nilotic groups, and among some hunters and gatherers like the Bushmen of the Kalahari desert in Southern Africa. However, it is practiced among the Pygmies of Equatorial Africa.

Although not commonly found among the native cultures of America, in South America circumcision is performed among the Moche and Mochita tribes of Peru.

Egyptian and Ethiopian Koptic Christians performed circumcision, but European and American Christians did not widely adopt the practice until the twentieth century. This practice also is not generally a part of the traditions of East Asia. In many Pacific Island societies, a practice known as *supercision* is performed wherein the foreskin is merely slit lengthwise but not completely removed. The purpose is to promote cleanliness and reduce odor.

Circumcision in infancy is now common among Jews and modern Western societies, but among most other societies, including those with an Islamic tradition, circumcision is not usually performed before the age of six, and in many cases is practiced as part of puberty rituals. The Konso of Ethiopia perform the surgery only some time after they have passed the age of 60, to mark the end of sexual activity instead of the beginning.

In the United States today, a small but growing number of parents who identify with the "organic" new-age subculture are insisting that physicians skip this surgery of their children.

Circumcised males may very soon be able to congratulate themselves on a sizable contribution to medical research. In a recent development, the American Cancer Society has begun underwriting experiments that aim at extracting interferon—a natural body protein thought to be of use in combatting cancer—from discarded foreskins. If the research succeeds, circumcision will have been put to use in helping cure cancer patients.

**Do circumcised penises feel more than uncircumcised penises?**
*No.*                              (References: 72, 85)
Myths have long circulated that tout the relative superiority of both circumcised and uncircumcised penises in sex. A foreskinned-penis may be less sensitive than a circumcised one, but at most this difference is minute.

A legal footnote is that in recent years we have witnessed law suits filed by sons against their parents for forcing circumcision upon them in their infancy. In general, the operation is performed within days after birth—long before the child could be capable of having a say in such matters. To our knowledge, all such suits have failed and for good reason. Not only is circumcision mandated by some religions (in Genesis, for instance, God commands: "And he that is eight days old shall be circumcised"), but an uncircumcised penis is more susceptible to disease and infection because the foreskin stands in the way of effective cleansing unless a male is diligent in his hygiene.

**How early can a man have his first orgasm?**
*As early as 2 months of age.* (Reference: 45, 76)

Even though preadolescents are able to achieve orgasm, and many have their first in infancy as early as the age of 2 months, the teen years are when most males initially have this experience. By age 16, more than 90 percent of men have had at least one bona fide orgasm.

A common confusion when it comes to male physiology is to equate ejaculation (the emission of semen from the penis) and orgasm. They are *not* identical. An orgasm, to define it technically, is a release of neuromuscular tension—something like a pleasant sneeze. It can be explosive in force and often causes shuddering. Some males, although not many, even faint during orgasm and nearly all report a momentary loss of consciousness ("the little death"). *No* ejaculation need accompany this process. Unless there has been cultural or psychological tampering, every man, regardless of age, is capable of achieving an orgasm.

**At what age do boys have their first ejaculation?**
*13.88 years is the average.*          (Reference: 76)
The initial ejaculation usually occurs during a male's middle adolescence (13–16). Although the norm is 13+ years, the first ejaculation takes place in some boys as young as 8, and unconfirmed research holds that a few boys ejaculate when they are 6; at the other extreme, some males enter their twenties before first ejaculating.

Infant sexuality is a cardinal tenet of Freudian theory. It is one that is well confirmed. Many are the instances of newly born babies seen fondling their own genitals. Disturbing as some parents find this child's play, there is no cause for worry; it is part of exploring and discovering one's own body. And the infant's genitals are closer to his exploring hands than are his distant toes.

Gender role, the awareness of being male rather than female, does not manifest itself so rapidly as does general sexual awareness. With most children, a few years pass before this knowledge is gained. Nor is a child unerringly right in deciding which gender he or she is. At the age of two or thereabouts, some male children begin to exhibit some feminine behavior, including a fondness for dresses. But because much of our gender-related behavior is culturally and not biologically determined, there is no physiological reason for males to avoid skirts and dresses, a practice common in Scotland as well as in many African and Pacific Island cultures. The causes of mistaken clothing choices in any society are apt to be learned and later unlearned through trial and error.

**How many men have had "wet dreams?"**
*83 percent.*                              (Reference: 47, 76)
By age 45, about five of every six men have experienced a nocturnal emission in which ejaculation occurs spontaneously during sleep. Even thought many writers prefer the term "nocturnal emission" and use that term exclusively, it is a bit misleading. It generally refers to all ejaculations during sleep, regardless of the time of day; and it also refers to emissionless orgasm during sleep. Because "nocturnal emissions" are so common, wet dreams are analyzed in the folklore and mythology of many societies; many primitive peoples believe that a succubus, a female demon, slides under a man during his sleep and prompts the ejaculation. The explanation for

wet dreams is far simpler. In most instances, nothing more mystical than an erotic dream, possibly accompanied by a little unconscious friction against the sheets, is at work.

**At what age do men have their first wet dream?**
*At 14.5 years of age on the average.*
(Reference: 76)

**How many men have multiple orgasms?**
*Fewer than 5 percent of men older than 35.*
(References: 47, 75, 76, 85)

Women (as we discuss in the next chapter) can easily have many orgasms within a single sex act. For men, because ejaculation and orgasm are effectively intertwined, the task is not so simple. When a male ejaculates, he usually discharges semen with the orgasm and most males require a recharging period in order to produce volumes of semen ample for another ejaculation. In addition, Masters and Johnson, in their detailed probing of the physiology of male sexuality, discovered what they call a "refractory period"—a period of time after ejaculation in which a man exhibits marked resistance to *all* sexual stimuli. Not always, however. Many young men, perhaps 20 percent of all adolescents and 9 percent of males between 26 and 30 years of age, report incidences of multiple orgasms. In the medical literature on orgasms an instance is recorded of a pubescent male who had 11 within four hours.

As a male ages, the reported incidence declines. Less than 5 percent of men over 35, for instance, report multiple ejaculations. Yet, devotees of group

sex sometimes report—regardless of age—a re
ability to achieve several ejaculations within a
time-span. Nonetheless, many men still will sm   at
the conversation of the city couple who, while visit-
ing the country, spied a rooster copulating five
times in rapid succession. "How come that tiny
rooster could do it five times in a row," asked the
frustrated wife, "and you can't manage to do it with
me more than once?" Her husband wasn't at a loss
for words: "My dear," he observed, "you'll notice he
isn't doing it more than once with the same hen."
There may be some validity to this story. The novelty
and uniqueness of each new body, group-sex participants concede, go a long way toward kindling the
steady sexual excitement they partially credit for
their multiorgasmic abilities.

#### How much semen is in a man's ejaculate?
*One teaspoonful.*          (References: 72, 94, 141)
That is the average, but there are, naturally, enormous variations in the size of ejaculations from man
to man. Even a given man's ejaculate can vary in
volume from time to time. A good part of the explanation relates to frequency of orgasm. Although a
man's ejaculate, a mix of semen and sperm, is continually replenished by the body, there are limits to
how fast it can be created. A man with many recent
orgasms probably will produce less ejaculate than
one who has not had sex in the near past.

#### How far does ejaculate spurt?
*12–24 inches. (0.3–0.6 meters)*
                    (References: 58, 72, 85, 111)
That answer of course is for an ejaculation that is

free of encumbrances such as a vagina. Variations in this average distance are common, too. In some men, the ejaculate literally dribbles out of the penis and travels essentially no distance. With other men, exactly the opposite is true, and distances of a yard or more are reached. One singer, Lou Reed, recently recorded his desire "to shoot twenty feet of jism." Although there's no confirmed instance of a male hitting that mark, differences in the distance semen travels do give natural rise to a prep school game where the winner is he who shoots the farthest. There is, however, no correlation between the distance potentially or actually traversed by an ejaculation and male potency.

Mohave Indian youths of the Colorado River Valley and Crow youths of Montana are reported to have contests to see whose ejaculate can travel farthest as a result of masturbation. The record for their contests is unknown. The Crow boys also contest the largest penis size and a boy's ability to drag a rock tied to his penis. Boys in the Marquesan Islands of the Pacific are reported to have contests for the fastest ejaculation. We would probably consider their winner to be our loser.

Semen is propelled out of the penis by muscle contractions. These powerful contractions aim at achieving release from the mounting sexual tension that precedes orgasm and ejaculation. Most men have several of these contractions during ejaculation,' which is why the seminal stream comes in spurts. The initial convulsions are often quite strong and arrive at intervals of about 0.8 seconds. Following the first three or four, the rate of occurrence and the force of the convulsions drastically diminish.

**How fast does ejaculate travel?**
*28 miles per hour (45 km/hr)*

(References: 72, 111)

"To bed! Aye, Sweetheart; and I'll come to thee," vowed Malvolio in Shakespeare's *Twelfth night* and his promise did not exaggerate. Ejaculate may not be as fast as a speeding bullet, but the relatively high speed of the initial spurts demonstrates the force behind them. Once the ejaculate enters the female vagina, however, the speed is abruptly and sharply reduced to a comparative crawl of 1–3 centimeters per hour (about a foot every half day).

**How many calories are in one ejaculation?**
*Five.* (Reference: 94)

This is good news for devotees of oral sex and great news for dieters. It is just about impossible to gain weight swallowing a man's ejaculate even though it is rich in protein. Many like the taste; others may find it unpleasant. But, like it or not, "I'm on a diet" is no excuse for omitting ejaculate from one's menu.

**How many sperm are in one ejaculate?**
*200 million.* (References: 13, 72)

Odd as it seems, there are more sperm packed into that teaspoon of ejaculate than there are people living in West Germany, Great Britain, and Italy combined. Furthermore, sperm constitutes only about 2 percent of the average ejaculate. The rest is semen, a mucuslike fluid.

Variations in sperm count from male to male are immense, with counts as low as 0 and as high as 700 million reported. Anything between 20 million and

300 million is considered normal and will effectively fertilize an egg.

Some unconfirmed research results maintain that the type of underwear a man prefers may affect his sperm production. The crux of the argument is that warmer testicle temperatures inhibit sperm growth; and, says this theory, men's jockey (or brief-type) shorts produce hotter conditions than do the boxer variety. But men who wear jockey shorts needn't worry. The correlation between underwear and sperm production is apt to be minute; otherwise, jockey shorts would be a recommended method of birth control.

**How long do sperm live?**
*Four days within a female's body, but only for a few hours when exposed to air.*

(References: 13, 72)

Once safely within a female's system, the hardiest sperm can live for several days as they make their climb toward the eggs. But they are fragile organisms when exposed to air, where most die within minutes and the strongest survive but a few hours. That mortality rate is slim consolation, however, for a female who unknowingly makes contact with still-living sperm—and more than one instance has been documented in which a pregnancy resulted.

**How many sperm generally must one ejaculation provide to impregnate a woman?**
*More than 18 million per ejaculate.*

(References: 13, 72)

Were most of us to have 18 million of anything, we would find the abundance staggering. Not so with sperm. When the sperm count dips much below 18 million, it is unlikely that a man could fertilize an egg. Of course, only a single sperm is needed to do that job, but the mortality rate for sperm after they leave the penis and commence their slow trek through the female's reproduction system is high indeed. For that reason, when the sperm count reads below 18 million, most physicians classify the man as infertile. As long as the reading is not zero, however, conception may still be feasible through artificial insemination, where the hit-and-miss route of coitus is abandoned in favor of a medically induced union of sperm and egg.

**At what age is a boy typically capable of making a girl pregnant?**
*At age 16.* (References: 72, 76)
Achievement of a fertile sperm count marks the last stage of adolescence—a time that also includes the first growth of facial and large amounts of body hair. The age range for this phase is 14–20, but most boys do not have a large enough and viable sperm count until the age of 16.

**Is ejaculation necessary in order to impregnate a woman**
*No.* (Reference:72)
Practitioners of premature withdrawal, who regularly remove the penis from a woman's vagina prior to ejaculation as a birth-control measure, should take particular note of the secretions from the Cowper's gland. So should those who try *coitus reservatus*, in which the penis is inserted into the vagina and intercourse proceeds normally but the

male, quite frequently with success, tries not to ejaculate. Those few drops from the Cowper's gland can thoroughly undo such plans. Although the liquid often is a harmless lubricant, it sometimes unpredictably contains sperm and can effectively impregnate an egg, making premature withdrawal and coitus reservatus nearly worthless methods of birth control. More bad news is that this juice can find its way into the vagina of a woman who pets or makes out with a partner when both are naked. The result can be a pregnancy without copulation.

How many men are infertile?
*Less than 5 percent.* (References: 13, 100)
Involuntary male infertility is relatively rare, as this incidence rate indicates. Curiously, some researchers now suggest that very high sperm counts —ones far above 200 million—too, may be infertile. The theory's root is that sperm crammed too densely into a space will lose their vitality. But this link between high sperm counts and possible infertility is still under investigation and no concrete conclusions can be stated.

We mention involuntary infertility, but many men now opt for *voluntary* infertility as a birth-control technique. This procedure, known as vasectomy, severs the tubes linking the sperm to the path it must travel to exit the penis. It is gaining increasing popularity owing to its low cost (no more than a few hundred dollars, often as little as $50); simplicity (the operation is painless, quick, and can be performed in a doctor's office); and effectiveness (almost 100 percent—in a very, very few cases the severed tubes spontaneously regenerate). A current estimate is that 15 percent—one in seven—of adult, married men have undergone vasectomies.

**At what age do boys begin sex play with girls?**
*8.81 years*                              (Reference: 76)
At a bit less than nine years of age, the average boy has played doctor or mommy-and-daddy or in some other fashion begun to explore prepubescent female bodies and to encourage exploration of his own by females. Such forays into adult sexuality may consist of nothing more than a quick peep into a girl's blouse or a hasty flash of a youthful penis. Although it is rare, some children perform full-fledged sexual intercourse long before puberty. If the male is prepubescent, pregnancy *cannot* result, since he lacks the sperm required to fertilize an egg.

**At what age is a boy considered an adolescent?**
*At 12–13 years of age.*          (References: 70, 76)
Adolescence is the physiological process in which a biologically immature boy grows into a man. It is a lengthy and complicated phase. Its first stage, marked by size increases of the testicles, scrotum, and penis, usually starts when a boy is 12 or 13. The range of normal ages is from 10 to 15.

When Kinsey asked his male respondents when their puberty began, the average answer was 13.7 years, about one year higher than the age we give. But there likely is no discrepancy. Kinsey's males, as is quite common, probably wrongly equated the initial growth of pubic hair with the onset of adolescence. A full third of these males indicated their pubic hair began to grow when they were 13 or 14.

There is no hard-and-fast rule about the sprouting

of pubic hair, but the normal age range is 11–18, with most males experiencing the first growth in the mid-teen years of 13–16. But some initially notice growth when they are as young as 9 (0.2 percent at age 9 or 10) and others lack hair until they reach their twenties (1.0 percent).

Middle adolescence, 13–16, is noteworthy not only for pubic hair growth. This period is generally accompanied by the teenage height spurt, in which several inches are rapidly added to a male's height; the change to a deeper voice; and the development of sperm, although this youthful sperm count may be too low to fertilize an egg.

**Is there a connection between hairiness and sex?**
*Possibly.*                        (References: 94, 98)
Hairiness in men is generally considered less attractive than the absence of body hair by both men and women because it is routinely viewed as less clean. Eugene O'Neil's play *The Hairy Ape* was not unusual in that it was largely based on the upper-class notion that hairiness and sweat were ugly qualities of the lower classes.

Another almost universal "hairy man" stereotype commonly accepted in the United States is that the hairy man is more masculine and more virile. In one study of college students in Illinois a man's hairy arm was perceived to be more masculine, harder, larger, stronger, and associated with a more virile man than an identical hairless arm.

Is beard growth heaviest when sex is anticipated? That is the conclusion of an anonymous anecdotal article that appeared in *Nature* magazine. The writer reported that he spent weekdays on a remote, deserted island and weekends on the populated mainland. He used an electric shaver daily and carefully weighed his beard shavings. The result, he reported, was that beard growth was demonstrably heavier on Fridays, when sex was in the immediate offing, than on other days. There may be some validity to this claim. Growth of facial and body hair is intimately connected with a male's sex hormones, which, of course, play a major role in regulating the quantity of semen in a man's system.

**At what age does a boy first caress a girl's breasts?**
*13.*                                    (References: 61, 76)
Petting, or "making out," is noncoital physical sex play, often involving fondling of the female's breasts and perhaps the genitals of both partners. Common in adult sex as part of coitus, among many teenagers it is an end in itself. In the latter cases, it frequently ends with one or both partners experiencing orgasm.

A few decades ago, only 12 percent of 13-year-olds had caressed a girl's breast. Now about 50 percent have. And 73 percent do so by the time they are 15. A full 90 percent have by 19 years of age. This experimentation with what is often a first stage of petting naturally coincides with middle adolescence and the accompanying changes in a male's physiology.

**At what age does a boy first fondle a girl's clitoris?**
*15.*                                      (Reference: 61)
Over half (55 percent) of all 15-year-olds have digitally probed a girl's vagina; 31 percent got their first touch by 13. By age 18, 77 percent have stroked a female's genitalia.

**How old is a boy when his penis is first stroked by a girl?**

*15.* (Reference: 61)

Here the girls return the favor—and the correlation between the age when a boy first touches a vagina and the first time a girl touches his penis is close enough to suggest that, in many cases, these forms of sex play are going on simultaneously. By age 13, 23 percent have had their penis touched; by 15, 49 percent; by 18, 68 percent.

**How many teenage boys have made love?**

*59 percent.* (References: 61, 66, 95, 131)

That's right: one in two teenage boys has "gone all the way," as the idiom puts it. By age 13, 18 percent have had coitus at least once. By 16, 43 percent have. By age 19, 59 percent—about six out of every ten—have had sex at least once. Do these numbers seem high? Consider this: only five percent of all societies that have undergone anthropological scrutiny place an outright ban on premarital sexual intercourse. *Seventy* percent generally allow it. In our society we're in the awkward position of officially condemning premarital sex—via statements made by many school and religious leaders as well as parents—while unofficially condoning it. Study after study drives this paradox home. And no study comes up with findings that differ significantly from the ones we cite. The U.S. House of Representatives, for instance, recently released documents showing that by their estimate 50 percent of teenage boys have had sex. Another current study pegged the number at 56 percent of 18-year-old boys. The point these numbers make is that premarital sex is deeply entrenched in our society.

### How often do teenage boys masturbate?

*2–3 times weekly.*          (References: 29, 30, 61)
Ask boys ages 17 and 18 how often they masturbate and 34 percent say two or three times a week. But 1 percent do it more than once daily, 13 percent do it every day, and 20 percent do it less than once monthly or not at all.

Among the ancient Egyptians the creation of the universe was believed to have resulted from the god Atum's masturbation, and his hand was considered his divine partner. One source claims that the Egyptian pharaoh was masturbated with the hand of the high priest of On (Heliopolis), who simultaneously sodomized pharaoh. The Sumerian priests are also believed to have masturbated as a ritual in honor of the divine masturbation of their god, Enki.

### How does a male learn to masturbate?
*In conversation and from printed sources.*
                              (References: 47, 76)
Only 25 percent of all males say they discovered masturbation on their own. The rest admit the initial clues and sometimes detailed instructions were provided by friends, relatives, or the media. Ironically, in years now past the very writers and preachers who strenuously protested "self-abuse"—as they were fond of calling masturbation—probably were instrumental in showing many boys the way, for such condemnation only seems to arouse a youth's curiosity.

**How many first ejaculations come from masturbation?**

*60 percent.*                    (Reference: 47, 76)

More than 6 males in 10 report that their first ejaculation resulted from self-manipulation or masturbation. It is importanut to realize that many of these males were masturbating without knowing exactly what they were doing. Ejaculation, in those instances, came as a surprise. Because the physical sensations are pleasant, even when the ejaculation is unanticipated, few boys express fear at the result. Now that our culture has largely abandoned warnings about the harmful effects of masturbation and has seen the condemnation of "playing with oneself" reduced, the anxiety associated with masturbation can be reduced even more. We are reminded, for instance, of one of our pubescent patients, a young man with considerable religious training, who reported that he often masturbated. When asked if he experienced any guilt about matsturbation, he rapidly replied: "Of course not. If God did not want me to masturbate, he would have made my arms too short to reach it."

For those males who first ejaculate *without* masturbating, nocturnal emissions ("wet dreams") are the most common cause. Nearly one third of all males first ejaculate in this fashion.

Other major sources include spontaneous ejaculations, where incidental friction (from climbing a tree or while wrestling, for example) triggers the reaction (2.8 percent); homosexual activities (2 percent); heterosexual petting (.06 percent); and coitus (0.6 percent).

**At what age does male masturbation result in orgasm?**

*13.*                    (References: 47, 61, 131)

By age 13, 75 percent of all boys have masturbated to orgasm with 12 percent doing it before turning 10; and 39 percent before turning 13. A few infants, some as young as 7 months, have been observed masturbating to orgasm. And, at the other extreme, some males wait until they enter their twenties.

**How many men have masturbated to orgasm?**

*97 percent.*           (References: 47, 58, 104, 112)

No, it will *not* make you or anybody else blind or insane. It won't even cause pimples. What masturbation will do is provide sexual relief, and almost every man you meet has tried his hand at it at least once.

How do men masturbate? Teenage tales of milk bottles or shoe boxes equipped with deftly measured holes notwithstanding, most men (60 percent) lie on their backs and 91 percent manipulate their penis with one of their hands until orgasm. A few do it while lying facedown on a bed and vigorously rubbing. In this substitute for solo intercourse, the penis is rubbed against the sheetcovered mattress. Other men stand or sit up. A small number do not rely on hands alone but explore a myriad of techniques including artificial vaginas made of pliable rubber that are sold in sex shops. "Love Dolls"—life-size plastic replicas of women, complete with breasts and a "vaginal" opening—also attract a following.

This is just a peek at the surface glimmer of the

amazing array of variations on this solitary theme. Masturbation, in most cases, is a self-refined skill; and, as any sex therapist can testify, there are no limits to the ingenuity that is applied to this skill. In one case, an ex-minister approached us with a desire to break his long standing habit of masturbating with coarse sandpaper. He was unable, he said, to reach orgasm and ejaculate in any other way, coitus included. The therapy, in this case, involved having him masturbate while gradually reducing the coarseness of the grade of sandpaper until he was happy using a grade which was almost as soft as velvet. After accepting that, the minister was induced to use just his dry hand, then a hand lubricated with KY ointment, and finally he successfully graduated to the moist, smooth environment of normal sex with a woman. Incidentally, the Marquesans of the Pacific masturbate with wet sand.

In another case, a senior executive from the South came to us for help because he liked to masturbate—but only with a martini stirrer, a technique he thought neurotic. Over time, with behavior-modification techniques, we gradually switched him from this prop to using his hand. Before coming to us, he was warned by a prominent Beverly Hills psychoanalyst not to proceed with behavior modification in this deeply entrenched case because of the danger of "symptom substitution," an erroneous belief that when one bad habit is broken, the root causes remain and as a result the former bad habit is replaced by a new but equally distasteful habit. After his problem had seen solved, our patient asked, "Considering that I consulted an analyst who believed in symptom substitution, some day can I expect to find that same analyst in a posh restaurant stirring his martini with his penis while whistling 'Dixie'?"

### How long does it take to masturbate to orgasm?
*2.8 minutes.*                    (References: 47, 76)

The hand may not be quicker than the eye but in this case it is mighty fast indeed. Although 2.8 minutes is the average, deliberate prolonging of masturbation beyond that time is common.

### How long does premarital foreplay usually last?
*32 minutes on the average.*    (References: 47, 76)

Foreplay is petting that culminates in sexual intercourse. When the partners are unmarried, their foreplay lasts about half an hour; over two thirds of the men finish their foreplay in 32 minutes or less, and 25 percent complete theirs in one hour or more. (See chapter 5 for women's surprisingly different report.)

Remember, however, that foreplay is a culturally determined and learned behavior. In some societies, for instance, nose kissing is considered far more erotic than kisses on the lips, and kissing is entirely absent among many primitive societies. It is not surprising, when matters are placed in this light, that many, many people approach sex with a ritualized order for foreplay's sequence—typically, kissing, petting, sometimes oral sex, and finally intercourse. Some studies elaborate upon this theme by pointing out that not only do many adolescents have in mind an order, but also a firm timetable—one that allows so many minutes for kissing, then so much time for fondling breasts, etc. A consequence is the development of the notion that some boys and girls are "fast" or "slow"—labels that do not so much refer to their willingness to have sex but rather the *speed* with which they like to progress through the foreplay sequence.

### Who is a man's first sex partner?

*A steady date.* (Reference: 2)

One man in four (25 percent) accomplishes his initial lovemaking with a "steady." "Someone you had known but not dated" accounted for the first time with 17 percent. Acquaintances or strangers obliged 15 percent. Small numbers of "firsts" are credited to prostitutes (12 percent); spouses (9 percent); fiancées (7 percent); and relatives (2 percent).

### How many men enjoyed making love their first time?

*72 percent.* (References: 2, 47, 61)

Men definitely do like their first sex, although 28 percent did report that they received no enjoyment whatsoever. Another 18 percent say they experienced "little" enjoyment and 14 percent received "some." But 40 percent experienced "much" enjoyment, they happily report.

As high as the number is for men who experienced no fun during their initial sexual encounter, it is not startling. Sex should be pleasureful, but one's first coitus often can be somewhat frightening. Many boys and men feel they are expected to know exactly how to do it when it comes to sex. Toss in the fear of causing pregnancy, the fear of infection from V.D., and the fear from moral strictures against premarital sex—and the results can be less than pleasureful. A beginning cook also has fears and cannot realistically hope to soon win a Cordon Bleu award; but a little success goes a long way in adding pleasure to the experience.

Men generally have sex with 7 or more partners before marriage. Men perhaps should count themselves fortunate. When a male bee has sex for the first time with his queen, his penis breaks off within her and he promptly bleeds to death. Sex for humans, happily, is not so final.

Nonetheless, 17 percent of males have premarital sex with but one female. Ten percent said they had two lovers. Another 24 percent listed the number of their partners at 3–6; and the largest group, 29 percent, reported seven or more. The remaining males in this survey either had not yet had *any* sex or had not had premarital sex.

Those number are for adults. Ask teenagers the same question and not only do the results differ, they provide a solid precursor for what future surveys of adults will reveal. Among male nonvirgins ages 15–16, 23 percent report they have had one partner; 54 percent have had more than one, but six or fewer; and 28 percent report more than six. Move up an age bracket to boys ages 17 and 18, and 19 percent report one partner; 60 percent say more than one but less than six; and 19 percent have made love with more than six girls.

**How many men have had sex with a prostitute?**
*30 percent.*                    (References: 58, 67, 124)

This number is a steadily declining one. A few decades ago, many males had their first coital experience with a "hooker," with the tab picked up, in many cases, by a sympathetic father, uncle, or older pal. Today, only 9 percent of males make this claim. This is not to say that the oldest profession is dying —a good estimate is that, adding up the takes of streetwalkers through highly paid call girls, a minimum of $100 million annually exchanges hands—but in a society that makes free sex widely available, paying for sex has become less common. In one recent survey, only 19 percent of the under-35 males with some college education had ever visited a prostitute. That compares with 52 percent of the college-educated males over 35. In another survey, this one of college students only, just 4 percent claimed to have paid for sex at least once. Certainly it is arguable that older, not younger, males have always constituted the major source of "johns" or "tricks" for "women in the life," as prostitutes themselves put it; and it can further be maintained that many of these now-young men who so far have eschewed paid sex may some day find themselves visiting a red-light district. This is an issue only future surveys can resolve.

Although considered "the oldest profession," prostitution has probably been around only a relatively short time within the 2.5 to 3.5 million years of human life. "Subsistence prostitution" (prostitution as the only source of income) is unknown among hunting and gathering societies. It therefore seems unlikely to date from before about 15,000 B.C., the earliest date that agriculture is believed to have come into existence, and probably came into full blossom with the flourishing of city life between 4,000 and 3,000 B.C.

In the Old Testament prostitution seems to have been permitted, but priests were forbidden from marrying harlots. Also, daughters of priests were prohibited from becoming harlots under penalty of death by fire. (*Leviticus* 21:7–9).

In pre-Islamic Arabia, prostitution was seen as a type of marriage for a short, specified period of time. This practice was also adopted by many Shi'ite Moslems and is still widely practiced in Iran. A marriage contract is agreed upon for a limited time, calling for a small dowry and no legal rights for the woman after the contract's expiration. This contract often is for only one night, although any children that result are considered legitimate.

For those enjoying this practice, these marriages are justified by the Koran "and you are allowed to seek out wives with your wealth in decorous conduct, but not in fornication, but give them their reward for what you have enjoyed of them in keeping with your promise." (Qur'aan 4:24)

**How many American men make love in the missionary position?**
*99.3 percent.*                           (References: 16, 17, 47)
Woman on the bottom, man on top remains the favorite position for coitus among American men. The name, according to Alex Comfort, was invented by Polynesian natives, who preferred a squatting sexual position, to describe the erotic conduct of Europeans in their midst. Other positions are more popular in other cultures, particularly in Asia where it is more common to find women on top and men below. Books such as *Joy of Sex* have aided many couples in discovering new positions. But good as

109

author Comfort is, he is no pioneer. The *Kama Sutra* enumerates dozens of positions, although many can be recommended only to those with the physical dexterity of a world-class gymnast.

**When making love how long do most men take to ejaculate?**
*Less than 6 minutes.* (Reference: 47)
Ask this question of randomly chosen men and they will tell you they ejaculate after initial penetration in times ranging from a few seconds to a few hours. But more than 60 percent of all men put their time at six minutes or less with most coming in close to the six-minute mark itself. Twenty-three percent say their coitus lasts longer than 10 minutes. But 18 percent say they ejaculate in less than two minutes.

How long should coitus be? With rattlesnakes, it often lasts 24 hours—or even longer. With humans sex should be a *mutually* satisfying and pleasant experience. At a minimum coitus should last long enough to satisfy both of the partners most of the time.

**How many calories are expended while making love?**

*150.* (Reference: 142)
What more pleasant way to work off an ounce of chocolate? Sex is exercise and by comparison is more rigorous than golf. Play 18 holes and you will burn up only 118 calories—and that is if you do not use a motorized cart. A single act of coitus consumes 32 more calories—enough to gobble an extra carrot or two between meals.

**How many men are impotent?**
5 *percent*                              (Reference: 47)
Almost all men have at one time experienced impotency. Anxiety, large doses of alcohol or other drugs from heroin through common prescription pharmaceuticals, and sexual satiation can all cause temporary impotency.

A shade over 5 percent of all males admit to being "more than incidentally" impotent. A cruel irony of impotence is its self-renewing nature. Because anxiety is a prime cause, a male who is anxious about getting an erection is more likely to fail than is a male with fewer gnawing worries.

**How many types of impotence are there?**
3.                            (References: 112, 128)
Incidental, primary, and secondary are the three basic types. Incidental impotence is the least troublesome from a clinician's point of view and probably from the male's as well. A man who, for instance, has drunk excessively and fails to get an erection need do little fretting about the cause. Nor is the occasional failure to get an erection, even without such obvious underlying factors as alcohol, uncommon. Fatigue, distraction, and fear can play roles in this type of impotence. The best advice for sufferers is not to worry; their predicament, while perhaps annoying, is normal.

Primary impotence is a different matter. This is when a male has *never* had an erection sufficient for entering a vagina. Many of these cases have physical roots; severe diabetes, for instance. A thorough medical probing of the male's sexual anatomy and health is in order for those experiencing primary impotence.

111

If no physiological cause is found, then the routine Masters and Johnson technique discussed below should work in a majority of cases.

The more common secondary impotence afflicts males who at one time achieved sufficiently hard erections but now no longer can. A full 97 percent of these cases are psychological in origin.

In the treatment of secondary and primary impotence it is always assumed that whatever the original cause of a man's impotent condition, the current dysfunction is maintained by the fear that if he attempts sex he will not be able to "perform" because of his previous impotence. Because fear inhibits sexual arousal, this "performance anxiety" is the immediate cause of his current impotence. Therefore the therapeutic object is to eliminate fear. Dr. Joseph Wolpe, the father of behavior therapy, observed that when sexual arousal occurs in the absence of fear, penile potency is restored.

Masters and Johnson theorized the problem differently. Their studies led them to believe that sexual functioning is the result of successfully completing a number of graduated sexual physiological stages.

B. F. Skinner's students theorized that all learning occurs in completing gradual behavioral (rather than physiological) steps of increasing difficulty, each of which is rewarded. Therefore adequate sexual behavior can be learned in the same way.

It is fascinating that all three theories lead to exactly the same treatment program, which is called "Desensitization" by Wolpe followers, "Sensate Focusing" by Masters and Johnson followers, and "Successive Approximations" by Skinner followers.

Put in easily understood terms, the program consists of gradually helping a patient succeed at completing several discrete steps that in life usually lead to intercourse but which in treatment are the ends in themselves: conversation without necking; necking without petting; petting without penetration; and finally penetration. The success rate of this treatment for incidental impotence is almost 100 percent, for secondary impotence about 80 percent, and for primary impotence close to 70 percent. Recently, some therapists have reported that they have been unable to replicate the results reported by Masters and Johnson. Our clinical experience with over 1,000 cases at the Center for Behavior Therapy in Beverly Hills consistently replicates Masters and Johnson's success rate, and we can only conclude that these other therapists wish to spend their time establishing a reputation as critics rather than in improving their clinical competence. Masters and Johnson were lonely pioneers in develping a successful treatment program that now alleviates the suffering of countless men and women throughout the world. Their achievements should remain untarnished by the criticism of less inspired sex therapists.

In cases in which treatment has failed or has not been tried in recent years, researchers have experimented successfully with surgical implanting of plastics into the penis. After the implant, the penis is always hard enough for penetration.

Ironically, however, researchers have long been plagued by cases in which it proved impossible to accurately determine whether the root causes were physical or psychological. But even that problem is nearing solution. A very inexpensive technique employed by some physicians and therapists involves tightly gluing a strip of postage stamps around the penis before the patient retires for the night. Odd as that may sound, evidence suggests that it works. The crux of the theory is that most males—including those whose impotence is psychological in origin—get erections during sleep. Thus, if the glue seal is broken in the morning, the researcher (and patient) are pointed in the direction of a search for underlying psychological matters. Granted, this technique is far from foolproof, but it is a very inexpensive way to get a feel for the problem's dimensions.

### How many men come too quickly?
*Answer unknown.*          (References: 47, 84)
There is considerable difficulty in defining what constitutes "too soon." With many men, "too soon" means ejaculating even before the penis enters the vagina. With others, it is having an orgasmic ejaculation within seconds after penetration. Other definitions are possible. Some researchers use time as the criterion, with men who are unable to control ejaculation for at least 30 seconds counted as premature. Eminent sex researchers Masters and Johnson, on the other hand, use a more sensitive definition. For them, a male whose partner does not reach orgasm in at least half their matings is a premature ejaculator. Although we do not know what constitutes "too soon," 0.5 percent of men routinely orgasm in coitus within 24 seconds of penetration, 3 percent climax in less than 1 minute and 18 percent climax in less than 2 minutes.

Fortunately for sufferers, new therapeutic techniques are many, and successes in curbing this tendency now are frequent. The most common of these methods is the "squeeze technique" in which the premature ejaculator's partner pinches or presses hard on his penis immediately after he achieves an erection. Sex play is interspersed with squeezing whenever the male senses an approaching ejaculation. Soon enough, the typical result of this therapy is a fully cured patient.

Another technique—this one developed at the Beverly Hills' Center for Behavior Therapy—revolves around masturbation. In questioning one premature ejaculator we discovered he never masturbated. We wondered, if in this case, the man's seminal vessels might be overfilling and if, as a result, his quick ejaculations were the body's way of relieving that pressure. So we suggested that he masturbate with some regularity and, in consequence, he happily reported back that his premature ejaculation had entirely ceased, a condition that was maintained throughout the four years of follow-up we did on this patient. With his success in mind, we began to recommend masturbation before intercourse to all premature ejaculators. In the process we discovered that many men avidly avoid masturbation before sex in the mistaken belief that they will not then be able to achieve another erection. Truth is, however, *a healthy man is ordinarily capable of almost endless erections* even if he has ejaculated two or three times, because erections (unlike ejaculations themselves) do not deplete semen. Remember, a concert pianist often practices immediately before a performance to improve the performance, and masturbating before coitus can be quite helpful in improving the staying power of many men.

**Are there men who fail to ejaculate during orgasm?**
*Yes.*                                          (Reference: 72)
Discounting men who use premature withdrawal or coitus reservatus and others who may occasionally get distracted during sex, about 1 in every 700 males consistently fails to ejaculate regardless of how hard he tries. As advantageous as this might seem, this disability is extraordinarily unpleasant for those who suffer from it. Their coitus never culminates in the intensely satisfying release that ejaculation brings. Due to the rarity of this disorder, reliable clinical solutions are still being explored—and the best success rates are found with males who can ejaculate in ways other than intercourse, such as masturbation or oral sex.

Another rare disorder is priapism, named after Priapus of Greek mythology. The son of Aphrodite (the god of love) and Dionysus (the god of wine), Priapus invariably is depicted in art with an erection. So it goes for those afflicted with the disorder that bears his name. Sufferers forever possess a hardened penis. Nor is this a boon. The condition can cause extreme pain, along with palpable social discomfort. Unfortunately for the sufferers, cures prove extremely difficult.

**Can a man die during orgasm?**
*Yes.*                                     (References: 85, 142)
Readers of English Renaissance poetry will smile at this question. In that era, "die" and its relatives

often found their way into poems as puns, as in this line from Shakespeare's Sonnet 146: "Death once dead, there's no more dying then." Know the Renaissance code and the way to parse that line is: Die and then there's no more sex, with *death* serving as a complex pun since it is used both literally and to make a smiling statement about the improbability of multiple orgasms in males.

That playful poetry aside, however, death in orgasm can be a serious and real concern. We are all familiar with reports and rumors of public figures who quite literally died in the heat of passion. Two who are known to have done so are Attila the Hun and Pope Leo VIII. These tales are not figments of crazed antisex minds. It is possible to expire in coitus, particularly for someone with a weak heart or circulatory system. During orgasm, a male's heart rate soars to as many as 160 beats per minute (60–80 is normal for a resting male). For some hearts, that strain is too much to take and the result can be a heart attack or stroke and possibly death.

Such fears should never, however, become a morbid concern for healthy males. A very few males do faint at the moment of orgasm. Frightening as that is for the partner, permanent physical damage does not usually result for either the fainter or the witness. But more than one male has been embarrassed when a solicitous partner hurriedly called paramedics to the scene. For those with heart troubles, however, a frank discussion with a knowledgeable physician is in order. Sex, in many ways, is a strenuous exercise. A heart patient would not take up rugby without first talking to his doctor, and the same precautions can be applied to bedroom sports, although sex can

117

be performed at a mild pace and give just as much pleasure to both partners even when one must be careful of his heart condition.

But to end on a lighter note, we are reminded of the story of a sultan who came equipped—as most do—with a sizable harem. One warm evening our sultan found himself in an especially amorous mood, so he summoned his eunuch to fetch and carry one of his wives to him for sex. The eunuch rushed to comply; the sultan had his fill, and then ordered the eunuch to carry this wife away and to return with another. So the eunuch did. When finished with this second wife, the sultan again commanded the eunuch to hastily carry that one away and to carry in yet a third. This done, the sultan again got down to sex and soon sated his appetite for this wife as well, but he wanted yet another. "Haul her away and bring me one more," he ordered. But as he struggled to lift the third wife, the eunuch suddenly dropped dead. This all goes to prove that it's not the fornicating that kills but the running around.

### Is there sex after death?

*Yes, but only for women.*                      (Reference: 58)

Yes, there is sex and even marriage after death. Ancient Egyptians refused to give the bodies of beautiful women to embalmers immediately after death for fear of the known practice of sexual violation (necrophilia). Among the Luo of East Africa, a stranger must have sex with the corpse of any girl who dies a virgin in order to pacify her spirit's desire to have children. Necrophilia is also known to be practiced by the Kainoutu of New Guinea's Eastern Highlands. No known counterpart for men exists

118

except the practice of "ghost marriage," where a childless man who has died will be married to a woman, who will then bear a child which can be credited to the deceased man's account. Nonetheless, it is an interesting note that Kinsey never met anyone that he regarded as a genuine necrophiliac in his surveys of American sexuality.

**On how many teenage boys has oral sex been performed**
*54 percent.*                    (Reference: 61)
Less than a generation ago, oral sex among teenagers was hardly practiced. There are few more graphic demonstrations of the extent of this culture's sexual revolution than the fact that one 18-year-old out of every two has been fellated by a female. And 33 percent of boys 15 and 16 make the same claim.

**On how many men has oral sex been performed?**
*77 percent.*                 (References: 2, 111)
Fellatio (oral-genital stimulation of the penis) is now very popular in the U. S. in spite of being condemned for centuries as immoral and even illegal. Thirty-four percent of all males cite it as a frequent part of their sex play. Only 3 percent say they have never had it and "would not permit it." But another 20 percent admit they have not had it, but would love to. And, incidentally, 0.5 percent of men say they have performed fellatio on themselves.

**How many teenage boys have performed oral sex on girls?**
*56 percent.*                    (Reference: 61)
We are talking of 18 year-olds—of whom more

than half have performed oral sex on a female. Among 15- and 16-year-old boys, 31 percent have.

What is significant in looking at the fellatio and cunnilingus numbers for teenagers is not the difference—the two-point spread between 54 and 56 percent is too small to be consequential—but the likelihood that the percentages are so close because the boys and girls are exchanging oral favors. Interesting as well is that the corresponding percentages for adults also differ by a scant two points although the adult numbers are significantly higher than those for teenagers.

**How many men have performed oral sex on a woman??**
*79 percent.*                              (Reference: 2)
Cunnilingus is the practice whereby the male uses his mouth and tongue to stimulate a female's genital area, sometimes to orgasm. Like fellatio, its popularity is increasing, and 38 percent of all males say it is a regular course on their sexual menu. Seven percent say it is "unlikely" they would ever try it; and 14 percent have not done it but desire the opportunity.

**How many men have particpiated in incest?**
*3.2 percent.*          (References: 47, 58, 67, 126)
In Western societies, no moral ban is firmer, more inflexible than the one against sex with relatives. Incest is prohibited in every known culture, although the boundaries of what constitutes incest vary considerably from society to society. In some, sex with any relative is banned. In others, only sex between adult relatives is prohibited. Some cultures permit

casual sex involving prepubescent children and adult relatives; they view this as solid sex education. In still others, the ban applies only to the immediate family—brothers, sisters, father and mother.

Incestual mother–son matings among primates have rarely been reported. Among the Masai of Africa the cure for a bridegroom's impotence is to require him to copulate with his mother. However, in all other situations mother–son relationships are universally prohibited.

Brother–sister marriages have been common in some societies, especially in ancient Egypt. Cleopatra was married to her brother, who was also her uncle. She had him murdered at the age of 12 so that she could court Julius Caesar and Mark Anthony.

Half brother/half sister marriages were common in the ancient mid-East, even though in *Leviticus* half-sibling marriages are prohibited. On the Pacific Isle of Bali brother–sister marriages are prohibited unless they are between twins, who are believed to have been intimate in the womb before birth.

Father–daughter incest has occasionally been institutionalized among ruling families in several societies. The Persian emperor Artaxerxes is reported to have married his daughter, and the Egyptian pharaoh Amenophis III married four of his own daughters.

A father is required to deflower his own daughter before her marriage among the Orang-sakai of Africa, the Eastern Mollucks of Indonesia, and several groups from Senegal.

In the United States, our taboo usually includes the immediate family plus aunts, uncles, first cousins, and grandparents. Only quite distant relatives such as second cousins are permissible sex partners. The United States, perhaps because of the rigidity and breadth of its ban, is generally considered to have the lowest incidence of incest among developed nations. New Zealand, by contrast, is cited as having the highest.

But incest definitely does occur in the United States. The most common partners for males are female cousins (with whom 1.6 percents of males have intercourse) and sisters (.06 percent).

Take a broader view of incest than just coitus, and the numbers of males who say they have tried it goes up accordingly. When *all* sex acts are counted (petting, fellatio, cunnilingus, etc.) 13.5 percent of males admit to past heterosexual incest. Another 0.5 percent acknowledge acts of homosexual incest.

No matter how we choose to precisely define incest, however, there remain solid scientific underpinnings for prohibitions against it when adults are involved. That is because inbreeding runs a risk that children born of such matings may exhibit marked genetic deformities such as retardation, hemophelia, and blindness.

**How many men have performed heterosexual anal intercourse?**
*60 percent.*                    (References: 67, 75)
Sodomy ("buggery") is another sexual activity that has been tried by the majority of men. (The term *sodomy* refers to anal intercourse and originated in the Bible when Lot refused to deliver two angels sent by God to the men of Sodom who wanted to gangrape them.) The anus sphincter muscle is ordinarily far tighter than the vagina's. Because the sphincter

is so tight, many couples prefer to make the going easier by first applying a few dabs of lubricant, such as KY, to the penis and to the anus. Penis insertion should proceed slowly and with considerable attention to the sensations both partners are feeling.

One worry those who try anal intercourse likely need not have is that the female partner's anal sphincter will collapse—although some who are repulsed by this recreation cite that as a contributing reason. It is true that some people do suffer from stretched or torn sphincter muscles but the cause is rarely if ever normal anal intercourse. Usually more exotic penetration is the culprit; with some couples (often homosexual) the sphincter collapses as a result of frequent "fist-fucking" (when a clenched fist is inserted into the anus). Bottles, whiskey glasses, baseball bats, and the like have all been inserted, at one time or another, into anuses. The results sometimes are catastrophic. But those are fears that need not worry couples who limit penetration to a penis.

**How many men have tried sadomasochism?**

*About 5 percent.* (References: 67, 143)

Sexual sadomasochism involves administering and receiving a stimulus that ordinarily would be thought painful but during sexual excitation may be experienced as decidedly pleasurable, for either or both parties. This is *not* the same as wife beating, where the motive for force is brutal intimidation, not sensual gratification. Sadomasochism, make no mistake, is a sexy experience for those who fancy it. Sadists were once thought to be exclusively on the giving end of pain; masochists on the receiving end. But those distinctions, while once believed to be hard and fast, are often blurred, with many individuals liking both. Major cities feature "S&M" parlors where, for a fee, a client can be whipped by the lady of his choice or sometimes whip a lady, although the latter often is a bit more difficult to arrange. Costumes ranging from police uniforms to Nazi garb are frequently part of S&M. So are mechanical props such as elaborately ornate whips, replicas of medieval torture racks, and mock jail cells. In the midst of these goings-on, many devotees of S&M routinely achieve orgasm.

In terms of incidence, about 10 percent of single men say they have engaged in sadomasochism at least once. Three percent of married men have. And, by a huge two-to-one majority, heterosexual men much prefer to give rather than receive in S&M play.

By contrast, sexual sadomasochism is very rare among primitive societies. Its popularity in Western societies may be related to the vivid tales of the sufferings of religious martyrs.

**How many men have reached orgasm with an animal?**
*5 percent.*                    (References: 58, 75, 76, 143)
The most common animal mates for humans have been four-legged, i.e., sheep, calves, burros, and dogs, although chicken hens have also attracted male sexual attention. Vaginal coitus is the most frequently used technique, although another popular method is to induce the animal—often an infant that is still suckling—to perform fellatio. While bestiality is severely frowned upon in our culture, in a few societies it is tacitly accepted and often is thought to be distinctly more acceptable than homosexuality.

Throughout most of the world, the practice of male sexual relations with animals usually is less related to a man's genuinely being turned on to animals than to either ritual behavior or the unavailability of human partners.

The Ijo of Africa required every boy to copulate successfully with a specific female sheep before witnesses, so that they could certify that his performance was adequate enough to enable him to marry. If his performance was not judged satisfactory, he was required to try again the following year.

The Yoruba of Africa have given up the ritual whereby an adolescent boy was required to copulate with the warm body of the first antelope he ever killed. A nineteenth-century naturalist, Richard Burton, described Middle Eastern male natives copulating with female crocodiles who were on their backs and in a position where they were helpless to defend themselves.

Although bestiality is condemned by most societies, among those who tolerate it are the Copper Eskimo of Alaska, the Hopi of the Southwestern U.S., the Kaisaians of Indonesia, and the Masai of Africa. When Kinsey first published his findings on the incidence of bestiality in his sample of U.S. men, his urban readers were shocked by the idea that so many men could have made it with animals, and they judged the figure 8 percent totally unrealistic and unreliable. This is because in Western culture bestiality is rare in urban areas, but is more common in rural areas where Kinsey found that 17 percent of boys had had some experience and at least one orgasm through animal contact.

A more recent survey posed precisely the same

question to its respondents as Kinsey had asked, and 5 percent of the males affirmed that they had reached orgasm with an animal on at least one occasion. Although that second figure is slightly lower than Kinsey's, there were probably fewer men of rural background in the more recent survey. This is attributable to the decline of the rural population from 12 percent of the U.S. population 30 years ago to less than 5 percent today; and to the geography of Kinsey's survey, which was conducted mostly in the then more rural Midwest.

**At what age does a man marry for the first time?**
23.                               (References: 58, 136)
In our society this average number creeps ever upward as the society lessens its pressures on young men and women to settle into a married homelife. One consequence of the increasing age at first marriage, however, is what we might term "quasi-marriage"— the increasingly popular arrangement in which a man and woman live together in a relationship that differs from marriage only by lacking official sanctions.

The Australian Aborigines and the Yanomano of South America would often betroth female children before they were even born. However, it is interesting that although in some societies female children are routinely married to mature or even aged men, in no society are male children ever married to older women.

**What is the largest number of marriages reported for one man?**
20.                                     (Reference: 88)
The greatest number of serially monogamous mar-

126

riages is 20, accomplished by an American, Glynn de Moss Wolfe. He seems to have been married twice to two of the women and was listed as having only 18 wives.

### What is the duration of marital foreplay?
*17 minutes.* (Reference: 47)
Men report that they spend an average of 17 minutes in marital foreplay. This compares to 32 minutes average for premarital foreplay, and only 5 percent of married men report a 30-minute or longer prelude to penetration.

### How frequently does a married man make love?
*2.5 times weekly.* (References: 47, 67, 138, 139)
Few questions are asked more often in sex therapy than this one. Several surveys provide firm statistical guides. In one, 32 percent of married couples make love 6–10 times monthly. Eight percent did it 20 or more times each month, but 2 percent did not do it at all.

Another survey uncovered similar responses. Its data show that the average weekly frequency for men ages 18–24 is 3.25 times; for those 25–34, 2.55 times; for those 55 and over, 1.00 times.

### How many married men have had sex before they were maried?
*90 percent.* (Reference: 67)
No matter how old a man is, odds are that he had sex before his wedding. But younger men, those 24 and under are the likeliest—95 percent made love at least once before marrying. In the 35–44 age bracket, 86 percent did. At 55 and older, 84 percent did.

127

**What was the most children fathered by one man?**
*888 (548 sons and 340 daughters).*

An incredible 888 children were born to Moulay Ismail "the Terrible" (1672–1727), sultan of Morocco. The Shah of Persia Fath Ali, is reported to have had 714 offspring (154 sons and 560 daughters).

**How many married men have had extramarital sex?**
*40 percent.*                                 (Reference: 2)

Adultery may be considered a sinful pastime by some people, but there are millions of participants. Fourteen percent have had sex with six or more extramarital partners; 6 percent did it with four or five; 10 percent with two or three; and another 10 percent with just one. And, of course, 60 percent have never wandered off the marital pasture.

**How long does the average marriage last?**
*6.6 years.*                                 (References: 4, 136)

**How many sex partners can a man expect after divorce?**
*8.5 per year.*                                 (References: 67, 143)

With one divorce for every two marriages and a rate nearer one-to-one in some states such as California, the nature of post-divorce sex life is on the mind of almost every man who is in the process of dissolving his marriage. But this is certain: there is plenty of sex afterward. *Every* man contacted in one recent survey found a post-divorce sex life and they had, on average, 8.5 partners per year.

**Are there aphrodisiacs for men?**
*Yes*                                 (References: 58, 72)

Aphrodisiacs are substances used to produce, heighten or sustain sexual excitement. The number of substances for which aphrodisiac claims are made are too numerous to list here.

Most of these substances are useless except for their "placebo effect"—the psychologically beneficial effect that any medication, no matter how inert, has on a user who believes that it will help his condition.

Most of the world's ineffective aphrodisiacs are derived from animal genitalia or penislike objects, such as the bull's testicles in Ancient Rome, the white rhinoserous horn in Asia, and the lion's penis in Africa. Some ineffective so-called aphrodisiacs have been derived from substances resembling female genitalia such as vanilla root in Ancient Rome, oysters in Europe and the U.S., and many varieties of eggs throughout the world. One interesting note: because of the similarity of the vanilla root to female genitalia, the word vanilla is believed to be derived from the Spanish word *vaina* which was derived from the Latin word "vagina." Even so, it has no known aphrodisiac powers. Some societies believe spicy hot foods can induce spicy hot passion, others prefer ground up spiders, crickets, or even a mixture of bat's blood and donkey milk.

For most of the active drugs used in our society for which aphrodisiac claims are made, we suggest that they be viewed as two separate groups: "sexual disinhibitors" and "sexual enhancers." No two people have the *exact* same inhibitions and associated anxiety responses to specific sexual practices, nor do any two people have exactly the same physiological responses to every drug. As a result, it is to be expected that different people report widely differing aphrodisiac or non-aphrodisiac reactions to the various disinhibiting drugs such as alcohol, tranquilizers, marijuana, opium, or heroin. All of these disinhibiting drugs when used in excess of an amount needed to reduce anxiety reduce sexual appetites and sexual functions.

The drugs that can be classified as sexual enhancers add some additional physiological or psychological responses to the normal sexual stimuli, such as enlarged blood vessels, faster heartbeat, increased adrenaline or an altered state of consciousness exemplified by hallucinations or euphoria. For many people these additional responses enhance sex and can therefore be classified as aphrodisiacs, but for other people there is a paradoxical effect. Those added physiological or psychological effects are perceived by many men as loss of control over the sex act. For these men any drugs which alter the exciting reality of sex in any way are distracting.

Among the sexually enhancing drugs which are believed effective, the best known is *cantharides*, "Spanish Fly," which is a powder made from ground-up Southern European beetles. Spanish fly works by dilating the blood vessels of the genital region in both sexes, thereby adding to sexual responses. In men its use can prolong erections; in women it can prolong excitation. Spanish fly is very dangerous and many people are reported to have died from its effects. Because different individuals respond differently to it, there is little knowledge about what constitutes a safe human dosage.

Among primitive societies, other drugs which may have some sexual enhancing qualities are *muriacithin*, derived from a Brazilian root, and *yoshimbine*, derived from an African tree bark, although aphrodisiac claims for both these substances have been challenged.

Other drugs reputed to be sexual enhancers and available to people in Western societies include: L.S.D., cocaine, L-Dopa, PCPA, and cyclazine. All are considered dangerous because of the unpredictability of human physiological response and behavior.

In the U. S. today sexual enhancing drugs known as poppers (amyl and isobutyl nitrite) are a current rage in many urban centers, and 500 million doses of these drugs were consumed for recreational purposes (often in connection with sex) last year. Poppers cause the body's blood vessels to dilate, yielding the sensations of a rush and dizziness, a sensation that many users believe heightens feelings of sexual pleasure. However, popper consumers often suffer from vicious headaches after their pleasure fades, and there is always danger that an individual's body may not be able to withstand the sudden physiological responses that poppers produce in the circulatory system.

**How many men find their sex life affected by alcohol?**

*87 percent.*                              (Reference: 2)

While Shakespeare's porter (in *Macbeth*) complains that drink "provokes the desire, but it takes away the performance," 45 percent of males say alcohol enhances their sex. Still, nearly as many, 42 percent, concur with the porter—for them, drinking decreases enjoyment. Thirteen percent claim no effect. In moderate amounts alcohol may well enhance sex by lessening inhibitions. However, because it is a depressant, in large amounts alcohol can ruin a man's sex life and can leave him unable to achieve an erection. In fact, in our practice, we have never seen a practicing alcoholic who had a satisfying sex life.

**How many men say marijuana enhances their sex?**
*80 percent of those who have tried it.*
(Reference: 2)

Anywhere from 25 to 50 percent of the United States's adult population has smoked marijuana. Marijuana serves as a disinhibitor and it may also function as a sexual enhancer for many people. Many like to combine their "weed" with sex and among those who have tried it, there are few who report unhappy experiences, although more than 10 percent report it has zero effect on them. The reasons that marijuana is more popular than other drugs in conjunction with sex are its relative safety and the predictability of physiological responses that it produces.

**How many males are gay?**
*13 percent.*                    (References: 2, 76, 99)

When Kinsey asked his male sample about their homosexual experiences, 37 percent reported they had had at least one homosexual orgasm. Does that mean one third of America's men are gay? It depends upon the definition employed. In the Kinsey sample, for instance, many of those orgasms were had when the males were boys. Other men had had only one adult experience. In another, more recent survey, 4 percent of the males said they have homosexual sex whenever they have sex; another 4 percent have it "frequently"; and 9 percent had it more than twice.

Tote up those figures, and are 4, 8, or 17 percent of American males gay? Johns-Hopkins Professor John Money, a distinguished sex researcher, is one of the few to use a precise definition. If a male has had more than 6 sexual experiences with other males, he is, says Money, gay. Here, too, there are admitted difficulties. A male who had dozens of homosexual experiences 10 years earlier but has had sex only with females since then certainly should not be counted as gay. So, to avoid this problem, in our clinical work we define gay as someone whose current sexual activities are *exclusively* homosexual.

**When does a gay male identify himself as a homosexual?**
*Between the ages of 15 and 24.*    (Reference: 21)
Our question does not imply that the male "comes out of the closet" or publicly proclaims his homosexuality. What it means is only that the gay male has identified himself to *himself* as gay. Not unexpectedly, gays take this route at widely differing ages. Twelve percent do it before they reach age 15. But 35 percent do so between 15 and 19, and another 31 percent make the decision between 20 and 24. Twenty-two percent wait until they are 25 or older.

In our clinical practice, we have encountered several males who identified themselves as gay but had never had homosexual contacts and currently engaged in heterosexual relationships, although unsatisfactorily. Their self-classification was based on their homosexual fantasies, which made them anxious and depressed. By way of a solution, we taught them to supplement their homosexual fantasies with heterosexual ones—an addition that subsequently

133

alleviated their anxieties and, in time, facilitated their enjoyment of heterosexual contacts.

In another case, a man came to us because he was disturbed that all his homosexual attempts ended in failure. The UCLA graduate student assigned to his case assumed he was a "latent heterosexual," due to his failure at homosexuality. But it ocurred to us that, since his contacts were exclusively homosexual, he might be better viewed as an impotent homosexual. With that diagnosis in mind, we treated him for impotence using techniques that before we had only applied to heterosexuals, and he shortly began pursuing a successful homosexual sex life.

**How many men have been approached by a homosexual for sex?**
*64 percent.*                              (Reference: 47)
Nearly two thirds of all men, whether gay or straight, have had this happen to them. Twenty-nine percent say it happens often. But much of this depends upon where one lives and the areas one frequents. Pass time in Los Angeles's West Hollywood or New York's Greenwich Village and the odds are higher. Spend days in a Southern Baptist town and the likelihood is less, but no place is a sure bet for either avoiding or inviting homosexual advances.

**How prevalent are sexually transmittable diseases?**
*Over 3 million cases annually in the United States.*
                          (References: 19, 72, 97, 115)
Herod, Pope Alexander VI, Goethe, and Al Capone all had venereal diseases. Today, venereal diseases are second only to the common cold as the most

common communicable diseases among teenagers. Among adults, the incidence rate is lower, but still enormously high. In a recent year, 620,000 causes of gonorrhea ("clap") were reported. Another 300,000 cases of Herpes Simplex II, a venereal strain, were also reported. The best estimate is that at least two million more cases of sexually transmittable diseases went unreported. At Rutgers University, 19 percent of its sexually active student body (which amounts to two thirds of the entire student population) admit to having had a sexually transmittable disease. But *another* 17 percent report having had symptoms that were never treated. Treatment, fortunately, is quick, painless, and simple in most instances, although Herpes II sufferers are still awaiting development of a cure for this increasingly common malady.

# CHAPTER 5

## I've Come a Long Way, Baby—
## Female Physiology

What happens to a woman's body during sex? How does she physically respond to excitement? Exactly what happens when she is turned on? How many lovers has she had? How often does she make love— and how frequently does she have an orgasm? Those are the types of physiological issues discussed in this chapter devoted to how and when a woman has sex. Female psychological and attitudinal data are discussed in depth in Chapter 7.

**How many erogenous zones does a woman have?**
*10 major ones and a number of minor ones.*

(Reference: 72)

For most females the principal erogenous zones (areas that quickly respond sexually to stimulation) are the mouth, the ears, the nipples, the inner thighs, the area between the anus and the genitals, the anus, the clitoris, the introitus (commonly known as the vestibule because it connects the outside of the woman's body to the vagina), the labia majora (large outer lips) and the labia minora (hairless folds of skin at the introitus's outermost opening).

A number of minor erogenous zones that are often sensitive during sexual foreplay and sexual activity are the eyelids, the tongue, the neck, the underarms, the inner crook of the elbow, the palm of the hand, the fingertips, the buttocks, the toes, and the area between the toes.

With the right partner it is possible for the entire female skin to react as an erogenous zone. However, not all women respond sexually to stimulation of the same area, and a caress that can sexually excite one woman can extinguish the flame for another. Knowing the map, in other words, is not enough to guarantee a happy trip— the traveling companion must, at every step along the way, tune in to a partner's feelings for signs of sexual excitement.

**When does a female grow aware of her sexuality?**
*At birth.* (Reference: 45)
Females begin to exhibit indisputable sexual feelings immediately after birth, and self-fondling in infancy is very common. Establishment of gender (sex) roles in females, too, parallels the male experience: a firm sense of being a female rather than a male is generally established in a child by age 2. It is then that the child begins to sense that the world is divided into *two* different sexes and she begins to act accordingly.

When is a woman's sexual peak?

*In her late 30s.*                    (References: 122, 135)

"Nature cares nothing for logic," wrote Russian novelist Ivan Turgenev. While a man is hitting his sexual peak at the age of 18, a woman is nowhere near her maximum sexual capacity and responsiveness at that age. In her late thirties she reaches her peak—and she maintains that level throughout her forties, into her fifties, and sometimes beyond.

Different women peak at different ages. There is a degree of uncertainty within the medical community about when the female sexual peak occurs. In a recent survey of the nation's psychiatrists, 2 percent said a woman reached her top sexual form before age 20; 24 percent pegged the age as 20–30 years old; 9 percent thought a woman peaked at 40–50; 1 percent thought 50+; and 9 percent saw no correlation between age and responsiveness. However, a clear majority, 52 percent, thought the age range for maximum female sexuality was 30–40.

The opinion of psychiatrists is interesting, but experience, knowledge, and sensitivity count as much as or more than pure physiological sexual prowess in accounting for satisfactory sex. In our practice we have also seen many successful relationships between younger men and older women. Physiologically, as the data indicate, these relationships are quite sound. It is strange that these relationships so often are misunderstood. It is far less often an attraction of youthful beauty and mature money and far more often a mutual attraction of youthful enthusiasm and mature wisdom. Young men frequently are attracted to women who are 10 to 20 years their seniors because these women often possess greater maturity, emotion-

139

al security, leadership, and a more solid sense of their place and function in the world than do younger women. The young men, for their parts, are often more energetic, flexible, and willing to learn than are older men. It is unfortunate that many women feel guilty about pursuing a serious relationship with a younger man even though sexually and emotionally he may be a better-matched partner than a man her own age.

### Can females be circumcised?
*No.*                                            (Reference: 28)

The clitoris may be the female counterpart to a man's penis, but it lacks a foreskin. Strangely, that essential anatomical difference has not prevented the development in some cultures of a cruel version of circumcision that resembles in name only the operation performed on men, and the name itself is used in error. The accurate term for this surgical technique is clitoridectomy and it usually involves cutting the female's clitoral glans (the visible tip) out of her body. In more radical forms of the operation, the entire clitoris is removed. Such operations, say international health authorities, are routinely practiced in at least 26 Middle Eastern, African, and South American societies. Females between the ages of 4 and 8 are typically the victims of these rites. Because the clitoris is richly endowed with sensitive nerve endings, this operation results in a diminution but not an elimination of a female's sexual response. The surgery is performed with the explicit aim of reducing a female's sexual pleasure, thereby enhancing the odds that the woman will remain a virgin until she weds and will remain faithful to her husband. Fortunately, this barbarity—one that is totally lacking in medical justification—has never been practiced to a significant extent in Western nations.

Clitoridectomies should not be confused with a procedure currently used in the United States by some sex therapists to *heighten* a woman's sexual pleasure. In this procedure, which often is erroneously termed "female circumcision," the clitoris is separated from the inner labia by removing adhesions. The technique is nonsurgical and is cited by some women as greatly increasing their sexual responsiveness.

**At what age does a female have her first menstruation?**
*12.5 years is the average.* (References: 47, 75)
This step, as indicated, is part of puberty's middle period, and the age range for first menstruation is 10–16. Sometimes the first menstruation does not occur until the female is 18 or older, however, and there are many recorded cases of women who have their first menstruation as late as 25. In other cases, preschool children have already had their menarche. The youngest confirmed menarche occured in a girl aged 3.

The first period, not surprisingly, is a shock to many females. Viewers of the movie *Carrie,* for instance, will not forget when Sissy Spacek's character, to her horror, began to first menstruate while showering in her high school locker room. Carrie thought she was hemorrhaging to death because she had not been prepared to expect the sudden vaginal bleeding which accompanied her first period. Few girls these days live in quite so thorough an informational vacuum as Carrie did. However, instructional pamphlets and hearsay from friends often do not provide sufficient emotional or informational preparation.

No sex therapist could fail to wonder about the connection between the lack of preparedness for a woman's first menstruation and adult sexual dysfunction. Fully 70 percent of adult women who come to us for therapy to resolve dysfunctions report they were unprepared for their first menstruations. We frankly do not know if the figure is so high for women without sexual problems, but we doubt it. It is unclear whether there is some cause–effect relationship or whether there is a correlation to indicate that both conditions are the result of a common cause such as early sexual repression by one's parents. Nonetheless, the relationship between shock at first menstruation and sexual dysfunction merits further study.

**What is the average length of the menstrual cycle?**
*28 days.* (References: 6, 47, 72)
During the complete menstrual cycle, the female reproductive system releases a mature egg from the ovaries into the uterus and, if the egg is not fertilized by a sperm, a short time later menstrual bleeding discharges the egg from the body. For the first few years after menarche, few women have regular periods; their bodies are looking for a cycle that is uniquely appropriate to them. Soon, an internal rhythm is achieved, which in 51 percent of women is 28 days. The shortest menstrual cycles are about 14 days; the longest sometimes exceed 51 days. Nonetheless, such large departures from the 28-day norm are rare. Nearly all women fall within a 20–36-day range.

It is not common, however, for a woman's cycle to occasionally or even frequently depart from its norm. Some women with regular 28-day periods will occasionally complete the lap in 25 days or in 31. Such irregularity, although wide spread, is not well understood. The woman's psychological state( Is she anxious about work? her homelife? Is she depressed?) is often thought to be a cause, but other factors, including hormone activity, may well be at work. In any event, menstrual irregularity is rarely a cause for concern, although good advice is for a woman to seek out gynecological counsel if the condition persists.

**How long does the menstrual period last?**
*5 days.*                    (Referenes: 6, 47)
Forty percent of all women cite 5 days as the duration of their menstrual bleeding, and the average is 4–6 days. But most gynecologists view periods that last as few as 2 or as many as 8 days as normal.

**How much blood flows during a woman's period?**
*2 ounces.*                    (References: 6, 72)
There are 5–6 quarts of blood in the average adult and the loss of a few ounces, about 4 tablespoons, poses no health risk in a normal woman. Women with blood disorders are faced with special problems that must be individually resolved.

**How many women experience pain during their periods?**
*57 percent.*                    (References: 47, 116)
Many women (43 percent) feel *no* pain during their periods. But the majority feel pain, usually

described as "cramps." "Little" pain is felt by 23 percent; 11 percent have "some"; and 23 percent experience "much." Perhaps as many as 5 percent (1 woman in every 20) have pain which is so severe it incapacitates them for several days each month.

While the cause of menstrual pain remains under research, some theorists argue that the severity varies in proportion to a woman's feelings about *being* a woman, with the female who has the greatest satisfaction in her gender having the least pain. But that theory is *not* supported by research findings and, in all likelihood, is untrue.

Importantly, the occurrence of pain is known to be irregular. A woman may feel great pain one month and none the next. Another fact about menstrual pain is that many women who use IUDs (intrauterine devices) find that, following insertion of the device, their pains increase substantially. Not all women find this is so, however.

### At what age does menstruation end?

*At 48 to 49.* (References: 6, 88, 126)

Menopause is the other side of the menarche coin; it signals a halt to the menstrual cycle. No longer is there monthly bleeding or discharge of eggs. A woman typically reaches menopause at age 48 or 49, and the range of average age is 40–55. But there are cases of women still in their teen years who have entered menopause; and at least one woman was still menstruating at age 104.

For some women, menopause comes as long-awaited relief from "the monthlies." For others, it seems a premature end to femininity. But it certainly is not the latter. Many women (as we detail in

144

later pages) continue to enjoy very active sex lives long after the onset of menopause.

What is curious about menopause is that there is no male physiological counterpart, although many men share with women a mid-life emotional crisis period. A healthy male can continue to father children throughout his life. That is not so for women. Menopause marks the end of fertility, and the oldest *confirmed* mother is Ruth Alice Kistler of the United States who gave birth at age 57 years and 129 days. Both medical and popular literature contain reports of older mothers, some as old as their seventies. But Kistler's claim is the only one that has stood up to scrutiny.

**After menopause how many married women have sex?**
*More than 70 percent.*   (References: 16, 17, 135)
There generally is no physiological reason for a woman's sexual feelings to decline after menopause. And 70 percent of married females age 60 and above regularly have sex. One study of still older couples found that of married men and women over age 78, 15 percent had regular intercourse.

**Is sex healthy during a woman's period?**
*Yes.*                          (Reference: 47)
Although some religious faiths (Orthodox Judaism, for instance) strictly forbid sexual relations with a menstruating female, there is no physiological reason for this rule. A few women (2.4 percent) report elevated sex drives during their periods and numerous couples find their sex at this time as satisfactory as at any other time during the month. Incidentally

145

the time of the month when most women (34 percent) claim they are most susceptible to sexual excitement is just prior to menses.

**At what age can a female have babies?**
*Usually by age 15.* (References: 70, 72)
When a woman becomes fertile she is capable of conceiving a child, and the typical age range for achieving fertility is 14–16. A few women do not become fertile until they are in their twenties. Others precociously do so when 10 or 11, but the youngest mother on record is far younger still. Lina Medina, a Peruvian, gave birth in a Caesarean section (a surgical procedure in which the abdomen is opened to remove the infant) at the age of five years and seven months. She had first menstruated at age three and became pregnant at four years and ten months. The infant, a full-term male, weighed six and one half pounds at birth. He lived, as did the mother. Lina Medina aside, however, few four-year-old girls need worry about pregnancy, no matter how playful the tots are.

**Does the beginning of menstruation mean that a female is fertile?**
*No.* (Reference: 70)

A female generally first menstruates several years before she is fertile. Her eggs need time to ripen into mature ova, a natural biological process that explains the time-lag between menarche and fertility.

**At what age is a female considered an adolescent?**
*10.* (References: 6, 70, 72, 116)

146

Around the age of 10, most girls find their hips becoming round and their breasts forming "buds." This first stage of adolescence is subtle, however, and a child could easily be unaware of the changes taking place. The more dramatic changes, the ones that are hard to ignore, come later. Naturally, there is no set rule making 10 as the starting point; for normal girls these changes commence as early as 9 or as late as 14.

Within a year or two of puberty's onset, the phase's middle period takes root and the girl notices a first growth of pubic hair and further breast growth. The menarche—the first menstrual period—is also part of these changes. The average age range is 10–16.

In the last stage of adolescence (14–16 years of age), a female literally rounds out her maturation. The breasts fill out, pubic hair is fully developed, and menstruation is solidly established. At the conclusion of this phase, which occurs in the age range 13–18, a female is biologically a woman and no longer a girl.

Before the onset of puberty, a female's endocrine system secretes only minute amounts of the two female sex hormones, estrogen and progesterone. When the body's inner clock signals that it is time for puberty to commence, the pituitary gland, often called the "master gland," significantly increases its output of FSH, so-called because it is the "follicle-stimulating hormone." FSH in turn triggers the production of increased amounts of estrogen in the ovaries. As that hormone flows throughout the body, it prompts the physical changes that occur during puberty, such as breast growth and rounding of the hips.

From the menarche onward, regular fluctuations in

147

the levels of sex hormones control the occurrence of a woman's menstrual cycle, a fact put to use by manufacturers of birth control pills (which contain synthetic sex hormones designed to alter the natural cycle).

On the whole, very little is known about the function of women's sex hormones. But researchers do know that once menopause occurs, production of the hormones slows to a trickle. Many theorists also suspect there is a connection between hormone levels and anatomical development—a point underlined by the experience of many birth control users who report sizable increases in their breasts.

Of the two chief sex hormones in women, progesterone is by far the more mysterious. Almost nothing is known about its physiological function except that it is closely associated with physical changes immediately before and during pregnancy.

**What is pubic hair's main function?**
*Decoration.*                    (References: 6, 72)
Variations in quantity and texture of pubic hair from individual to individual are enormous. Some have a few strands; others, a dense thatch. Some women shave their pubic area, although with the skin-folds present in this region, most women find shaving a delicate procedure and the *au naturel* look is far and away more common.

**At what age do girls first pet?**
*14–15.*               (References: 47, 61, 75, 131)
By age 15, over one half of all females have "made out" with a boy, with this sex play usually involving hugging, kissing, caressing, etc. By age 16, well over

two thirds of the females have petted, and over one third have achieved orgasm by this route.

**How old is a girl when a boy first caresses her breasts?**
*13.* (Reference: 61)
Breast manipulation is a standard part of many teenagers' "making out," and by age 13, 31 percent (nearly one third) of females have experienced this. By 15, 69 percent have; and by 18, nearly all (91 percent) have had their breasts fondled by a male.

**How old is a girl when a boy first fondles her clitoris?**
*15.* (Reference: 61)
A second step along the making-out route often is digital caressing by the boy of the girl's vagina, and by age 13, 15 percent of all girls have experienced this. By 15, about half (49 percent) have. By age 18, 83 percent (about five girls out of every six) have.

**How old is a girl when she first caresses a boy's penis?**
*16.* (Reference: 61)
Probably because males traditionally assume more aggressive sexual roles and females more passive ones, girls take a year or two beyond the initial time their genitals are touched before they first fondle a boy's penis. Perhaps a shade less than half have done so by age 16; by age 18, more than three fourths (78 percent) have.

**How many females blush when sexually aroused?**
*75 percent.* (Reference: 85)

A "sex flush" is one sign of sexual excitement, although women who do not blush also attain high levels of sexual arousal. In the 75 percent of women who display a blush reaction, the flush generally begins on the skin covering the upper abdomen and spreads until it covers the chest, neck, face, thighs, arms, and sometimes the buttocks.

Although many men (roughly 25 percent) show signs of a sex flush, its extent often is less on a man. Why men blush less and also why proportionately fewer men blush when aroused is not presently understood by researchers.

**How much do a female's breasts expand when she is excited?**
*Their size increases by 20–25 percent.*

(Reference: 85)

This answer must be qualified. Current research suggests that an increase in breast size is common in women as they near orgasm but *only* if the breasts are unsuckled, that is, have never fed an infant. Suckled breasts do not exhibit marked size increases. The explanation for this difference is unknown.

Incidentally, when there is a size increase, it is very temporary. Most breasts return to their normal state in about 5 to 10 minutes following orgasm.

**How big do a female's nipples become when she is sexually excited?**
*¼–½″ longer and ¼″ wider.* (Reference: 85)
*(.62–1.25 cm. longer and .62 cm. wider)*

Not all women get nipple expansion when aroused, although most do. Nor are erect nipples a sure sign that a woman is turned on—a chill can prompt the

150

same physiological reaction, a fact used to advantage by models for men's magazines. During photography sessions, many insure erect nipples by rubbing ice cubes on their breasts. It works.

**How many teenage girls have made love?**
*44 percent.* (Reference: 61, 66, 75, 131, 139)
Premarital sex is blossoming. Half of all women are sexually active before turning 20. Perhaps one in five has "made it" before age 15.

Premarital sex, as we discussed in the preceding chapter, is well entrenched in many cultures. Perhaps 70 percent of the world's societies condone at least some forms of premarital intercourse. Although some parents and educators in the United States rail about "deteriorating" morals and too much sex exposure, this condemnation has obviously done little to reverse the trend. A legitimate topic for rational debate is whether or not teenage sex is harmful to the participants. Answers, it seems to us, can be provided only on a case-by-case basis. Some teens surely are not emotionally prepared to accept the implications and consequences of a deeply romantic entanglement. Others are as ready as their parents and may even be better equipped.

**How many sex partners does the average teenager have?**
*1–5.* (Reference: 61)
Of those teenage girls who have had intercourse, 84 percent have had between 1 and 5 sex partners. Just 7 percent of girls 15–16 years old have had more than 10 partners; and 5 percent of girls 17–18 have had more than 10.

How many non-virgin teenage girls have had an orgasm during sex?

*73 percent.*                    (References: 61, 139)

Whereas only 27 percent of experienced teenage girls have never had an orgasm in intercourse—only 6 percent always have orgasms. Twenty percent reach orgasm 75 percent of the time; 19 percent do so about half the time; 25 percent have an orgasm in perhaps one intercourse out of every four; and a final 6 percent estimate they reach orgasm about 10 percent of the time.

Some light is thrown on these findings by the results of another survey that asked adult women about their orgasms in premarital sex. Of the women who reported that their affairs consisted of a string of "one-night stands," 77 percent—more than 3 in every 4—reported they had *never* reached orgasm in coitus before marriage. Only 23 percent of the women who reported having lengthy premarital affairs with one partner had never had a coital orgasm. The rest—again, 77 percent—said they had reached orgasm at least once, although many had far more. What these data strongly suggest is that repeated sex with a single partner is a far more likely way for the woman to reach orgasm—perhaps because such long-term relationships usually feature enhanced mutual concern on the part of both partners as well as a more relaxed and comfortable approach to sex than the quite frequently tense "one-nighter."

By what age will most women have had an orgasm?
20.                       (References: 45, 75, 126)
More than half (53 percent) of all women have

reached orgasm by their twentieth birthday. Twenty-three percent are more precocious—they had their first by age 15; and some women (about 10 percent) achieve orgasm before they enter puberty. At least one four-month-old infant, according to medical reports, achieved a bona fide orgasm.

Males, on the other hand, are on average more precocious still. By age 17, 90 percent have had at least one orgasm. Women are 29 before reporting the same percentage. Huge as that difference is, the explanation is not difficult. Masturbation, typically the source of many first orgasms, has traditionally been more common among young males than young females. Furthermore, triggering a male orgasm is a more straightforward affair than eliciting a female's. With a female, neither the area to be stimulated nor the procedure is so evident for the novice. Beginners often need considerable experimenting through trial and error in order to successfully achieve orgasm by self-stimulation.

Importantly, too, it has only been in recent years that encouraging female sexual responses has achieved widespread acceptance. Even in the recent past, a woman's sexual role was depicted as limited to procreation; enjoyment was for males only. Many females found themselves inhibited by unavoidable feelings of shyness and guilt when it came to exploring the dimensions of their own sexuality. Happily, that has all changed in recent years and women now are at last granted equal billing with men on the sexual stage. As a result, a valid suspicion, even in the absence of hard research numbers, is that the age by which 90 percent of all females have reached orgasm has declined considerably.

**Do women really "come" during an orgasm?**
*Maybe.*                                   (Reference: 161)
Sorry, but that is as good an answer as can currently be provided. The centuries old theory that women do not ejaculate is now undergoing serious challenge. One research team currently insists that the women they have studied regularly emit an urethral ejaculation during orgasm, the nature of which they have yet to identify. They claim that women ejaculate a substance similar to spermless male semen and that the source of this fluid is a tiny organ within the vagina which is similar to the male prostate. A major problem in confirming this research is the difficulty in distinguishing between a female's vaginal lubrication and whatever ejaculatory fluid there might be. While we hesitate at this point to accept these tentative research conclusions as fact, this area of research is one that is certain to undergo intensive investigation in the coming years.

**How many women have had "wet dreams"?**
*21 percent.*                         (References: 47, 75)
Hold on. We know that, taken literally, "wet dream" cannot be used in describing female sexual response unless the previously mentioned research into possible female ejaculations during orgasm is confirmed. But women, like men, sometimes achieve orgasm during sleep. There is nothing known to be "wet" about this process except internal vaginal lubrication, but the name sticks anyway.

Although about 21 percent of women say they have reached orgasm during sleep, the true incidence probably is higher and perhaps hits the 83 percent incidence reported by men. The suspicion is that because the telltale evidence of wet-dream semen deposits on night wear and sheets is lacking, many women might not be certain what transpired during their sleep. Unless a woman had awakened, an admittedly common reaction, she would not likely be aware of a wet dream. Even if she did awaken, there is no assurance that she would fully remember what had happened during sleep.

What causes female wet dreams? *Not* the "incubus" of ancient myth. That creature (analagous to the male's succubus) supposedly visited sleeping females and lay upon them to produce their orgasm. Amusing as that flight of fancy may seem, it is not necessary in explaining this simple phenomenon. Couple a particularly erotic dream with a bit of friction caused by rubbing against a mattress, and the ingredients for prompting an orgasm are in ample supply. The average age at which women first say they experience wet dreams is a relatively late 30.2 years. Half of the women who have wet dreams experience their first one after the age of 25.

**How fast after stimulation does a receptive woman show signs of sexual arousal?**
*Within 10–30 seconds.*          (References: 72, 85)
Present a woman with erotic stimulation and within a half minute her vaginal walls will begin to moisten, which commonly is the sure sign that she is turned on. Even though both the exact internal source (it is thought to be the walls themselves) and nature of this lubricant remain under study, it is known that this moistening of the vaginal walls acts as a lubricant to make passage of the penis into the vagina a bit easier.

**How much does a woman lubricate**
*Unknown amount (data are insufficient).*

(References: 47, 85)

Women are baffled and sometimes worried about their lubrication: Am I too dry? Too wet? Scientists are just as confused. Although researchers suppose that a "few" drops of the lubricant are produced to coat the vaginal walls, that answer is of little help to the concerned woman. A guide of sorts is provided by one study that asked women to gauge the volume of their own lubrication. Their answers are inconclusive: None—13 percent; Little—7 percent; Some —10 percent; Average (moderately wet)—66 percent; Much—5 percent. There are two enormous problems with this series of responses. For one, few of these women had any experience with even *one* vagina other than their own and they consequently lacked a standard for comparison. Another point to remember is that lubrication occurs internally. Lacking sophisticated equipment, it is impossible to come up with better than a vague approximation of the volume.

**How many types of female orgasm are there?**
*Possibly two.*          (References: 8, 72, 85, 161)

A concept of female sexuality, held by Freud, is that there are two distinct types of female orgasm: clitoral (centered in the clitoris) and vaginal. In elaborating upon this theory, Freud argued that the clitoral orgasm is inferior to the vaginal, and supported his position with somewhat convoluted argumentation. Given Freud's dominance in psychiatry's early stages, this notion quickly received wide spread acceptance within the clinical establishment; but lost support during the 1960's. Masters and Johnson and most other serious sex researchers believe that there is only one type of orgasm, that begins in the clitoral region, quickly spreads throughout the pelvis and from there to the whole body.

However, a growing number of sex therapists are now claiming that, indeed, there are two types of orgasm, one clitoral and one triggered by penetration of the vagina and stimulation of a sensitive area within called the "Grafenberg Spot" or "G" spot. Advocates of the "G" spot contend that it is associated with the female counterpart of the male prostate, and that stimulation produces not only an orgasm, but also an ejaculation of fluid as well.

**How many mature women have never been sexually aroused?**
*2 percent.*                                    (Reference: 75)
Many women—ones who cling to Victorian or Puritan notions about sex—find any kind of sex to be unseemly or even unladylike. This factor alone could explain why 2 women in every 100 have never experienced sexual excitement. In addition, serious diseases (such as diabetes), hormone irregularities, and genetic and anatomical abnormalities can significantly impede and even eliminate sexual responsiveness.

**How many women have never had an orgasm?**
*8–10 percent.* (References: 58, 75, 84, 85, 127, 139)
Among nonhuman primates, female orgasms are considered unusual. Furthermore, failure to achieve orgasm by women of most human societies is not

157

usually viewed as dysfunctional. As an example, among the Kyika of Tanzania and the rural Irish, female orgasm reportedly is very rare.

In perspective it must be realized that the inability to have an orgasm is not actually a loss of capacity but the failure to develop an ability. Nonorgasmia in women appears to represent a normal variation in the sexual responsiveness of the world's women viewed as a group. The women who are nonorgasmic in the U. S. today appear to be suffering from a failure to experience the sexual zenith of our cultural expectations, rather than the normal routine bodily response to lovemaking.

Although all women are believed to be capable of orgasm by the Mangaians of Polynesia, that society also believes that the ability to achieve orgasm must be learned. This is our position as well. Failure to achieve orgasm is not an illness requiring treatment; the ability to orgasm can be learned by almost every woman who desires the experience. Some women learn how to have orgasms on their own or with a partner by trial and error, and for the woman who has not acquired the ability in that manner she can be taught to orgasm by a sex therapist using behavior therapy.

Religious orthodoxy also is often cited as an important factor in female dysfunction. Of the 29 vaginismus cases (cases in which the vagina's sphincter muscle has been tightened to the point that penile entry is very difficult or impossible) treated by Masters and Johnson, 12 reported backgrounds of serious religious orthodoxy; 6 were from devout Roman Catholic backgrounds, 4 were from orthodox Jewish backgrounds, and 2 were from strict Protestant Fundamentalist backgrounds. Perhaps that a woman's non-orgasmia is dysfunctional is more related to the *changing beliefs* of those who were once religiously devout. Certainly there are some deeply religious non-orgasmic women in the U. S. today who are quite satisfied with their non-orgasmic sex lives.

**Can physical conditions prevent a woman from reaching orgasm?**
*Yes.*                          (References: 60, 112)
Many prescription drugs—depressants, for example—can reduce a woman's interest in sex to nil. So can some illicit drugs such as heroin. Illness can do the same. Among women who have *never* achieved orgasm, current research suggests that in some cases there may also be an anatomical reason for this inability. In one study it was claimed that one third of the non-orgasmic women had clitoral adhesions—extra skin on the clitoris—and that following removal of the adhesions a third of these women become orgasmic. Nonetheless we believe in perhaps 97 percent of all cases of non-orgasmic women, *psychological,* not physical, factors are at work.

**How long does a woman's orgasm last?**
*5-6 seconds.*                    (Reference: 125)
Brief as six seconds seems it is longer than a male's orgasm by a second or two. That is an issue that fascinates sex researchers. Likely as not, the time difference derives from nothing more mystical than a female's sexual anatomy, which differs in hugely important respects from a male's, as we dis-

cussed in earlier chapters. Because the systems are far from identical, it should come as no surprise that there are differences in the orgasmic responses and experiences of men and women.

### Does the anus respond during orgasm?
*Yes.*                                    (Reference: 85)

The anal area is rich in nerve endings and is, as we have noted, an erogenous zone. Its most overt sexual responses occur during orgasm when many women and men have involuntary contractions of the anal sphincter muscle. During an especially intense orgasm, there might be 2 to 5 contractions which come at intervals of roughly 0.8 seconds; or there might be no contractions at all. Though many sexual responses occur uniformly—at least in a given person —such is not the case here. Sometimes the contractions occur; at other times they do not.

Intriguingly, some people—men and women both —can reach orgasm by stimulation of the anal area alone. This response, common among male homosexuals, usually occurs in connection with anal intercourse.

### How many women have an orgasm when their breasts are caressed?
*Less than 1 percent.*              (Reference: 92)

It is possible but not common. Fewer than 1 percent of women can achieve orgasm as a result solely of breast and nipple play. Intriguingly, of those women who do achieve orgasm this way, most express a strong preference for orgasm achieved in sexual intercourse.

**How many women frequently have more than one orgasm during a single sex act?**

*14 percent.*                    (References: 47, 75)

Unbelievable as it might now seem, a few decades back eminent scientists, all men by the way, stridently argued against the physical possibility of multiple orgasms for a female. Women who thought they achieved them, in fact, did not, these men asserted. What they were actually experiencing, the theory continued, were "incomplete" orgasms—a common symptom, the men concluded, of "nymphomania." Do it right, they insisted, and one is all you get.

That theory is nonsense. A healthy, sexually excited woman can easily have two, three, even ten or more orgasms in the course of a single sex act. A few women even report achieving 100 and more orgasms.

Interestingly, women generally report that each succeeding orgasm in a multiorgasmic experience is both easier to achieve than its predecessor and more pleasurable. This stands in marked contrast to the multiorgasmic episodes of men, in which it typically is reported that each succeeding male orgasm is less pleasant and far more difficult to achieve.

Such differences, we have found, have enormous therapeutic significance in the treatment of both sexual dysfunction and claimed sexual incompatability. When a woman tells us that she routinely takes "too long" to reach orgasm or that her mate reaches orgasm "too soon," we often recommend that she masturbate, use a vibrator, pet, or receive oral stimulation of her genitals to at least two and sometimes three orgasms before proceeding to insertion of the penis. After taking those steps, most women

161

happily find they are quickly achieving satisfying orgasm in intercourse, even if their partner might tend to be a mite "fast on the draw."

A lesson we learn from such cases is that resolution of marital sexual incompatability often requires little more than designing techniques to speed up a woman's orgasm or delay her partner's ejaculation so that they can both achieve the same level of pleasure at about the same time during lovemaking (the techniques for prolonging a man's coital performance are discussed in Chapter 4).

One in every seven women says she regularly experiences multiple orgasms. Many more do so irregularly. Remember, too, that for a woman to have multiple orgasms she ordinarily requires a partner who is willing to sustain the sexual play long enough for her to proceed beyond her first.

### How many women masturbate?

83 percent.                (References: 61, 65, 75, 139)

Masturbation is a practice that takes hold early. Medical literature is crammed with reports of female infants masturbating, some as young as a few months. Others come to this practice later. Importantly, during the past few decades, ever more American women have discovered masturbation. In a survey three decades ago, for instance, 62 percent of all adult females had masturbated, with 58 percent having achieved orgasm by this route at least once. But more recent research points to a far higher incidence rate. Among married women, 74 percent masturbate, and 16 percent do it frequently. Among teenagers, more than half (52 percent) masturbate. With older single women, the practice is nearly universal, perhaps because their sexual outlets are a bit more limited than are those of their married counterparts.

**At what age does the average female first masturbate?**

*At 17–18 years of age.* (References: 61, 131)

A good indication that women are becoming sexually more adventurous at ever earlier ages is provided by this answer. By age 18, about half of all teenage girls have masturbated at least once. And, by age 13, more than a third of them (37 percent) have. But this is far from the youngest reported age. Perhaps one girl in six starts masturbating by age 10.

**How often do teenage girls masturbate?**

*Once a week or more.* (Reference: 61)

Most teenage girls who masturbate (51 percent) do it once or more a week. About 1 percent masturbate more than once a day; another 6 percent do it daily; 22 percent regularly masturbate 2–3 times each week; and 24 percent masturbate at least once weekly. Another 12 percent enjoy masturbating, but on average do it only once every month. Finally, 35 percent of the teenage girls who masturbate do so less than once a month.

**How does a female learn to masturbate?**

*Self-discovery.* (Reference: 75)

Over half of all women (57 percent) who masturbate learned how to do it on their own. Other major sources of learning about masturbation include verbal and printed information, observation, and petting.

Interestingly, only one fourth of all men make the discovery of the solitary joys of playing with one's

163

self. Most males learn about it from word of mouth or reading. Can we conclude that men are less sexually inventive than women? Probably not. A more likely explanation is that male masturbation has long played a more prominent role in our culture. "Jerking off" jokes are common among teenage boys; far less so among girls. Some prep school boys even explore "circle jerks," a communal form of masturbation. And the Roman Catholic Church, perhaps the globe's chief anti-masturbation institution, has itself evidenced ambivalence about female masturbation because there is no "wasting of seed" as in an ejaculation, no destruction of "potential" life in a female's orgasm. The Church, consequently, has energetically spoken out against male masturbation and largely ignored female masturbation. A result is that many an alert boy has scampered away from a sermon or confessional bent on finding out just what sinful pleasures the Church is castigating. Few girls have been afforded these Providential clues. They must tough it out on their own, as most quite successfully do.

**How many female masturbations result in orgasm?**
*95 percent.*                                    (Reference: 75)
Masturbating among both women and men is the surest route to orgasm. But that is not unexpected because a key ingredient of successful sex is understanding a partner's needs. Affairs are naturally simpler when one is one's own sex partner.

What causes failure to reach orgasm by masturbation? A loss of interest, distractions, interruptions—all can derail the masturbator's enthusiasm for the project at hand. Nonetheless, no other sexual practice has nearly so high a rate of orgasm.

**At what age do most women have their first orgasm while masturbating?**

*17–18.*                    (References: 47, 61, 131)

More than 10 percent of masturbating women first had an orgasm by masturbation when they were 12 or younger. Over 40 percent have by age 15; and by 18, more than half have had an orgasm.

**How long does it take a woman to masturbate to orgasm?**

*4.5 minutes.*                    (References: 47, 75)

Some 70 percent of all females report that masturbation leads to orgasm within 5 minutes; more than half say within 4 minutes; and a few report times under 1 minute. Most males, by contrast, do it in 2 to 3 minutes. What is important, however, is not the difference but the similarity. Women are as sexually responsive as, although a minute or two slower than, men.

**How often do women masturbate to orgasm?**

*About once every 3 weeks.*         (Reference: 75)

Ask this question of more mature women and the answers range from "several times daily" to "once a month" through "never." Generalizations are possible, however. Married women masturbate somewhat less frequently than do singles. Once wed, the average incidence of masturbatory orgasms drops to about once per month. While single, a woman typically reaches masturbatory orgasm every two weeks or so. The difference is generally explained by the easier access to sexual intercourse which most married women have.

**In what manner do most females masturbate?**
*With manual stimulation while lying flat on their backs.* (References: 58, 65, 87, 148)
Dildoes (penis-shaped devices used by women for masturbation) date from the ancient world and were used by the Babylonians, Greeks, Indians, and Chinese. They were made from a number of different materials: clay, bronze, gold, silver, ivory, ebony, horn, glass, wax, leather, resin, rubber, and (more recently) plastic. A number of plant materials have also been used. The Tikopean of the Santa Cruz Islands and Zanda women of Africa use bananas and phallic-shaped roots. Chukchi women of the Arctic region use the calf muscle of a reindeer.

Certainly many contemporary American women praise dildoes and vibrators, but most females rely upon their trusty hands, with the clitoral and vulval regions as targets of choice. Yet the use by females of "sex toys" is increasing and can only vault still higher with the new involvement by huge, brand-name beauty and health companies in the sale and manufacture of vibrators, which these firms delicately term "massagers." Although almost all women rely on manual stimulation, many now supplement this technique, with 30 percent sometimes using water spray (from a hand-held shower head, for example) and 28 percent occasionally using vibrators. Soon enough, vibrator advertisements will be a television staple and, with their relatively low price tags, such gadgets look destined to take their place in the well-equipped home along with electric shavers and blow-dryers.

### Who is a woman's first sex partner?
*A steady date.*                                    (Reference: 2)

Over a third (37 percent) have their initial sex with a "steady." Other "firsts" include fiancés (17 percent); "someone you had known but not dated" (15 percent); casual acquaintances or strangers (6 percent); and relatives (1 percent). Husbands account for a mere 12 percent of first coital experiences.

### How many females bleed at their first lovemaking?
*50 percent.*                                       (Reference: 47)

It is an even split: half the females bleed, half do not. The cause of bleeding is that the membranous hymen, discussed in the anatomy section, ruptures. Among those females who do not bleed, the absence of blood is explained by either prior breaking of the hymen in nonsexual exercise or the easy, bloodless penetration of a very thin hymen. In any event, the amount of blood lost usually amounts to little more than a tablespoon's worth.

Two conclusions are readily drawn from this information and both are contrary to widely held beliefs. For one, the lack of vaginal bleeding can in no way be taken as a sign of virginity's absence. Many, many virgins just do not bleed, no matter how chaste they have been. Nor can the presence of blood confirm virginity. Many other factors, including the menstrual period or preperiod "spotting," can account for blood.

**How many women enjoy making love their first time?**

*43 percent.* (Reference: 47)

Granted, over half (57 percent) say they received no pleasure at all from their first sex, but that leaves 43 percent who did get pleasure—20 percent received "much"; the rest say "little" or "some."

What accounts for the dismal experiences of the majority? Lack of skill on the part of both partners and uncertainty about what to do explain some of the lack of pleasure. In many other instances, the female likely "gave in" in order to satisfy (not "lose") a pressuring boyfriend. Often, too, the expectations associated with sexual intercourse are high and the quality of the first sex act in terms of technical performance is quite low. Such results, given those high expectations, can be disappointing. Nonetheless, unfortunate as it is that a woman's initial sexual encounter so often is disappointing, most usually learn that a good way to insure more fulfilling sex is to take more time in a more comfortable setting.

**How many women enjoy making love?**

*97 percent.* (Reference: 148)

Almost all American women enjoy sex. Almost none dislike it and only a few claim neutrality on the issue.

**How many women have had a virgin man?**

*32.9 percent.* (Reference: 47)

**How long does premarital foreplay usually last?**

*26 minutes on the average.* (Reference: 47)

Foreplay is petting that culminates in sexual intercourse, and 44 percent of all females (and 40 percent of males) say their premarital foreplay lasts about a half hour. Another 15 percent said 13–17 minutes. And 12 percent said it routinely exceeded an hour.

It is interesting to note that when compared to men's answers to the same question, women report a shorter duration of foreplay. This may be due to distorted perceptions by men who think their foreplay takes too long and women who do not think it lasts long enough.

**How many women have never had an orgasm during sex?**
*7–10 percent.*　　　　　　　　(References: 2, 139)

Different surveys arrive at different numbers, but all come up with about the same answer: one woman in ten has never reached orgasm in intercourse. Certainly intercourse without orgasm can be a very pleasant experience, but most of us on most occasions would hope to have an orgasm. While some of the coitally non-orgasmic women may have physical or psychological factors that interfere with their sexual satisfaction, quite a few could benefit from the introduction of changes in their sex practices. New partners or changes in a present partner's bedtime habits often bring pleasing results. Different positions, use of sex toys (vibrators and the like), exploration of noncoital sex (cunnilingus, for instance), can easily enhance a couple's mutual enjoyment. So can sex therapy, many American couples can testify.

**How many women have orgasms at the same time as their partners?**
*35 percent.*　　　　　　　　(Reference:41)

Simultaneous orgasms may be a goal for many couples, but it is one that most find difficult to achieve. Only 35 women in 100 regularly reach orgasm when their partners do. When the rest of the women reach orgasm in intercourse, 41 percent generally do so before their mates do; and 23 percent do so afterward.

**While making love, how many men have an orgasm within 6 minutes as reported by women?**
*69 percent.*                                    (Reference: 47)
When females report on their mates' performances, nearly half say their partners ejaculate in under 4 minutes; 69 percent say he takes less than 6 minutes. At the extremes, 1 percent say their sex lasts a half minute or less; and 3 percent regularly enjoy intercourse that lasts 20 minutes or longer.

**While making love, how many women have an orgasm within 6 minutes**
*28 percent.*                              (References: 120, 139)
Even though 28 percent of women reach orgasm in less than 6 minutes, a large majority take longer. Thirty-seven percent say intercourse must last 6–10 minutes before they have an orgasm; 20 percent peg the necessary time at 11–15 minutes; 9 percent says 16–20 minutes; 3 percent look for 21–25 minutes; and the remaining 3 percent say they need intercourse to last more than 26 minutes.

An unavoidable implication in comparing these times with the ones for males is that coitus alone is not generally the surest route to a female orgasm. When intercourse is coupled with other techniques (cunnilingus, lengthy foreplay, etc.), the effectiveness of the coital route dramatically escalates.

Another implication, according to a broad survey of the nation's psychiatrists, is that the failure of a woman to reach orgasm in sex play can, as a rule, be traced to male ignorance of effective sex techniques. At least that is the view of 77 percent of the psychiatrists. And good advice for a couple who want to put more orgasms into their relationship is mutually to explore any of the new and good technique books that now are widely available (such as Alex Comfort's *Joy of Sex*).

**How many women prefer the missionary position for lovemaking?**
*60 percent.* (Reference: 148)

**How many women prefer to be on top during sex?**
*25 percent.* (Reference: 148)
Although the missionary position (man on top, woman below) ruled supreme for generations, alternative lovemaking postures now are making major inroads, with women on top, man beneath starting to loom as a major challenger. Other favorites preferred by many include (in order of popularity): the man entering from the rear, side-by-side (the spoon position) and standing sex.

**On how many teenage girls has oral sex been performed?**
*About 50 percent.* (Reference: 61)
Long rare even in adult bedrooms, cunnilingus currently is experiencing great popularity among teen-

agers and 34 percent of 15–16-year-old girls have tried it at least once. Well over half (59 percent) of 17–18-year-old girls have also tried cunnilingus.

**On how many married women has oral sex been performed?**
*93 percent.* (References: 2, 139)
In the conjugal bedroom, cunnilingus now is a nearly universal sex practice. For good reason: the tongue and lips are extremely sensitive and prove especially adept at stimulating the clitoral region. Not a few women far prefer cunnilingus over coitus, although 7 percent of adult females insist they would "never permit it" to be performed on them. But 39 percent of married women experience it "often."

**How many teenage girls have performed oral sex on a male?**
*59 percent.* (References: 61, 126, 131)
The Arab women of Northern Africa, according to several anthropological studies, come to "giving head" or fellatio when they are still prepubescent— and as many as 80 percent, some estimates have it, have performed fellatio (typically on a relative) at least once by age 5. While that is far removed from the American norm, 30 percent of this nation's 15–16-year-old females report they have fellated at least one male. And more than half (59 percent) of 17–18-year-olds have.

**How many married women have performed oral sex on a male?**
*91 percent.* (References: 2, 55, 75, 126, 139, 145)

Fellatio is an integral part of the sex lives of many married couples. As with cunnilingus, some use fellatio as a form of foreplay; for others, it is an end in itself. About 40 percent of all married women do it often and 34 percent find it "very enjoyable." Seventy-five percent of all married couples explore fellatio at least once yearly.

Nor is fellatio confined to the conjugal bedroom. Centuries back, Egypt's Queen Cleopatra, so the tales go, performed fellatio on at least 1000 men. Although few can rival that claim, a recent survey of affluent, educated, and unmarried young women found 100 percent—every woman who responded—had fellated at least one man. For 80 percent, it is a regular course on their sexual menu.

There remain hold-outs, however. Twelve percent of all women in a survey of a broad cross section of American society insisted they had never "given head" and likely never would.

**How many women have had incest?**
*9 percent.* (Reference: 67)

Construe incest as including *all* sex acts (from petting through intercourse), and 8 percent of women have partaken of heterosexual varieties; another 1 percent have had a homosexual incestuous relationship. The major partners are brothers (4 percent of females have some form of sex with them); male cousins (3 percent); sisters (0.7 percent), uncles (0.6 percent); and fathers (0.5 percent).

Limit incest to coitus alone, and the numbers tumble. About 2 percent of all women have had incestuous coitus, with brothers (0.8 percent) and male cousins (0.5 percent) serving as chief partners.

Are these numbers accurate? That is a question we could ask about *every* percentage in this book; but just about every other number, we think, is well founded and amply coincides with our clinical experience. The reported incidence for incest is a different matter. Many researchers suspect the true rates are considerably higher (perhaps double or greater still), but social and family pressures work to inhibit females from revealing incestuous experiences even to sex therapists and researchers who guarantee anonymity. The taboos, in other words, are so powerful that getting merely a slender grip on the dimensions of incest in America proves difficult, perhaps even impossible. What we do know for sure, however, is that many females have had such experiences.

**How many married women have tried anal intercourse?**

*43 percent.*                    (References: 139, 143)

Actors Marlon Brando and Maria Schneider aroused millions of viewers and maybe turned off a few with their buttered-up anal sex bout in *Last Tango in Paris*. The anus, as has been stated earlier, is richly endowed with nerve endings and rapidly responds to sexual stimulation. That is what paves the way for the increasing popularity of anal intercourse among married couples. Not as widespread among unmarried couples, anal sex nonetheless still has been tried by about 25 percent of *all* adult females.

**How many women have played the aggressor during sadomasochistic sex?**

*2 percent.*                    (Reference: 67)

Very few women have engaged in active S&M. Only 2 in 100 *ever* have assumed the active role in S&M.

How many women have played the victim during sadomasochistic sex?

*5 percent.*                                    (Reference: 67)

More than twice as many women have assumed the more passive role in S&M than have tried the active, but overall, few have tried either.

How many women have had sex with more than one partner at a time?

*23 percent of young unmarried women.*

(Reference: 148)

In a recent survey of largely young and unmarried women, 23 percent reported they had had sex with more than a single partner at least once. The bulk of these had tried sex with two males simultaneously; many fewer had had sex with a man and another woman. But 18 percent overall reported they had participated at some point in orgies or partner-swapping parties.

How many women have had sexual contacts with animals?

*5 percent.*                                  (References: 72, 75)

Cats and dogs are the animals of choice (if only because of their availability) and 1.5 percent of preadolescent females have had sex with beasts. Some 3.6 percent of adult women have too. Intriguingly, fewer than 1 percent of all women report having reached orgasm with an animal while 8 percent of all males have. The reason for this large difference?

Perhaps it can be struck up to the differing techniques of the sexes. Men, in most cases, have achieved orgasms with animals in vaginal coitus. For women, that option is less appealing and some might erroneously fear they could become pregnant as a result. But that is a physical impossibility when sex partners are so biologically different.

For those women who have tried sex with animals, preferred techniques cover a large spectrum. Common favorites are fondling the animals genitals and encouraging the beast to do the same to them with its tongue or paws.

**At what average age does a woman marry for the first time?**
*21.*                                    (References: 70, 136)

This number, along with its male counterpart of 23 years of age at first marriage, has increased steadily. Only a few decades ago 19 was the female norm, with 21 the norm for men. We are marrying at a later age and some reasons are the changing attitudes and career expectations of women. Another reason is our society's decreasing inhibitions about premarital sex. Not long ago, the only respectable relief for a woman's sexual needs and wants was to dash to the altar. That is no longer a prerequisite for an active and socially accepted sex life. We can now more easily find our sex without the sanction of marriage. Add these factors up, and the reasons are evident for our delay in tying the nuptial knots.

Just as men tend to first marry when they are 2 years older than the first-time brides, only 15 percent of the marriages in this nation feature a wife who is older than her spouse. In another 12 percent, the couple are the same age. In the other 73 percent, the man is older—1 or 2 years senior in 26 percent of the marriages; 3–4 years in 20 percent; 5–9 years older in 17 percent; and 10 or more years senior in 7 percent.

**How many American women are "virgin brides"?**
*4 percent . . . and going down.*
(References: 136, 139)
The virgin bride is no more. Certainly she once was (survey a cross section of all ages and at least 12 percent say they were virgin when they first spoke their wedding vows). Limit the survey to brides age 20 and under, however, and just 1 female in 25 makes that claim.

**How many premarital sex partners does the average woman have?**
2–6. (References: 2, 47, 139, 148)
The answer to this question hinges upon the respondent's age. A few decades ago, a major sex survey discovered that 53 percent of mature females had premarital sex with only 1 partner. Not so today. Only about 25 percent of young women currently limit themselves to a single partner. Twelve (12) percent have 2; 21 percent have 3–6; and 19 percent have 7 or more. Intriguingly, no survey and, in particular, none of the teenagers and their sexual practices supports the fears expressed by some groups that unbridled promiscuity is sweeping the nation's young. A rough rule of thumb, based upon contemporary findings, is that the overwhelming majority of young women have perhaps a half dozen premarital lovers.

And only 1 percent or so of women have more than 20 premarital lovers (although by contrast about 1 percent of men have premarital sex with over 100 women).

**What is the largest number of marriages reported for one woman?**
*16.*                                            (Reference: 88)
Beverly Nina Avery holds the record, with 16 marriages to 14 different men. Ms. Avery was divorced for the sixteenth time in 1957. Incidentally, she claimed that five of the fourteen husbands had broken her nose.

**How long does marital foreplay last?**
*14 minutes on the average.* (References: 47, 75)
Once a couple marries, the average time devoted to foreplay tumbles from 26 minutes to only half that figure. Granted, 22 percent usually put in more than 20 minutes. But 31 percent spend 11–20 minutes; 36 percent engage in foreplay for 4–10 minutes; and with 11 percent , it is 3 minutes or less. Why the overall decline? With unmarried couples, intercourse often is not seen as a necessary or certain step in their play. It is arrived at gradually and, quite frequently, spontaneously. Married couples, on the other hand, know where their foreplay is heading and they typically get there in a hurry.

**How often does the average married couple have sex?**
*Twice weekly.*                                  (Reference: 139)
How old are you? That is important because the exact answers to our question show considerable variation with the age of the couple. Young newlyweds,

for instance, often consummate their marriage with hundreds of sex acts within the first month. Older couples generally go about their sex with a trace less fervor. But our answer is an approximation based upon the experiences of couples of all ages. More specifically, 8 percent of American married women report they routinely have sex 5 or more times weekly; 11 percent say 4–5 times; 21 percent say 3–4 times; 32 percent say 1–2 times; 26 percent just a single coitus monthly and 2 percent *never* have intercourse.

**How many married women regularly experience orgasm when making love?**
*63 percent*                              (Reference: 139)
Masturbation may do the job almost every time, but intercourse is demonstrably less effective in prompting female orgasms. Still 15 percent achieve orgasm all the time; 48 percent usually do; 19 percent reach orgasm sometimes; and 11 percent have a coital orgasm "once in a while," less frequently than, say, 25 percent of the time. A final 7 percent *never* have orgasms in intercourse.

**Do married women have sex as often as women who live with male partners?**
*No.*                                     (Reference: 148)
Daily intercourse, for instance, is three times more common among unwed live-in couples than among marrieds and a full half of the unwed pairs have sex 3–5 times weekly, compared to 41 percent of the marrieds. The familiarity marriage provides, this evidence suggests, sometimes breeds sexual indifference. But it need not and does not always. Every sex ther-

apist has encountered long-married couples by the hundreds who find their sexual pleasure increasing with every passing year. But, as with much sex, the outcome in specific cases hinges for the most part on the attitudes and wants of the partners.

**How many women have had extramarital sex?**
*29 percent.* (References: 2, 67, 75, 120, 139)
What is remarkable about this number is that despite the "sexual revolution" we have passed through in the last decades, the incidence of female extramarital sex has remained steady. When Kinsey asked married women about their out-of-wedlock affairs, 26 percent had had at least one experience. Years later, a current survey posed the same question and turned up our 29 percent figure, only a few notches higher than Kinsey's.

What prompts extramarital affairs? In later pages we will probe what women have to say about this. But survey the nation's psychiatrists, a range of explanations is offered. Many (29 percent) strike extramarital sex up to hostility the adventuring spouse feels toward the other. But the concensus is far from clear. Another 25 percent say the predominant cause is when an easy and safe opportunity presents itself; 24 percent put the stress on sexual dissatisfaction within the marriage; and 20 percent say the wandering mate feels a need for sexual variety that the new partners afford.

**How many extramarital sex partners do women have?**
*1–5.* (References: 67, 75, 139)
Responses to this question run the gamut. Exactly

half (50 percent) of all women who have had extramarital sex limited themselves to a single partner. Forty (40) percent had 2–5; 5 percent had 6–10; and a final 5 percent had more than 10 partners. About 2 percent report having several dozen or more partners.

**How many women regularly have an orgasm during extramarital sex?**
*39 percent.*                    (References: 2, 139)
Over half (53 percent) of women regularly have an orgasm in their marital intercourse. But that number topples 14 percentage points to 39 when extramarital affairs are involved. Another 12 percent reach orgasm about 75 percent of the time; 7 percent do half the time; and a final 7 percent do about one-quarter of the time. A scant 7 percent never reach orgasm in their mutual sex; but that number leaps in out-of-wedlock doings. More than one third (35 percent) of women with extramarital experience say they rarely or never have an orgasm. Why the disparity? As we saw earlier in connection with premarital sex, regular sex with one partner usually is the surest route to coital orgasm. Much the same can be said here. When an extramarital affair is brief (and 26 percent of women *never* made love to any extramarital partner more than 5 times; 6 percent made love just once), the odds of reaching orgasm decline.

**What is the largest number of children reported for one woman?**
67.                              (Reference: 88)
The first wife of Russian peasant Fyodor Vassilet

(1816–1872) is said to have conceived 69 children in 27 pregnancies all involving multiple births (16 pairs of twins, 7 sets of triplets, 4 sets of quadruplets). The maximum number of recorded pregnancies was 39; that woman had 32 daughters and 7 sons.

**How many women have had abortions?**
*About 33 percent.*                          (Reference: 148)
In a recent magazine survey of women fully one third reported that they had at least one abortion and 72 percent viewed abortion favorably.

**How many fertile women practice birth control?**
*84 percent.*                          (References: 22, 72, 148)
The pill is used by 40 percent; diaphragms by 19 percent. The rest use, at about an equal incidence rate, IUDs, condoms, foam, rhythm, and withdrawal. Only a handful cite vasectomies or tubal ligations. And 16 percent use nothing at all.

Taken collectively, birth control measures reduce a woman's chances of becoming pregnant to about 1 in 20. Bad as that arithmetic may sound to some sexually liberated women, there are ways to make the odds far better. Scratch the rhythm method from the repertoire for starters. Although rooted in sound physiology (during a normal 28-day cycle, a woman is apt to get pregnant on only eight or so days) even slight irregularities in the cycle throw the calculation of "safe" days into chaos. Popularly known as "Vatican roulette" because it is the only birth control method endorsed by the Roman Catholic Church, the rhythm method is appropriate only for women who like gambling in bed.

Spermicidal foam, cream and jellies (when used alone) are relatively ineffective. So are vaginal suppositories where the active ingredient is a spermicide. Sperm are devious organisms; there is no safe charting their course once they enter a female's reproductive system. No spermicidal method can claim higher than 70 percent effectiveness.

What is left? Excellent birth control odds (99 percent effectiveness) are to be had by users of intrauterine devices (IUDs) and birth control pills. Yet both these methods have health-risk drawbacks and, superbly effective as they are, are slipping out of favor as awareness grows of their potential side-effects.

Two old standbys now are claiming allegiance from many who have abandoned the pill and IUDs—the condom (or rubber) and the diaphragm. Three quarters of a billion (750,000,000) condoms are annually sold in the United States and, although many surely go to waste in the wishful wallets of teenage boys, millions are put to good use in preventing pregnancies. Another benefit is that a condom prevents transmission of sexually transmittable diseases such as gonorrhea. Estimates of the condom's effectiveness range from 67–97 percent but, when properly used, it is nearly perfect. It is not foolproof, however. Violate the basic rules by, for instance, lubricating a condom with petroleum jelly (it eats through the thin fibers), using a condom for more than one ejaculation, or using one only when the mood strikes, and significantly reduced effectiveness is an understandable result. When used correctly and consistently, on the other hand, this time-tested device—the first ones were made in the early eighteenth century

—is extremely reliable and, importantly, it has no medical side effects.

The diaphragm too lacks side effects. Invented in 1882 (although the storied lover Casanova earlier applied the same idea by inserting half a lemon peel into a lover's vagina prior to copulation), a diaphragm works on the principle that if a sperm cannot enter the cervix and begin its trek up the woman's reproductive system, then pregnancy cannot result. Thus the diaphragm, a dome-shaped piece of rubber, is inserted into the vagina before sex. For added protection, gynecologists strongly urge users to coat their diaphragms with spermicides before insertion. Used in this fashion, the effectiveness is high—about 98 percent. As with the condom, however, effectiveness strongly correlates with correct insertion and use of the device. Fail to put it in properly or ignore using it from time to time and, certainly, decreased effectiveness will result.

Want to have no chance of getting pregnant? The best odds (almost 100 percent) are enjoyed by women who opt for sterilization, a route that 16 percent of all adult women choose.

**Without using birth control, how many women would become pregnant during a year of sexual relations?**

*60–80 percent.* (References: 19, 72)

Were no contraceptives used, it is estimated that 60 to 80 sexually active women in every 100 would become pregnant in the course of a year. Confirmation of a sort is provided by teenagers, who now account for over one million pregnancies yearly. A chief factor behind this high birth rate, according to many experts, is that fewer than 20 percent of sexually active teenagers use *any* kind of contraceptive. However, some 10–15 percent of all pregnancies are terminated in naturally occurring spontaneous abortions (miscarriages) which usually occur in the initial trimester of pregnancy.

### How many couples are sterile?
*10–15 percent.*                    (Reference: 72)
In about 60 percent of these cases, the infertility is traced to the woman. In the other 40, it is the man who is infertile. Why the greater rate of incidence of infertility in women? A suspicion, still to be confirmed, is that the relatively greater complexity of a woman's reproductive system heightens the chance of biological miscues.

### What are the odds a pregnancy will result in twins?
*1 in 90.*                    (Reference: 72)
Statisticians are fond of such calculations and their equations are of more than passing interest to any pregnant woman. Odds are also available on triplets (1 in 9000) and quadruplets (1 in 5,000,000).

### How many sex partners can a woman expect after divorce?
*3.5 per year.*                    (References: 67, 143)
An overwhelming majority, 91 percent, of all divorced women establish active sex lives soon after termination of their marriages. The average number of partners yearly is 3.5 (compared to 8.5 annually for men).

**Are there aphrodisiacs for women?**

*Yes, at least two.* (Reference: 148)

In Chapter 4 (Male Physiology) there is a full discussion of chemical aphrodisiacs and how they affect both men and women. In addition, in a recent survey of women it was determined that two more powerful aphrodisiacs were available for women. The playwright William Congreve, in one of the most consistently misquoted lines, opined, "Music has charms to soothe the savage beast." And, in the minds of 80 percent of women, music *is* a potent aphrodisiac, outpointing alcohol, marijuana, all other chemical substances, and erotica. Nevertheless the aphrodisiac listed by 95 percent of American women as the most powerful is "love."

**Does alcohol affect a woman's sexual pleasure?**

*Yes.* (References: 2, 119)

For many women (68 percent), alcohol "greatly or somewhat" enhances sex. Only 11 percent report no effect, and another 21 percent say it decreases their enjoyment. Women, in other words, find that sex and drink mix better than do men. In large measure that is because sizable quantities of booze can make it extraordinarily difficult for a male to achieve an erection. Not so for women, of course, although some do report that when intoxicated they have a far harder time reaching orgasm. A pleasant side effect for many women is that alcohol significantly decreases inhibitions, which makes the exploration of new or more imaginative sexual techniques easier.

Intriguingly, a recent survey of the nation's psychiatrists reveals that the health-care professions concur with much that women suspect about the interplay between alcohol and sex. The use of relatively small amounts of alcohol (an ounce or two) prior to lovemaking, say 63 percent of the psychiatrists, definitely enhances pleasure. However, 64 percent of the psychiatrists also warn that half or more of chronic alcohol users suffer from sexual dysfunction.

**Does marijuana affect a woman's sexual experiences?**

*Yes.*                                    (References: 2, 119, 139)

Rough estimates hold that anywhere from 25–50 percent of the nation's adult population has smoked marijuana at least once. Among women who have mixed "grass" and sex, 63 percent report the drug definitely added to their sexual pleasure. Sixteen (16) percent said it sometimes did, and 21 percent said marijuana definitely did not help their sex.

The previously mentioned poll of psychiatrists found them in substantial agreement with these surveyed women. Over half (52 percent) of the psychiatrists thought grass would increase sexual performance or pleasure, and 18 percent voted that it would diminish the sexual experience.

But the psychiatrists added another word of warning, one that applies to alcohol and marijuana both. The "female sexual symptom" they thought most associated with use of such substances is poor judgment in choice of partners (or so said 72 percent of the psychiatrists). Another 28 percent thought that women often failed to reach orgasm when mixing sex with any "recreational" drug.

187

**How many women get turned on to other women?**

*28 percent.*                    (References: 2, 75)

And 22 percent of all women have "thought of" having sex with another female. Harshly as old moralities would deal with these women, there is nothing whatsoever odd about getting turned on by a member of the same sex or fantasizing about sex with another woman. Imagination is a key to all satisfying sex. No harm befalls those with the most active imaginations—and much pleasure may.


**How many women have been raped?**

*24 percent.*                    (Reference: 148)

We are extremely tolerant of any sex act practiced by consenting adults. Rape is another matter. It is *not* a sex act; rather it is an act of violent aggression.

Over 50,000 rapes are reported yearly. But only a small fraction, suspect law enforcement agencies, are reported—perhaps 10–25 percent of the actual total. Even so, a reported rape occurs every 17 minutes in the United States. It should be sobering to hear that 24 percent of the *Cosmopolitan* women in a recent nationwide survey reported they had been raped. Of these, 51 percent said their rapist was a friend; 37 percent was raped by strangers; 18 percent by relatives; and 3 percent by husbands.

It is clear from the questions and the choice of answers offered by *Cosmopolitan* in that recent survey that the connotation of the word *rape* has changed in common usage. This in turn is largely responsible for much of the apparent increase (from 1 in 25 a few years ago to 1 in 4 today) among surveyed women. For in years past few women would have been presented with a choice of answers which included "friends" and "husbands" as rapists. This is not to say that friends and husbands who force entry on a woman are not guilty of "rape," but only that it would not likely have been called rape by women themselves until recently.

During the past five years we have all become more enlightened about the crime of rape and the impact it has on its victims. In the process we have also gained empathy with the badgered and embarrassed victim who must face the court when attempting to bring the rapist to justice. However, the victim's courtroom ordeal today cannot compare to the ordeal of rape victims trying to bring a rapist to justice in the past. According to eighteenth century Welsh law a woman could assure a man's conviction of rape only by holding a religious relic in her right hand while grasping the rapist's penis in her left hand and swearing that the penis in her hand was the one that raped her.

**How many women have experienced a homosexual overture?**
*22 percent.*                          (Reference: 47)
About three times as many men have been "cruised," as the language goes. Among women, the experience apparently is somewhat rare. Only 9 percent say it happens "often"; another 2 percent say "sometimes." The rest who have had this experience say it is rare.

**How many women are lesbians?**
*7 percent.*                      (References: 75, 99)
Define a lesbian as an adult female who has had

more than six sexual experiences with other women, as John Hopkins Professor John Money does, and 1 woman in 14 is a lesbian. Useful as this definition is (and no matter what definition is used, all surveys peg the U.S. incidence of lesbians at 5–10 or so percent), there are problems with it. Certainly a woman who had, say in her early twenties, dozens of lesbian contacts but now have passed several years in an exclusively heterosexual life-style should not be counted as a lesbian, although this definition would view her as one. That is why in our clinical work we consider a woman to be a lesbian only if her current sexual activity is exclusively homosexual. Other categories we use include: exclusively heterosexual, bisexual with largely heterosexual preferences, and bisexual with mainly homosexual preferences.

Arguments about definitions aside, however, some 19 percent of American women have had at least one sexual contact with other women. A full 13 percent have achieved orgasm in the process.

**When does a woman identify herself as a lesbian?**
*In her early twenties.* (Reference: 18)
Mind you, self-identification does not imply stepping "out of the closet" and publicly proclaiming one's homosexuality. What our number refers to is when a woman is apt to decide that her orientation in matters sexual is lesbian.

# CHAPTER 6

## Wasn't It Good?—Male Psychology

"The mind," wrote British philosopher Bertrand Russell, "is a strange machine which can combine the materials offered to it in the most astonishing ways." So it is with men and their psychology when it comes to sex. We have seen, in previous chapters, how men's bodies work and what their sexual practices are. But how do they feel about sex? Women? Love? It is in this section that men speak their minds on these and many other subjects.

**How many men worry that their penises are too small?**

*17 percent.* (Reference: 138)

Virtually all such worries, as we have discussed earlier, are unfounded. Nonetheless, 1 man in 6 fears his "manhood," as chaste fiction writers of earlier eras delicately put matters, is too tiny to do its job. But reassuring news is that an overwhelming majority, 83 percent, are confident about and satisfied with the size of their erect penises.

**How many men think they are good lovers?**
*73 percent.*                    (Reference: 138)
About one quarter (24 percent) say that they are very good lovers; another 49 percent say they are good in bed; 25 percent say they are "fair"; and 2 percent are sure they are poor.

Self-descriptions aside, what makes a man a good or even a great lover? Not anatomy or physiology—most men are pretty much alike in those regards anyway. Mental attitude, in our clinical experience, is far more important.

How a man approaches making love is critical. Is he giving or selfish? Sensitive to a partner's desires? Put in this perspective, no man who genuinely wants to be a good lover need resign himself to being "fair" in bed. An attitudinal overhaul—one geared to stressing sensitivity and sharing—can put matters straight.

**How many men think sex is very important?**
*49 percent.*                    (Reference: 105)
American men regard sex as an important part of their lives and happiness. But ask men to rank their priorities and love beats sex hands down. Eighty-five percent of all adult men say love is "very important" —nearly twice as many as those who put sex in that slot. Nonetheless, health is accorded the highest ranking; 89 percent of men deem it very important. List the top 11 concerns of men and sex manages but a

ninth place finish. Only religion, considered very important by 41 percent, and money, much valued by 39 percent, fall below it in importance.

**How many men think sex is the most important pleasure in life?**
*20 percent.*                                    (Reference: 102)
Sex may not be a man's most important pleasure (only 1 man in 5 accords it this elevated rank) but 98 percent of all men agree it is certainly a pleasure they want to enjoy. Only 1 percent say it is not important; another 1 percent dismiss it as "something you have to do."

**How many men think sex and love are linked?**
*Only 17 percent.*                                (Reference: 2)
A full 83 percent of men think sex and love need not be linked. Certainly, most men (76 percent) think love makes sex better; but even when love is absent, all but 17 percent still are eager to "make it" when they can. A flat 7 percent see no relationship whatsoever between love and sex.

**What is love?**
*Discussion follows.*
Love is a word used in many contexts. How do people use it? Some people love a particular food, parents love their kids, kids love pets, some teachers love their students, sometimes a person loves his or her garden. Husbands, wives, and lovers love one another, and many people love God.

In most of these cases love can be thought of as appreciating, caring for, nurturing, and enhancing the growth of the love object. In all cases love can be defined as the receiving or the anticipation of receiving such intense pleasure from the love object or relationship that one desires to perpetuate this pleasureful sensation. These feelings of love can vary in intensity from mild to addictive; and when people speak of being "in love" or experiencing "true love" for someone, they are usually describing *an addiction to the love object's company*.

So far nothing has been said about sex in this discussion of love. That is because sex is not necessarily a part of love, even "true" (addictive) love. People can fall in love with other people and become addicted without any sexual relationship whatsoever.

Then what role does sex play in a love relationship? In rare cases sex itself may be the sole source of the pleasure which produces the addiction and the feeling of being "in love." However, more commonly sex adds pleasure to an already pleasureful relationship to produce the "in love" addiction or it adds pleasure to what would be an intense, pleasureful addiction in the absence of sex.

At times love and sex are even incompatible. Many *macho* men suffer from a "Madonna/whore" complex, feeling that love should be reserved for Madonnas (chaste women) and sex should be practiced only with whores (all women who are not chaste). These unhappy men unceasingly attempt to seduce virgin women to prove to themselves that these women are not chaste and therefore are not worthy of their true love. Their unhappiness is a product of their constant unresolved quest. They want what they cannot have and when they get it they no longer want it.

For these men even marriage to a Madonna rarely results in happiness for them or their wives. They often expect to have sex with their wives only to produce children, and the slightest sign of sexual arousal in their wives is cause to suspect she is no Madonna and may not be trusted in the presence of other men. These men, in turn, expect to get all their sexual pleasure with prostitutes or other unchaste women.

In a tender Italian film titled *Il Bell' Antonio*, Marcello Mastroianni played the title role of a man who was madly in love with the nonsexual qualities of the beautiful woman he married. Although before marriage he had a reputation for being a great lover in the best Italian bordellos, he was incapable of having sex with the wife he adored and worshiped. For him "true love" and sex were incompatible and he experienced impotence in her presence. Unfortunately, for his wife "true love" without sex was unthinkable. The story ended tragically in annulment, and a broken heart for Antonio who believed in sex without love and love without sex.

**How often do men think "true love" comes?**
*1. 2 times in a lifetime.*          (Reference: 136)
Few men do not cherish, however secretly, the feeling that somewhere in the world there is the perfect mate for them. Centuries back, the Greek philosopher Plato built this notion into his *Symposium* where, Plato theorized, each male and female are but half a perfect organism and for love to be "true" we must discover the one "other half" that makes an exactly perfect pair. Today many of us still speak of a

spouse as our "better half." Valid or not—and there is ample evidence to suggest that a man or a woman could easily find happiness and contentment with many different mates—this Platonic theory obviously claims numerous adherents.

**How many men think love comes by the fourth date?**
*20 percent.*                                    (Reference: 136)
If lights are not flashing and feelings of love not stirring in their hearts on the first date with a woman, some men suspect it is a match that will never result in love—for them it is love at first sight or not at all. But most men are more patient. Twenty percent expect love to bloom by the fourth date; 30 percent said it would take at least twenty dates to be sure; and most of the remainder fall in between.

How fast *should* love come? Lively a topic as this question provides for living room analysis, it is one that defies answering. Love is like the mail. Neither's arrival is predictable.

**How many men are indifferent when a love affair ends?**
*10 percent.*                          (References: 102,144)
Macho myths notwithstanding, most men admit to sadness and pain when an affair or marriage falls apart. This unhappiness, many men (37 percent) say, will pass quickly; but 22 percent feel hurt enough to want to avoid women for a while—a number that is nearly matched by the 20 percent who say they will immediately pursue a new relationship. One in 20 (6 percent) admit that in the aftermath of a roman-

tic breakup their work suffers; and a final 2 percent say they are close to a mental breakdown.

The collapse of a marriage or love affair is traumatic for both partners. A step-by-step 12-week program for overcoming postlove suffering and developing the self-assurance and strength required for achieving satisfactory relationships in the future is outlined in *Letting Go,* the book which presents an action program for moving beyond a broken heart.

**How many men approve of premarital sex?**
*91 percent.*                                   (Reference: 2)
But the unwed should wait before cracking open the champagne: Many men among the 91 percent who express approval do so with string attached to their opinion. Only 28 percent give premarital sex their unequivocal approval with another 27 percent giving the nod only when adults are the lovers. Thirty-three percent believe it is acceptable if the couples "share affection" or are in love, and 3 percent limit it strictly to engaged couples.

**What is a boy's chief source of sex information?**
*Friends.*                            (References: 2, 67, 156)
Locker-room chatter and street-corner talk, say 59 percent of adult men, provided them with the bulk of their sex education. Reading did the job for another 20 percent. The rest turned to scattered sources: fathers (6 percent); mothers (3 percent); other adults (6 percent); and brothers and sisters (4 percent). A bare 3 percent say that school afforded them their main source of sex education. Only 20 percent

of men reported that their parents told them anything about sex.

**Who do men think should provide sex education?**
*Parents.*                    (References: 2, 61, 67)
Their friends, most males admit, were not the ideal sex educators—only 6 percent deem this the best way to get information. Nearly half (45 percent) think parents should do the job. Another 28 percent would send children to a solid sex education class in school and 15 percent more think books are the best source.

Why the switch away from friends when we shift from practice to theory? It is perhaps because, as many men discover in maturing, the "facts" and theories on sex offered by teenage boys often are thoroughly erroneous. Many boys, for instance, continue to think that premature withdrawal is an effective contraceptive technique. It is not. In addition, about 30 percent of adolescents believe that a female who does not *want* to become pregnant won't, no matter how sexually active she is. False as such notions are, learning these lessons can be a sad education for many a young man—and sad, too, for his female companion.

**How many teenage boys tell their parents "almost everything" about their sex lives?**
*9 percent.*                        (Reference: 61)
Kids are generally mum about sex when it comes to discussions with parents. Forty-five percent talk with Mom and Dad about sex only in the most general way, never about the specifics in their own lives. Twenty-six percent say almost nothing. And another

20 percent tell their folks "only what they would approve."

**How many teenage boys believe they need not be "romantically involved" with a female before having sex with her?**
*59 percent.* (Reference: 61)
Just as adults are ambivalent about the need for love in a sexual relationship, kids are skeptical, too. Only 41 percent insist romance must come before lovemaking.

**How many teenage boys say they have been in love?**
*82 percent.* (Reference: 61)
Kids may be silent with their parents, but they eagerly talk with researchers, and only 18 percent of boys 15–18 say they have never been in love.

**What qualities do teenage boys most value in a girl?**
*Good looks and a good body.* (Reference: 61)
In appreciating girls, teenage boys have physical priorities. Other factors listed by the boys are: friendly; not conceited; intelligent; sense of humor; honest; good conversationalist; similar interests and values; sexually open; outgoing; and mature. What is intriguing about this list is the proportionately greater stress on female physical qualities among boys when compared to the female qualities appreciated by adult men.

**How many teenage boys approve of premarital sex?**
*83 percent.* (Reference: 61)
Not surprisingly, younger men are enthusiastic

about premarital sex, with only 1 in 6 expressing disapproval.

**How many teenage boys believe a man should be a virgin when he marries?**
*8.5 percent.*                              (Reference: 61)
Only 8 percent of boys ages 15–16 think they should be virgin grooms; and 9 percent of boys 17–18 think they should.

**How many teenage boys believe men should be sexually experienced before settling down with one person?**
*62 percent.*                              Reference: 61)
In light of our previous question about teenage boys' feelings about virginity at the altar, their attitudes about sexual experience before settling down (not marriage) with one person are more conservative. This is because many teenagers believe couples should live together before marriage. Sixty-five percent of boys 15–16 think a male definitely should be experienced; and 59 percent of 17- and 18-year-old males agree.

**How many teenage boys believe girls should be sexually experienced before settling down with one man?**
*55 percent.*                              (Reference: 61)
With cohabitation rates rising, this question explores another dimension of teenage attitudes. Not unexpectedly, more boys prefer chastity in their prospective live-in partners than in their brides. Almost half (45 percent) want their "steadies" and other

"serious" women in their lives to be sexually inexperienced at the relationship's onset. This is probably indicative of the fact that many teenagers want to be their wife's first lover, but also want to play that part with someone else before marriage.

**How many teenage boys believe a girl should be a virgin when she marries?**
*15 percent.*                          (Reference: 61)
In this instance, 13 percent of boys ages 15–16 want a virgin bride. But 17 percent of 17- and 18-year-olds do.

**Of the teenage boys who have fondled female breasts, how many enjoyed it?**
*99 percent.*                          (Reference: 61)
There is near unanimity here, with 60 percent finding this fondling to be very pleasant and 39 percent saying it was "moderately" enjoyable. Just 1 percent had no fun at all doing it.

**Of the teenage boys who have caressed a female's vagina, how many enjoyed it?**
*99 percent.*                          (Reference: 61)
Near unanimity once again—but with a slight shift in the responses. Here, 68 percent found this digital exploration to be very enjoyable and 31 percent received moderate enjoyment from their experience.

**Of the teenage boys who have had their penis caressed by a female, how many enjoyed it?**
*98 percent.*                          (Reference: 61)
In this case, 73 percent thought it "very" enjoyable,

with 25 percent finding it "moderately" so. Only 2 percent say it was not fun at all.

**How many teenage boys fantasize while masturbating?**
*91 percent.*                    (Reference: 61)
And only 9 percent approach masturbation with a clear head.

**How many boys approve of receiving oral sex from a girl?**
*92 percent.*                    (Reference: 61)
Teenagers, in the main, hold to liberal attitudes about sexual expression—a point vividly underscored by the refusal of only 8 percent of young males to grant approval for this type of oral sex.

**How many teenage boys approve of giving oral sex to a girl?**
*91 percent.*                    (Reference: 61)
A variation of 1 percentage point in a survey's responses, most statisticians admit, is not meaningful— a caveat that may apply to the 1 point difference between teenage males approval rates for fellatio and cunnilingus.

**How many teenage boys fantasize about sex?**
*84 percent.*                    (Reference: 61)
Besides having a fair amount of sexual activity, most boys admit to whiling away at least a portion of their time with fantasies and other thoughts of sex. That is not unusual, however. *Most* of the adult population does also.

**How many teenage boys approve of sex between a white man and black woman?**

*65 percent.* (Reference: 131)

Boys, interestingly enough, grow more accepting of this kind of sex as they mature. Almost half—46 percent—of 13–15-year-olds deem such coupling "immoral," and only 54 percent of them give their approval. The attitudes of older boys, in the 16–19-year-old bracket, are strikingly different. Only 23 percent of these teens believe that sex between a white man and a black woman is immoral and a full three quarters (76 percent) approve, with only 1 percent expressing uncertainty.

**How many teenage boys approve of sex between a white woman and a black man?**

*69 percent.* (Reference: 131)

If teenagers are the harbingers of our society's future, this nation soon will be fully accepting of interracial sex—with more than two thirds of all teenage boys now giving their hearty approval. Twenty-nine percent think it is "immoral" and another 2 percent are not sure where they stand.

**How many men approve of sex with older women?**

*84 percent.* (Reference: 102)

Only one man in six (16 percent) firmly eliminates older women from the list of potential lovers. Of the remaining 84 percent, however, most attach a variety of conditions to their approval. Thirty-eight percent say age is not relevant to sex, but another 13 percent say a sex partner could be any age as long as she does not *look* older. Sixteen percent will take a lover who's up to five years older, and 11 percent allow a decade's difference but no more. Finally, 4 percent say they invariably prefer older lovers.

**How many young men have ever been asked out on a date by a woman?**
*89 percent of college men.* (Reference: 52)
More than half (51 percent) said it was "great" to be approached by a woman, and 45 percent thought it was "O.K." Only 4 percent admitted to feelings of discomfort.

**How many college men insist on paying all expenses on dates?**
*28 percent.* (Reference: 52)
Another wrinkle to the caveman stereotype is the notion that man is the provider and that by extension, it is the man who pays all the bills of socializing. In some elegant restaurants, in both France and the United States, waiters enforce this custom by distributing menus lacking prices to all women they seat. Only men, in those establishments, are privy to the evening's tab. However, if the current practices on campus are an indication of coming developments, such customs appear to be doomed. Among college men, only a trace over 1 man in 4 holds to the practice of paying all. More than two thirds (68 perment) say they "usually" pay, but certainly do not always pick up the tabs on a date. And 4 percent go further still, these men insist on splitting all bills with dates, making every evening a dutch-treat.

**How many men believe their dates expect to have sex on the first date?**

*8 percent of college men.*        (Reference: 52)

Over half of the men (53 percent) believe women are in no particular rush to have sex; for these women, say the men, the right time for sex is "once we know each other." Another 39 percent of men say their dates have "no expectations" at all about when to have sex—it will happen for them when the physiological and psychological chemistries are right.

**How many men do not think masturbation is wrong?**

*80 percent.*        (Reference: 67)

Almost all men enjoy this normal sexual outlet, and, to massage the old Gallic saying, can 100 million American men be wrong? Certainly not in the eyes of younger men, whose sexual outlets typically are limited and may consist solely of masturbation. A scant 15 percent of males ages 17 and 18 have any qualms about masturbation; and the same 15 percent of men ages 19–24 also have qualms. Only 16 percent of men 25–34 see anything wrong with this playful stroking. At the other age extreme, among men 55 and older, 29 percent believe in the sinfulness of masturbation.

**How many men disapprove of their son's masturbating?**

*57 percent.*        (Reference: 136)

Psychology unearths many paradoxes and this surely is one of them. These fathers, odds are, tried their hands at masturbation, and did so much more frequently than once. Their sons are doing it, too—of that there is no doubt. Even so, over half the men disapprove of this practice for their sons.

**How many men disapprove of their daughter's masturbating?**

*65 percent.* (Reference: 136)

When the sons do it, it is not considered good. When the daughters masturbate, it is even worse, say fathers. Nearly two thirds would like to deny their daughters a free hand in exploring their female sexual anatomy.

**How many men fantasize while masturbating?**

*72 percent usually do.* (Reference: 102)

An absolutely clear head, say most men, is not a masturbatory aid. Fantasies of sex play are an effective tool in enhancing the enjoyment of self-stroking. In addition to the men who usually fantasize, another 17 percent "sometimes do." Only 11 percent of all men say they *never* fantasize while masturbating.

**What do most men fantasize about while masturbating?**

*Their current sex partners.* (Reference: 102)

About two men in three (64 percent) say they are loyal to their partners even while fantasizing. Eleven percent favor dreams that incorporate past sexual experiences; another 11 percent think about other persons such as movie stars and acquaintances; and 4 percent try thoughts of group or other exotic kinds of sex. For younger men and those lacking current partners, the fantasy objects of choice often are acquaintances and celebrities, from TV stars through models in magazines.

**How many men sleep in the nude?**

*10 percent.* (References: 58, 136)

That's the bare fact. In-the-buff sleep simply is not popular. Most men prefer a bit of clothing at night, with preference ranging from briefs alone through complete pajama outfits.

Nudity does not always accompany sex. Some extremely Hasidic Jews must copulate through a cloth with a hole in it so that the act is devoid of nudity. In addition, Mormons require the wearing of a sacred garment during sex, and Christ is always depicted wearing a loin cloth on the cross even though his crucifixion was conducted in the nude.

The Menomini Indians of Wisconsin would prevent nudity and direct skin contact during sex by covering the women with a deerskin blanket having a hole in it. These decorated blankets, which were considered sacred, were owned by only a few members of each band and were rented out with extra charges for damages if the blankets were returned soiled.

Several Christian sects have been known to embrace nudity during mass because they believed Adam and Eve originated in that condition before sin. These Christians believed that Christ had succeeded in returning their sects to that sinless condition. Appearing in the 2nd century A.D., these sects —including the Adamiani, Carpocratons, Encratites and Marcosians—disappeared by the beginning of the fifth century. During the Middle Ages similar groups made their appearance in Europe, but they too died out.

Among some more recent Christian groups like the Franciscans, penance was often performed in nudity, and among several eastern religions nudity is often considered a sign of piety.

How many men enjoy hugging and kissing if intercourse will not follow?

*71 percent.* (Reference: 102)

Many women complain that men are excessively "goal oriented," too interested in climbing into bed and immediately engaging in sex. Valid as that complaint may be with some men—only 19 percent of men find terminal hugging and kissing to be frustrating or distasteful—most men are quite happy to partake of these simple pleasures. One man in ten even says he has "a real need for it," and mounting psychological evidence suggests that caressing is an integral part of every healthy person's life. There is an apparent need to touch others and to be touched. Chimpanzees, denied such intimacy, often exhibit increasing signs of mental instability.

What form of foreplay do men most enjoy?

*Kissing and caressing.* (Reference: 102)

Given the preceding answer, this response is unsurprising, and it is offered by 37 percent of men. But praised as kissing and caressing are, they have a strong rival—oral sex, which is favored by 27 percent. Showing in third place is fondling a female's breasts, an activity much favored by 22 percent. The remaining men divide their allegiance between caressing their partner's genitals (19 percent) and simply gazing at their lover's nude body (11 percent). Mathematicians in our readership likely have noticed that our numbers total more than 100 percent. No matter. A few men cite co-favorites and, furthermore, an additional 2 percent insist they do not like foreplay in any manner, shape or form.

**How many men prefer the lights on during sex?**
*45 percent.*                              (Reference: 47)

Lights on or off? That's a major etiquette question for many couples. Twenty-four percent of men definitely prefer lights on, probably because it is all the better for viewing a partner's body. Another 21 percent like at least some light shed on the subject, a dimly romantic one perhaps? Twenty-nine percent, however, emphatically want their sex in the dark. The rest have no preference.


**How many men think it should always be their job to make the first sexual move?**
*That depends on age and education*
                                           (Reference: 67)

The number of birthdays a man has counted as well as the number of years spent in school determines the answer to this question. Forty percent of males over 35 who have never attended college think it is unacceptable for a woman to make the first move. Among college-educated men under 35, only 16 percent have any problems with sexually assertive women. As a rule, college-educated men, no matter their age, are more accepting of sexually-assertive women than are noncollege-educated men; and younger men are usually more receptive to women's advances than are older men.


**How many men are turned on when a woman takes the sexual initiative?**
*80 percent.*                              (Reference: 136)

In yet another male endorsement of the revolution in female attitudes, the caveman stereotype activity of carrying off a shy woman to have sex is fast disappearing. Men are now eager to be on the receiving end of sexual overtures, from invitations to dinner dates through outright requests for sexual favors. If a woman wishes to take the sexual initiative, she is certainly no longer restricted by male antagonism.

**How many men communicate their true sexual desires during sex?**
*53 percent.* (Reference: 102)

Men are relatively quiet when it comes to talking about sexual matters with their partners. Only 28 percent say they discuss such issues while having sex and 16 percent more say that, after considerable experience with a particular partner, they might discuss such matters. A final 9 percent talk before or afterward. That leaves nearly half of all men (47 percent) who simply do not talk with their lovers about sex. But communication is an integral key to good sex. Statisticians have calculated over 14 *million* possible sexual positions involving a man and a woman, and given the magnitude of that list, no lover can always be expected to magically know exactly what will turn you on at any given moment. If you would like to have your ear kissed during orgasm, tell your partner; better yet, beg for it during the throes of passion. She will probably be delighted to oblige you. No matter what your desires are, a very few words to a caring and loving partner can bring new luster to any sexual relationship.

**How many men want sex more than once daily**
*13 percent.* (Reference: 102)

210

About 25 percent opt for 5–7 times a week. The simple most common desire, a response offered by 35 percent, is for 3–4 times weekly; 18 percent opt for 1–2 times a week; and the rest would be satisfied with intercourse every other week or so—except, that is, for a reluctant 0.4 percent who *never* want sex.

**How many men are satisfied with their sex lives?**
*69 percent.*                          (Reference: 2)
Two men of every three utter nothing but contentments when it comes to rating their sex lives. Twenty percent describe their sex lives as "very satisfactory," and a shade less than half rate theirs "satisfactory." Among less happy males, 23 percent report their sex is unsatisfactory and 8 percent are sure it is even worse than that.

What makes one man's sex life satisfactory and another's not? Part of the answer may be rooted in physiology (points probed in earlier sections), but the major factors typically are attitudinal. Two men could have identical sex lives in practice, yet offer radically different ratings. Expectations are the key. Some men are eager adventurers into new sexual territory. Unless they find willing partners in these treks, their satisfaction level may be disappointing. Other males, thoroughly content with regular episodes of largely predictable sex, may be somewhat easier to please, although demands made by more adventurous women might frustrate these same men.

**How many churchgoing men find sex pleasureful?**
*40 percent.*                          (Reference: 67)

**How many men who don't attend church find sex pleasureful?**

*78 percent.*                    (Reference: 67)

More than three fourths (78 percent) of all men who do not attend church report that their sex during the past year was pleasurable. Among regular churchgoers, the pleasure rating dips to a relatively meager 40 percent. We mention this difference on sexual matters between the churchgoers and non-churchgoers because it is a factor that affects answers to many of the questions in this book. In every instance, the regular communicant reports receiving less pleasure from sex and to being less adventurous in his sex life. One reason for this may be that many religions preach against non-procreative sex, i.e., sex for sheer physical excitement, or for love and communication between partners. Regardless of cause, however, we mention the church/unchurched chasm in order to provide perspective.

**How many men have changed their attitudes about sex during the past five years?**

*74 percent.*                    (Reference: 102)

Only one man in four reports that his feelings about sex have remained unchanged during the past half decade. For most of the rest, matters have changed for the better. Over 40 percent are enjoying sex more than ever; 11 percent happily report they vary their practices and positions more these days; and another 13 percent are happy *but* they would like more experimentation. A final 11 percent report their sex is now more humdrum and less enjoyable.

What is the clear conclusion? Most men, as they themselves testify, find their sex lives more fulfilling with every passing year. One explanation for this may well be we are now considerably more open and frank about our sexuality. Needs and wants are candidly discussed and, in the process, many find that as knowledge, understanding, and communication increase so do enjoyment and satisfaction.

**How often do men think their sex partners have an orgasm?**
*Most of the time or always.*    (Reference: 138)
Women have already had their say on this; now it is the males' turn. Twenty-one percent of men are certain their sex partner(s) always reach orgasm. About half (48 percent) think their partner does most of the time. Twenty-three percent say "sometimes," and the remaining 8 percent don't know or else suspect their partner never reaches orgasm.

**How many men deliberately try to delay their orgasms during sex?**
*84 percent.*    (Reference: 102)
A physiological fact, as we have examined earlier, is that on average men climax a shade faster than women. With most couples that time difference is small, but it looms large to many. To help ensure an orgasm for their female companions, many men explore all manner of delaying tactics, from using local anesthetics—widely available in sex shops—to mulling over the Dow Jones Index for industrial stocks. Where thoughts are the tool of choice, many men find nonsexual ones to work more effectively than sexual ones. But a more sexual approach we often recommend to clients when an orgasm is in the immediate offing is to interrupt intercourse and turn to

213

other sexual play—oral sex, fondling, etc. Another tack is to try a change of positions or perhaps to pause for a glass of wine or warm conversation. Fear not. Erections have a way of returning on their own.

**How many men think sex ends after both partners have orgasms?**
*41 percent.*                                       (Reference: 102)
The beginning of sex is easy to define. When it ends is far more controversial. However, 41 percent of all men agree the happiest ending is when both the male and the female climax. Not all men are so magnanimous however; for 18 percent, sex ends when *they* have an orgasm and for 5 percent more it's when they have two orgasms. Another 11 percent say it stops when they want it to stop.

A considerate 18 percent say it is time to call a halt when the woman wants to stop. Another 10 percent say intercourse ends when the woman has had an orgasm or two.

**What is the most common reported feeling of men after climaxing?**
*Contentment.*                                      (Reference: 102)
The Rolling Stones may have paved their way to rock success by complaining "I Can't Get No Satisfaction," but the average man is certain that sex is a good route to providing him with a healthy share of contentment. Following orgasm, 45 percent usually feel a satisfied contentment and another 24 percent say they typically feel quite loving toward their partners. Sixteen percent feel exhilarated; yet, paradoxically, 16 percent feel drowsy. This evidence suggests most men conclude a sex act with strong feelings of

happiness. Not so, however, for a handful. Two percent feel depressed, another 2 percent feel guilty. Younger males, in particular, are acutely prone to feelings of guilt and fear until they become comfortable with integrating sex into their personal value systems.

**How many men would like to try different positions more often?**
*54 percent.*                                    (Reference: 102)

To improve their pleasure, 54 percent of men are keen to explore new ways of lovemaking. But second on the list of men's wants is more oral sex, which 22 percent mention. Eleven (11) percent would like group sex with multiple female partners; 4 percent would like more anal sex; 2 percent vote for homosexual pursuits; and 1 percent say sadomasochism is their answer. A final 11 percent want no change in their current sex practices.

**How many men want their sex partners to be more active during sex?**
*34 percent.*                           (References: 67, 102)

This answer underlines men's criticism (seen in later answers) of female unresponsiveness, and 34 percent of men definitely want their partner to be more active in bed. Other favorite desires are for more oral sex (24 percent) and for their partners to caress their penises more (18 percent). Sixteen percent want their partner to wear sexy lingerie; 11 percent are hoping for a longer display of her nude body; and 7 percent want her to use exciting words. A final 3 percent, presumably men whose lovers provide complete contentment, offer no answer at all.

**How many men enjoy giving oral sex to a woma?**
*55 percent.* (References: 67, 102)

Giving oral sex to a woman is a mountingly popular sexual pastime and, in addition to the majority of men who positively like it, another 23 percent do not mind getting their licks in. That leaves 15 percent who do not engage in cunnilingus; 5 percent who insist "it is unnatural"; and the final 3 percent who dislike it.

Intriguingly, the question affords a significant perspective on the relationship between sexual attitudes and race. Black men, on the whole, are far less enthusiastic about giving oral sex to women than are whites. Thirty-three percent of black men do not practice cunnilingus but otherwise offer no explanation for their reluctance. Other blacks who refuse to do it are more informative: 11 percent more will not do it because it is unnatural; and 5 percent more hold out because it is boring. Put another way, twice as many male blacks as whites think the vaginal area is no place for a man's tongue.

A chasm also arises when age is correlated with attitudes about giving oral sex. Younger men, 89 percent in the 25–34 age bracket, support giving oral sex. Older men are far more reserved. In the 45–54 age group, only 56 percent give cunnilingus even a mild endorsement; and in the 55 and up group, that number declines to 48 percent.

**Do men become excited while giving oral sex to a woman?**
*Yes.* (Reference: 118)

That is the answer given by most of the nation's psychiatrists. But they are of several minds as to why men employ their tongue in oral sex. Forty-seven percent say the act is exciting for men, but 43 percent think it is done to enhance the partner's pleasure. Three (3) percent say men perform cunnilingus to "appear sophisticated," and the rest of the psychiatrists in this poll offered no firm opinions.

### How many men think anal sex is acceptable?
*59 percent.*                                   (Reference: 67)
"Going in the back door"—as a common idiom puts it—is another sexual pursuit that is rapidly winning afficionados. A full third of all men think it is fine; 26 percent say it is "somewhat" O.K.; and 14 percent express no opinion. Only 27 percent insist anal intercourse is unacceptable. Physiologically, the anal opening is a richly sensitive erogenous zone, a fact that is ample explanation for why many couples find this version of sex pleasurable.

### How many men have fantasies during sex?
*58 percent.*                                   (Reference: 133)
While 41 percent never have fantasies in the midst of intercourse, 5 percent almost always do and 53 percent sometimes do. Why put your thoughts elsewhere during sex? Often, say 38 percent of the men who have fantasies, such thoughts heighten their interest in and enthusiasm for the sex at hand by increasing their overall level of excitement. Thirty percent more say such imagining increases the partner's attractiveness; 18 percent think about sexual practices that their partner isn't using and 3 percent are seeking to diminish boredom. Another 10 percent confess they do not know why they fantasize.

**What do men fantasize most during sex?**
*Oral sex.*                           (Reference: 133)
Fellatio and cunnilingus, say 61 percent of men, often are on their minds when having fantasies during coitus. Other main fantasy paths include: having women find them sexually irresistible (55 percent); imaginary lovers (44 percent); former lovers (43 percent); and others giving into you after first resisting. (Percentages exceed 100 because the men were free to check off as many items as they wished.)

**How many men while masturbating fantasize about being raped?**
*18 percent of males under 35 have; 5 percent of older males have.*          (Reference: 67)
Sadistic fantasies may win few male fans, but masochistic ones score even lower. Again, our numbers do not suggest these men always have such thoughts; just that they sometimes do.

**How many men while masturbating fantasize about rape?**
*30 percent.*                           (Reference: 67)
This is not to say these men *always* have such fantasies; just that they have done so at least once.

**How many men have ever fantasized about raping a woman?**
*30 percent.*
      (References: 37, 38, 72, 82, 90, 91, 93, 138)
Broaden the scope of the question to include rape fantasies in any context and nearly 1 man in 3 says he has had such thoughts at one time or another. But most qualify their admission by noting that at

no time do they actually wish to physically hurt a woman. What they want instead, these men say, is to conquer her. Even so, 9 percent of men say they have at least once used force or its threat to compel a woman to have sex.

That men are more aggressive than women is not disputed by scientists. Certainly there are aggressive women (and, among praying mantises, the female often eats the male while he is copulating her). But among humans, males generally are decidedly more aggressive. Three, *not* mutually exclusive, factors have been articulated by researchers as possible explanations.

First, as our anatomy section underscores, men tend to be physically larger than women. They are, on the whole, also more muscular and stronger. Although relative smallness need not rule out aggressiveness, it frequently makes it a less-than-effective course of action.

Other researchers argue in favor of socialization and conditioning. To a large extent, most of our tastes, likes, and dislikes are products of social forces, and not of instincts. Males, this theory continues, are raised in environments that approve of their aggressiveness and condemn a female's. The young boy who comes home with a "shiner," a blackened eye, is often greeted with parental praise. A girl who did this, on the other hand, probably would be treated either as a "wounded flower" or as a pariah.

Although not denying the importance of either of these theories, much current research actively explores a different avenue—hormones. As previously noted, a great deal remains to be discovered about hormones and their roles in human behavior. Although most researchers now concur that hormones are critical, even instrumental factors in determining behavior, few specific implications have emerged. Nonetheless, work with lower animals (typically monkeys) leads to numerous interesting conclusions. Androgen deficiencies in animals, for instance, make them far more docile and less aggressive than their normal relatives. In other studies, androgen inhibitors—drugs that block hormone activities—when administered to humans result in lower sex drives, overall decreases in sexual activity, and declines in aggressiveness. Another case in point is that when pregnant female monkeys are administered high levels of testosterone, their female offspring exhibit traces of male anatomical features and dramatically elevated levels of aggressiveness.

Add these findings up and there emerges a clear link between hormones and sexual behavior. Androgen (testosterone), the chief male hormone, in particular appears related to aggression; increase its levels to a certain point and sexual behavior increases. Increase it further and sexuality is reduced while aggression is induced. Still to be discovered, however, are the precise threshold levels. When, for instance, do androgen levels dip low enough to effect behavior changes? Needless to say, such issues now are chief among the concerns of many researchers.

### How many men can ejaculate by fantasy alone?
*1 in 1000.* (Reference: 126)
The no-hands and no-physical-contact route to orgasm is successfully pursued by but 0.1 percent of men. There is ample reason to suspect many more men *could* ejaculate just by fantasizing, except other

forms of sexual expression are generally faster and more reliable, so most males simply never give this technique a thought.

**How many men have voluntarily viewed erotic or pornographic materials?**
*92 percent.* (References: 2, 110)
Just about all adult males have had at least one glimpse of erotica. Within the past two years, 40 percent have seen pictorial descriptions of intercourse. Among males under 21, 80 percent say they have seen visual or textual descriptions of intercourse at some point; more than half have their first peek by age 15.

**How many men are aroused by erotica?**
*73 percent.* (References: 2, 138, 139)
These are the men who admit to arousal. Not willing to accept such wholly subjective reports, researchers have devised experiments employing sophisticated devices for detecting and gauging arousal. In this work, which did *not* ask for self-description of responses by the research subjects, 86 percent of men evidenced moderate to strong reactions to erotic films and slides. The yardstick used in determining if arousal existed was simple but effective: penis erection. Thus, no matter what men say they feel about erotica or pornography, all but a few respond by getting turned on.

**How many men are turned on by being bitten during sex?**
*44 percent.* (Reference: 47)
Here, it must be remembered that bites include

"hickies" (suction kisses). Eleven percent of men report decided and frequent erotic responses to toothy caresses, while 33 percent report "some" response. Mind you, in both instances we are talking about gentle nips. Add up the ones who like biting, however, and the majority of men abstain: 56 percent who say, "no, thank you," even to deftly delicate nips.

For the woman with a desire to put her teeth to good use in the bedroom, these findings admittedly leave her without much to hold on to. Half her partners will like her biting; the other half think such activities are best restricted to the dinner table. Best advice, as always when there is cause to doubt, is to ask. If the response is encouraging, work up to full-fledged biting gently.

**How many men are attracted by women's breasts?**
*50 percent.*                                     (Reference: 138)

The surprise is that when asked to list *all* the very important qualities they are looking for in a woman, just one man in four checks off "large breasts"—*and exactly the same number are looking for a woman with small breasts!* Other physical characteristics and the number of men who want them in a woman are shapely legs (70 percent); slim hips and rear (35 percent); and a pretty face (25 percent). (An unknown number of men in this survey put no stress on physical qualities.)

This same survey also asked men to pick nonphysical qualities they would like to have in a woman, and the greatest number of men (85 percent) think it is very important that their partner love them; 80 percent think intelligence is important in women; 65 percent want a woman with a sense of humor; 55 percent would like her to have a career of her own; 45 percent want her to be self-confident; and about 10 percent think it would be very nice if she were wealthy.

We are reminded in this context of Follies impressario Florenz Ziegfeld's legendary "10 Commandments of Female Desirability": native refinement; poise; health; strength; symmetry; spirit; style; appeal to both sexes; femininity; and glory.

**How many men are aroused by lacy lingerie?**
*75 percent.*                                    (Reference: 136)
The utilitarian long johns of yesteryear are out, and over the past decade clothing manufacturers have kept themselves busy developing and selling an array of erotic underwear for both men and women. According to the testimony of men, it is a marvelous change for the sensuous better.

**How many men are turned on by the natural fragrances of their sex partners?**
*40 percent.*                                    (Reference: 136)
Vaginas, even when freshly cleansed, often have their own unique fragrance. And a sizable number of men report that these fragrances are potent aphrodisiacs. In our clinical experience, we have discovered, too, that a fair number of men report adverse reactions to these scents. But in many cases, more potent scents are associated with minor vaginal infections which require hygienic care.

Pheromones (scents that are emitted by many

species), although important for sexual attraction throughout much of the animal kingdom, are not significant in human sexual attraction. Although vaginal fragrances are detectable to humans, they are cross-culturally considered unattractive; however, a minority of men in any society may find fragrances of undergarments to their liking. Nor is there evidence that men or women can determine the time of a woman's ovulation by her vaginal fragrances.

**How many men are turned on by perfumes?**
*77 percent.* (Reference: 136)
A man's nose is one kind of erogenous zone and Shakespeare as well as other Renaissance writers often used "nose" to mean penis. Puns aside, most men find an exotic-smelling woman to be erotic. A man's proboscis may not be the quickest route to his heart, but it definitely leads directly to his brain, where a perfumed fragrance may be a signal for sexual arousal.

**How many men are turned on when a woman uses sexually explicit language?**
*45 percent.* (Reference: 136)
Four-letter words are a turn-on to many men, particularly during sex. For them, the use of four-letter words by the woman to whom they are making love is a sign that their lovemaking has swept away all of her "proper" conventional behavior, and that they have succeeded in awakening the fierce animal within. Nonetheless, about as many men are turned off by a woman's use of explicit language during sex.

**What most irritates men during sex?**

*Trying to make love to a cold or disinterested woman.* (Reference: 102)

The bored or unresponsive woman is classed as the bane of many a man's sex life, which is why 60 percent gave this response. But men denounce other irritants, too. A woman's criticism is offensive to 12 percent. In a minor paradox, 5 percent are upset if the woman is "too easy" and another 5 percent are put off if the woman makes demands. Three percent more are irritated when the woman makes the first advance. But not all men are complainers: 17 percent *never* get irritated in bed.

**What is the most common turn-off for men?**

*An unresponsive sex partner.* (Reference: 102)

According to 46 percent of men, the most sexually inhibiting factor in sex is an unresponsive sex partner. But that is not the only outstanding turn-off in men's eyes. Others (18 percent) cite quarrels; physically unattractive women (13 percent); a partner who wants to control things (5 percent); and, the first time in bed with a particular partner (3 percent). However, an eager 16 percent say, no matter what, they are ready. These men insist they are never totally turned off.

**What quality in a woman makes a man feel most nervous?**

*Physical beauty.* (Reference: 102)

One quarter (25 percent) of men recoil with fright when meeting a beautiful woman. Intelligent women fare but little better—21 percent of men admit they are intimidated by these women. Fourteen percent find virgins scary; 13 percent fear females with voluminous sexual experience; 12 percent are put off by wealthy women; and 9 percent are nervous around a woman who holds a high-paying job. The rest, only 6 percent, claim they are never nervous in any woman's company.

**How many men are turned off by heavy makeup?**
*80 percent.* (References: 58, 136)
Most women know applying makeup is a delicate task. It is an art form. Bombarded by cosmetic advertisement, some women come to believe that more is better. It definitely is not, say most men. However, an interest in good looks in women rather than in men is characteristic of all societies, and in most societies women attempt to improve their appearance in some way.

It is interesting that concepts of beauty are constantly changing. Few better examples exist than Western society's attitude toward suntan. In past ages, ladies of quality usually avoided the sun to distinguish themselves from women who worked in the fields. However, during the past few decades the tan has become a symbol of beauty and an indication that a woman had the time and money to leisurely follow the sun. This is in spite of the fact that the sun ages the skin faster and increases the likelihood of skin cancer.

**How many men find hair on a woman's legs or underarms unattractive?**
*70 percent of American men.* (Reference: 136)
European men do not agree; for many of them, a

woman's hair is extremely erotic. This is indicative of the fact that the American man's aversion to naturally growing female hair is culturally imposed.

**How many men find women less attractive during menstruation?**
*42 percent.*  (References: 102, 136)
For many men, "that time of the month" means no sex. Among Orthodox Jews this ban is explicity incorporated into their religious canon. But most men find that menstruation has no effect on their sex drives or their attitudes. And a few men admit to finding menstruating women particularly exciting.

**How many men say fear of pregnancy has prevented them from free sexual expression?**
*31 percent.*  (Reference: 2)
These men are fearful that sex without contraceptive precautions can lead to unwanted pregnancy. Guilt (23 percent), social pressures (20 percent), religious training (17 percent), and fear of diseases (14 percent) have also inhibited male sexual expression. A final and hardy 31 percent say nothing has ever inhibited their sex lives.

**How many men find a pregnant woman less sexy?**
*50 percent.*  (Reference: 136)
Although half the nation's men express negative sexual feelings toward a pregnant woman, most of the other half offer no opinion.

**How many men are aroused by watching animals have sex?**
*32 percent.*  (References: 75, 76)

Many, perhaps even most of us, have witnessed animals engaged in sex. Urban alleys are a common setting for copulating cats and dogs and rural areas offer even a wider variety of animal lovers. Many men frankly say these sights and sounds are a turn-on. Is this interest prurient or unhealthy? One would be hard pressed to classify the sexual interest shared by a third of the adult male population as sexually deviant. More importantly, perhaps one might ask, what harm might befall an occasional enthusiastic observer of nature?

**How many men are happy with today's contemporary woman?**
*58 percent.* (Reference: 102)
There may be grumbles about the dramatic changes in the roles of women that the last decade or two have witnessed, but the complainers are a minority. Most men are well pleased with the new woman. Asked to pick a single description of her, 23 percent say she is better company; 18 percent praise her for being more intelligent than ever; and 17 percent are convinced she is now more loving and caring.

But the ledger, in men's views, has a debit column too. First, 23 percent decry the increased independence of today's woman. Another 11 percent say females expect too much from men, and a final 8 percent say women, in their sexually liberated stance, are "too fast." Tote it up, and 42 percent have something negative to say about today's woman.

**What do men most look for in a potential wife?**
*Concern for a man's needs.* (Reference: 102)

Offer men a list of personal characteristics that mates should have and 28 percent hurriedly check off their favorite as the woman who is concerned with her mate's needs. Twenty three percent are in quest of a sincere woman; 21 percent look for an affectionate spouse; and 12 percent most prize self-confidence. A sexy woman fares less than stupendous—only 12 percent establish that priority. Bringing up the rear, only 11 percent most want a woman with a good sense of humor.

Sift through these responses and what emerges is a clear correlation with other findings in this book—in particular, that most men put the primacy on love, not sex. Affection, sincerity, and concern for another are all characteristics that are intertwined with their concept of love.

**How many men believe their first sex partners were virgins?**
*27 percent.*                          (Reference: 47)
Tests of virginity in females are always inconclusive as we have discussed, and this question explores what men believe about the female with whom they lost their *own* virginity. Besides the men who were confident of their partner's virginity, another 2 percent thought she was "probably" a virgin. But 1 percent said she was "probably" a non-virgin and 69 percent were confident she was not.

**What besides love do men think is the main reason for getting married?**
*Companionship.*              (References: 102, 136)
Marriage provides a man with far more than a lover, and 47 percent of men cite the companionship

a wife provides as the most important reason for getting married. Having a homelife is the answer of 24 percent, and 14 percent say that having children is the main reason in their view. Only 7 percent say marriage definitely is out for them, a figure that closely parallels the census statistics that show 90 percent of all adults get married at least once.


## How many men consider monogamy to be the ideal sex life?

*51 percent.* (Reference: 102)

In a survey of both single and wed men, a majority (51 percent) cast their ballots for sex exclusively with a wife. Another 20 percent want marriage with occasional outside partners. Eleven percent want monogamy but outside the conjugal framework. The rest agree about avoiding marriage, and 6 percent of them are actively hoping for countless casual love affairs.


## How many men say it does not matter what sexual experience a wife had before marriage?

*34 percent.* (Reference: 102)

When asked to specify the kind of sexual experiences they would prefer a wife to have had, a full third of men (34 percent) say her experiences would not matter. But 32 percent would have preferred their wives to have had sex with no man other than themselves. Twenty-one percent say "one or a few men she really loved"; 12 percent give a nod to a few "casual" affairs; and a final 2 percent want a wife who has had sex before marriage with many men.

**How many married men say their sex lives have improved since their honeymoons?**

*65 percent.* (Reference: 138)

Although one scholarly study suggests there is a slight but demonstrable diminution of passion between partners as the duration of marriage increases, this finding does not jibe with the testimony of men themselves. Nearly half of all married men—45 percent—report their sex lives are *much* better now than when honeymooning. Another 20 percent enthusiastically say matters are "somewhat" improved and 11 percent see no difference. Only 23 percent feel their erotic activities have deteriorated since marriage.

**How many children do men want to father?**

2. (References: 39, 136)

Just a decade ago, four kids were considered the ideal by many. Now that number is cut in half. An intriguing sidelight to the cohabitation issue, however, is that 70 percent of men are united in disapproving of having children out of wedlock.

**How many young men definitely do not want children?**

*Only 2 percent of college men.* (Reference: 52)

In this survey of college men, 55 percent definitely want to be fathers and another 29 percent say they probably do. Just 3 percent say "probably not," and 2 percent are sure they do not want children. Eleven percent are uncertain.

**How many young men expect to become fathers by the age of 30?**

*88 percent of the college men who expect ever to be fathers.* (Reference: 52)

Of those college men who indicated parenthood was a likely entry on their personal agenda, 67 percent expect to father their first child when 26–30 years old and 21 percent think they will do so when 20–25. A final 12 percent say 31–35.


**How many men believe women alone should shoulder the responsibility for birth control?**
*Only 20 percent.* (Reference: 102)
A majority of men admit they prefer to see a woman take charge of contraception, but only 20 percent insist it is her job exclusively. Another 36 percent say it is the man's responsibility to have protection, usually a condom, at the ready, but if these men had their druthers the woman would already have assumed control. About one third of men see birth control as a two-way street: both partners should take precautions (as in a condom–diaphragm tandem).


**How many college men say that, were a safe and effective birth control pill for men available, they would use it?**
*48 percent of college men.* (Reference: 52)
Although researchers are actively searching for a male "pill," none has yet met the approval of the federal Food and Drug Administration, which must approve all drugs before they enter the marketplace. Researchers— whose search is concentrated on developing a hormone-based pill that will eliminate or severely restrict sperm production—remain confident that a viable formula will be in production before this decade closes. If that prognostication pans out,

nearly half of college men appear willing to use a male pill. Another third (36 percent) are uncertain what they would do, only 16 percent say "No."

**How many men disapprove of homosexual activities?**
*78 percent.*                    (References: 53, 136)
Although only about 50 percent of American men want to keep homosexuality in the closet of illegalities, seventy-two percent say it is always wrong; 6 percent say "almost always"; and 8 percent think it is wrong "sometimes." Only 14 percent say flatly that it is *not* wrong and in fact is OK.

**How many men approve of extramarital sex?**
*82 percent.*                    (Reference: 102)
But the 82 percent who approve have their conditions. About 6 percent say, no matter what, extramarital sex is all right; whereas another 2 percent who adore double standards say it is fine for men *only*, never for women. The rest attach strings that vary from unspecified "very special" conditions (24 percent) and prior mutual agreement by the spouses involved (23 percent) to a caveat that it is OK if the consequences are recognized as potentially disastrous. Five percent give their approval only if one remains silent about it.

**How many men intend to cheat on their wives?**
*12 percent.*                    (Reference: 102)
Bring the extramarital sex question down from the abstract to this personalized question and male enthusiasm decreases sharply. Thirty-four percent

say, regardless of circumstances, it is out for them. Only 12 percent take the other path—no matter what, they *intend* to cheat to add spice to their sex lives. The rest say maybe ... *if* they were separated from their mate for a lengthy period, fell in love anew, or if their conjugal relationship went sour. Tote these numbers up, however, and the inescapable conclusion is that men are generally more tolerant of extramarital sex in other homes than they are in their own.

**What is the chief cause of extramarital sex?**
*Sexual frustration in the marriage.* (Reference: 57)
In a survey of married couples who had entered into extramarital sexual relations, the most commonly cited cause—mentioned by 70 percent—was sexual frustration. Other major reasons, and the number who cited them, are curiosity (50 percent); feeling of revenge (40 percent); or boredom (30 percent); and a need for acceptance and recognition (20 percent). These, it must be stressed, are the conscious and stated reasons mentioned by married individuals in talking about their extramarital sex.

**How many men would be tempted to cheat by a "beautiful woman?"**
*25 percent.* (Reference: 102)
All but 25 percent pride themselves on their willpower in the face of feminine allures. But poor sex or fighting at home will succeed where beauty fails: these conditions would propel 45 percent of men into the arms of another woman. Nineteen (19) percent cite a variety of conditions, from the availability of a woman at work through finding a woman who

understands them better. Only a final 16 percent say, come what may, they would not be tempted into an extramarital relationship.

**How many men approve of unmarried couples living together?**
*52 percent.*                          (Reference: 136)
Cohabitation has increased 200 percent during the past decade, with an estimated 1.3 million unmarried couples living together in the United States—and, suspect social scientists, the wave has yet to crest. But although it may appear that every new couple you know is living together minus the benefit of matrimony, it is not so. Seventy percent of males over 18 are married, which proves that the conjugal institution is far from finished.

**How many men favor group marriage?**
*12 percent.*                        (Reference: 2, 102)
As far as the testimony of men goes, group marriages do not have many supporters. A full 41 percent disapprove of group marriages, and another 47 percent have no opinion or are neutral about the notion. This clearly is not an idea whose time has come.

# CHAPTER 7

## Great Compared To What?— Female Psychology

On sexual matters, attitudes and psychology are what set American women apart from their international sisters. There is not much difference in sexual anatomy and physiology between the women of one society and those of another. However, U.S. women have unique attitudes about sex. Not only are the attitudes of today's U.S. women different from those held by women in other societies, but they are different from those held by U.S. women only a decade or two ago. Are women satisfied with their sex lives? Do they want more sex? What do they most enjoy about sex? What do they least enjoy? In this chapter you will find the answers.

**How much is female sexual pleasure affected by penis size?**

*Very little.* (Reference: 122)

That's what 70 percent of the nation's psychiatrists surmise. But 27 percent think female pleasure is "somewhat" influenced by penis size, and 3 percent think there is a "considerable" influence.

### How many times do women think they will fall in love?

*At least six times.* (References: 70, 136)

Half of all women (52 percent) expect to be in love at least six times. One third (33 percent) say they expect to be in love three to five times. The remaining 15 percent anticipate fewer than three serious love relationships.

What is love? As discussed much more fully in Chapter 6, love can be defined as the receiving or the anticipation of receiving such intense pleasure from the love object or relationship that one desires to perpetuate this pleasureful sensation. Furthermore, these feelings of love can vary in intensity from mild to addictive, and when people speak of being "in love" or experiencing "true love" for someone, they are usually describing *an addiction to the love object's company.*

### How often do women think "true love" comes?

*1.3 times in a lifetime.* (References: 70, 136, 144)

Women continue to believe that true love is very rare. Many women believe that there will be only one "true love" in their lives. The belief is so prevalent that the .3 increment, taking the average above 1, probably represents those who have loved and lost and believe that true love will come once again. We suspect that most women define "true love" as a one and only "right man." Before he comes along, however, they expect to be in love six or more times.

This unrealistic belief in one "right man" is one of the most difficult notions that must be overcome in treating people for the loss of love. If the concept of only one "right man" is allowed to remain unchallenged, and a woman loses that "right man" through estrangement, divorce or death, then very often she can see no more purpose in life. Suicide sometimes can seem a logical alternative to a loveless life. As pointed out in the book *Letting Go*, people who lose a loved one must recognize that there are many other "right people" in the world. They must then channel part of their energy into an outreach for these other potential "true lovers."

**How many women think love comes by the fourth date?**
*15 percent.* (Reference: 136)
A small percentage of women, as the figure indicates, are impatient for love to bloom. For them, it must germinate no later than the fourth date or they feel it will never grow. But 85 percent of women are more willing to bide their time. They will cultivate a relationship through five, ten, or twenty and more dates to determine for certain if a relationship will bear the fruits of love.

**How many teenage girls tell their parents everything about their own sex lives?**
*11 percent.* (Reference: 61)
Nearly all girls express reluctance to talk to their

239

parents about sex. Fifty-one percent of girls will talk to their parents in only the most general and theoretical ways about sex; 23 percent tell their folks nothing about their sex lives; and 15 percent tell only about the activities they anticipate their parents will approve.

**What is a woman's chief source of sex information?**
*Her friends.*                                    (Reference: 2)
About half (46 percent) of all women cite their friends as the providers of most of their sex education. Reading accomplished the mission for 22 percent; mothers handled it with 16 percent. The rest received their tutoring from scattered sources: siblings (6 percent); school (5 percent); and adults outside their homes (4 percent). Few women, it seems, turn to their fathers for an explanation of the facts of life—only 1 daughter in 100 gets her sex education this way.

**What do women believe is the ideal source of sex information?**
*Parents.*                                        (Reference: 2)
Mom and Dad may not have provided tutoring for them, but most women (56 percent) say the task of providing sex education would be best performed by parents. School climbs to second place as a preferred place for learning about sex, with 20 percent of females choosing it as the ideal. Books are touted by 14 percent and religious institutions are the choice of only 1 percent. Five percent cite "other" places— adults other than parents, siblings, etc.—and friends, the *actual* providers of most sex learning, attract only 4 percent of the vote.

Why the lack of confidence in the teaching skills of friends? As they mature, many women discover that the "facts" bequeathed to them by their friends are far from true. Legions of adolescent girls, for instance, still believe that soda-pop douches are effective contraceptives. They aren't. As a woman matures, she discovers she often must unlearn all the erroneous "facts" taught her by her teenage peers.

**How many women openly talk about intimate sexual matters with a person other than their lovers?**

*61 percent.* (Reference: 139)

Only 39 percent keep reticently mum on the subject. Among the talkative ones, many of whom recorded more than a single response, female friends head the bill—42 percent speak to their female pals about sexual wants and needs. Another 13 percent talk with female relatives, often their mothers and sisters. Male friends are included in conversations by 9 percent and another 8 percent consult professionals (psychologists, physicians, sex therapists). Not surprisingly, among the women who can provide the prerequisite, "other lovers" are privy to intimate details with 12 women in 100.

Should one talk with others about these matters? In discussing sex there are distinct advantages to candidness. Communication of any form tends to clarify our thoughts; we learn better what we mean by attempting to explain our thoughts. Then, too, many of us fear our "private" sexual desires—ones we many never have expressed even to a lover—are "kinky" or bizarre. Likely as not, they aren't. Many people beginning sex therapy are convinced there is something radically disturbed about their ideas —only to find through discussion and counseling that what they desire is ordinarily quite normal. For many, that simple discovery is an enormous relief. And it can be a key that opens the door to fuller and more enjoyable human sexuality.

**How many teenage girls have ever been in love?**
*79 percent of those over age 14.* (Reference: 61)
If the requirement of love is all that prevents most teenage girls from having sex, there does not appear to be much to stop them. So many teenage girls claim to have been in love that their basic requirement for having sex seems to have been fulfilled. More than three fourths (76 percent) of 15- and 16-year-old females believe they have been in love at least once; 82 percent of 17- and 18-year-olds also believe they have experienced love.

**What quality do teenage girls most value in a boy?**
*Intelligence.* (Reference: 61)
When sizing up a boy as a potential date, girls report they fasten first on his mind. The other qualities valued by teenage girls are (in order of importance): good looks and body; ability to converse; sincerity and honesty; confidence; sense of humor; good grooming; romantic and affectionate; popular; and gentle.

**How many teenage girls approve of having sex?**
*59 percent.* (Reference: 61)
As girls grow older, they grow increasingly permissive about the role of sex in the lives of teenagers. Among girls ages 15–16, only 54 percent say they

think intercourse is fine for teens. But ask girls 17–18 the question and almost two thirds (64 percent) say it is all right.

**How many teenage girls think a female should have sexual experience before settling down with one person?**
*52 percent.*                                    (Reference: 61)
Mind you, this question does not imply marriage, which will be discussed later. "Settling down," in this context, can run the gamut from entering into a cohabitation arrangement through simply going steady. Even so, more than half of all teenage girls think a girl ought to have a variety of sexual experiences before tying however loose a knot with a male.

**How many girls think a male should have sexual experience before settling down with one person?**
*61 percent.*                                    (Reference: 61)
Girls are a bit more permissive with boys than with themselves when it comes to granting a sexual license before settling down. Only 39 percent think a male should enter into the arrangement while still sexually inexperienced.

**How many teenage girls believe they should be virgins when they wed?**
*24 percent.*                                    (Reference: 61)
Only a few years ago that number stood at 41 percent; now it is 17 points lower. Most girls, it seems, do not share their parents' strictures regarding premarital sex: most teenage girls have no intention of being purely chaste at the altar.

**How many teenage girls want to marry boys who are virgins?**

*16 percent.*                                    (Reference: 61)

Girls, not suprising, impose somewhat higher standards of chastity upon themselves. But, in any event, most want a husband who has had a bit of sex before the ceremony begins.

**Among the teenage girls who have had a male fondle their breasts, how many enjoyed it?**

*97 percent.*                                    (Reference: 61)

But the degrees of enjoyment varied. A trace over half (51 percent) of these teenagers found the experience "moderately" enjoyable. And 46 percent thought it was "very enjoyable"—leaving only 3 percent who received no fun whatsoever from this fondling.

**Among the teenage girls who have fondled a boy's penis, how many enjoyed it?**

*89 percent.*                                    (Reference: 61)

Although 28 percent thought this penis fondling was "very enjoyable," more than twice as many (61 percent) said it was merely "moderate" fun. The rest, 11 percent, thought it was no fun at all.

**Among the teenagers who have had their vagina touched by a boy, how many enjoyed it?**

*96 percent.*                                    (Reference: 61)

More girls enjoy getting their vaginas touched than like fondling a boy's penis. Only 27 percent described it as "moderate" fun. The remainder, 69 percent, say it afforded "much" enjoyment.

**How many teenage girls fantasize while masturbating?**
*75 percent* (Reference: 61)
Teenagers fantasize for exactly the same reasons that adults do. And, perhaps even more importantly for teens with relatively limited sexual outlets, this is a valid way to explore—mentally at least—untraveled sexual territory.

**How many teenage girls approve of giving oral sex?**
*72 percent* (Reference: 61)
Again, older teenage girls, in the 17–18 age bracket, are a bit more permissive than younger ones. Seventy-two percent of the older ones give their approval to this form of sexual expression. However, 67 percent of 15–16-year-olds do.

**How many teenage girls approve of receiving oral sex?**
*74 percent* (Reference: 61)
Again, it is the older girls who are a shade more liberal, probably because of increased enjoyable experience. Among 15- and 16-year-olds, 69 percent say they enjoy that type of intimate kiss, whereas 76 percent of 17–18-year-olds do.

**How many teenage girls fantasize about sex?**
*73 percent.* (Reference: 61)
Just about all of us, teenagers as well as adults, sometimes daydream about sex and only 27 percent of teenage girls say they never do.

**How many teenage girls want to live with a man before marrying him?**

*42 percent.*                              (References: 61, 136)

Cohabitation is a relatively new living option, and what we see here is that large numbers of girls are eager for a trial before plunging into matrimony. They believe living together is a good way to get a fix on what married life would be like.

**How many teenage girls approve of sex between a white woman and a black man?**

*73 percent.*                              (Reference: 131)

Teenage girls ages 16–19 are more permissive than their elders. Older women are much more evenly divided on this issue.

**How many teenage girls approve of sex between a white man and a black woman?**

*72 percent.*                              (Reference: 131)

A few decades back, approval rates for this form of interracial sex were lower than those for Herbert Hoover during the last months of his Depression-era presidency. But times change; so do attitudes. Ask teenage girls ages 16–19 this question, and they have no doubts—about three fourths say it is O.K. Ask middle-aged women, however, and the result is nearer an even split.

**How many women prefer older lovers?**

*90 percent.*                              (Reference: 148)

But they don't want their lovers to be very much older. The vast majority say desirable potential mates would be one to five years their elder. Most of the rest like lovers to be the same age; a bare minority of a few percent like younger lovers. Yet this report is what women see as most *desirable*. Their actual practices may, in numerous instances, vary widely from what they say they most prefer.

**How many college women have asked men out for dates?**

*82 percent.*                                                  (Reference: 52)

The assertive woman thrives on college campuses. Just 18 in 100 co-eds have never popped the dating question to a man.

**How many college women feel fine asking men for dates?**

*44 percent.*                                                  (Reference: 52)

Assertive they may be, but college women ask men out with some trepidation. Forty-five percent, the biggest group, are a "little" hesitant, and 11 percent more are "very" hesitant about taking this first step.

**How many college women always pay their own way on a date?**

*2 percent.*                                                   (Reference: 52)

But the financial and social independence of college women definitely is making itself felt on campuses: 71 percent "sometimes" pick up a date's tab; only 27 percent say the man always pays.

**How many college women resent paying for themselves on dates?**

*16 percent.*                                                  (Reference: 52)

The vast majority are comfortable in paying the check. Over half (62 percent) feel fine about paying;

11 percent feel "great"; and a final 11 percent say they wish they paid even more often than they do.

**How many men, according to young women, expect to have sex on the first date?**
*10 percent.*                              (Reference: 52)
The overwhelming majority of men, according to the young women they date, are in no urgent rush to make love. For 49 percent, they will wait "until we know each other." And another 41 percent say there are no expectations at all in this department.

**How many women approve of masturbation?**
*The percentage varies greatly with age.*
(Reference: 67)
Nearly all younger women (78 percent) have no reservations about this auto-sex. Ask women 55 and older for their opinion, however, and only 52 percent give masturbation their approval. Women, as they age, do not generally become restrictive about sex. In large measure, the reason younger women are generally more permissive about sex of all kinds is that our culture no longer is as embarrassed or uninformed about sex as it was a generation ago in the pre-Kinsey days. When today's young women age, they will likely remain open to and accepting of a wide range of formerly *verboten* sex practices.

**How many women enjoy masturbation?**
*80 percent.*                              (Reference: 139)
There is near unanimity about the enjoyment, but the degrees of enthusiasm vary. For 31 percent, this self-sex *always* is satisfying. With another 49 percent,

it sometimes is. And there is a final 20 percent who never get joy from masturbation.

### How many women have fantasies while masturbating?

*64 percent.*                    (References: 75, 139)

Half of all women, exactly 50 percent, almost always masturbate to a fantasy serenade. Thoughts of past or present lovers may flick through their minds, or of acquaintances with whom they have never made love. Another 14 percent also fantasize, but only "sometimes." Only 36 percent invariably approach masturbation with utterly clear heads.

It is normal to fantasize while masturbating—most women do. But some women are troubled, because their fantasies are not of their current lover, but of other men—of, for instance, an attractive co-worker. Such fantasies need not imply you actually want to make love with the person. Fantasy is simply a harmless way of trying on new clothes: you needn't buy them just because you wanted to get a feel for how they might fit.

### How many women use mechanical sex aids?

*21 percent.*                    (References: 139, 148)

Vibrators, massagers, and other sex toys may be popping up in supermarkets, but nearly 8 women in 10 still prefer their sex without mechanical accompaniments. For those thinking of giving it a whirl, however, here are the preferences of the women who specify what gadgets they use: 8 percent opt for vibrators; 5 percent use oils; 4 percent give the nod to dildoes and other penis-shaped objects;

and 1 percent like feathers. Feathers? No, these aren't necessarily passionate Audubon members. Feather-devotees swear that tickling is *not* the result. Deftly and delicately apply this avian friend, users say, and the result is a deliciously subtle sensation, a sensual tickle, if you will.

**How many women sleep in the nude?**
*2 percent.* (Reference: 136)
Going *au naturel* at night claims few enthusiasts among women. Ask why and the answers range from "it's too cold for that" through "I'm more comfortable" in clothes. And the styles of preferred night-time wear vary greatly. T-shirts, often borrowed from a male lover, are favored by many. Classical pajamas adorn a few females' bodies. So do more exotic lingerie items and peignoir sets.

**How many women prefer sex with the lights on?**
*17 percent.* (References: 47, 75)
Only 8 women in 100 adamantly want lights-on sex. Another 9 percent like to throw at least some brightness on these proceedings. But a full 54 percent prefer darkness. Twenty-eight percent like it either way.

**What factor most influences a woman's desire for sex?**
*The emotional climate of her relationship.*
(Reference: 122)
That's the answer offered by 87 percent of the respondents in a nationwide poll of psychiatrists. Four percent stressed the woman's menstrual cycle and her attendant hormone changes; 4 percent cited

her husband's desires; and a final 4 percent struck it up to living routines.

### When do most women become sexually excited?
*34 percent answer: Immediately prior to the period.* (Reference: 47)
Most women have a natural body rhythm, but the beat differs widely from woman to woman. Just prior to her period is preferred by many women (34 percent) as the time when they are most receptive to answering sexual overtures. Most of the rest offer various responses. Immediately after the period is cited by some; a few say during their periods. But for 25 percent, any time of the month is fine.

### How many women think any time is appropriate for sex?
*67 percent.* (Reference: 139)
Sextime, two thirds of all women say, is whenever the mood strikes. But ask the ones who hold out (the remaining 33 percent) for their favorite times and the evening emerges the clear favorite, with 23 percent of all women preferring sex after dark. Five percent like to do it bright and early in the morning; 4 percent opt for weekends, although a handful of churchgoers grumble about sex on the sabbath; and 1 percent like to have their sex by the calendar, with particular days (say, the first, tenth, and twentieth of the month) firmly programmed for their erotic adventures.

No matter the time preferences, what is important is for the partners to be aware of each other's preferences. Match an A.M. woman with a P.M. man and compromise must follow as the partners learn to give and take pleasure at various times of the day and night.

**How many women think there's a "most" appropriate place for sex?**
*50 percent.*                    (Reference: 139)
For the 50 percent who have definite preferences, the bedroom tops the list—24 percent of all women prefer the comfort of their beds. Another 22 percent opt for anywhere in the house—outside, for them is out of bounds. Not so for the remaining 4 percent who offer a multitude of choices—the beach; a boat; a car; the woods. The other fifty percent have no preferences for an ideal place to make love.

**How many women ever initiate sex?**
*96 percent.*                    (Reference: 139)
Most women occasionally are sexual aggressors, and are quite comfortable in that role. Two percent are *so* comfortable, they always do the initiating; and another 9 percent usually do. But most women are a bit more laid-back. Forty-four percent say they are the initiators about half the time; another 42 percent, a somewhat more timid group, are the initiators "sometimes." How many women never take matters into their own hands? Just 4 percent.

Should a woman initiate sex? A century ago, even asking the question would have been deemed scandalous, which is not to say all women in those days were happy to wait until their lovers roused them. Some women have always succeeded in taking the lead in sex. Nor is there any reason a woman shouldn't take the sexual lead. Many men, as discussed earlier, are turned on by a passionately assertive woman. Even more to the point, if a woman feels like having sex, why should she feel uncomfortable in telling her lover? If your sexual pace is a bit faster than your partner's, there's good cause to hasten his when you have the urge.

**What are the two most important factors women cite as facilitating their sexual response?**
*Privacy and freedom from intrustion, and a good relationship with her mate.* (References: 41, 122)
Although those conditions are the most frequently cited by women, many mention a wide variety of other factors. Other common responses include: not feeling tense or tired; lack of a time limit; having eaten a good meal or had a few drinks; and soft music.

When asked the same question, however, the nation's psychiatrists offer somewhat different opinions of what they think most contributes to good sex for women. Over half (57 percent) strike it up to sound emotional interaction between the partners. But 26 percent think the woman's intrinsic level of sexual interest or responsiveness is the key. And 16 percent believe that the quality of the physical stimulation she receives is most important.

**How many women think they are very good at sex?**
*83 percent.* (Reference: 148)
About 5 women in 6 are convinced they are very good at sex. This exceptional display of sexual confidence on the part of women is reassuring because confidence in one's sexual ability is one of the most important ingredients necessary for a satisfying sex life.

**How many women think they get enough sex?**
*58 percent* (Reference: 148)

**How many women want more sex than they are getting?**
*38 percent.* (References: 2, 139, 148)

More than half of all women (58 percent) are content with how often they engage in sex. Another 38 percent want more sex than they are getting. Only 4 percent want less. However, this issue is not the same as female satisfaction with sex in general. Certainly frequency is more than incidentally correlated to overall happiness and, not suprisingly, these current numbers parallel closely the percentages of how women rate their sex lives (which we cite in the next answer). Nonetheless, their lovers' techniques, amount of variation in types of sexual encounters, and personal enthusiasm all influence a woman's overall feeling about sex. Frequency pertains to only one issue—how often she has sex. And the majority are happy in this regard.

**How many women are satisfied with their sex lives?**
*73 percent.* (Reference: 2, 84, 85)

Although researchers Masters and Johnson estimate that only 40 percent of America's adult females have fully happy sex lives, the women themselves offer a different report. Nearly three out of four rate their sex lives with at least a "7" on the proverbial scale of 10. Twenty-seven percent are "very satisfied" and another 46 percent, about half, are thoroughly content. What about the unhappy ones? Eighteen percent report their sex is "unsatisfactory"; the other 9 percent say theirs is even worse.

What makes one woman's sex life pleasant, another's less so? Physical performance of the lovers is a consideration, to be sure. But expectations also play a key role. A woman who desires frequent or virgorous sex, but is not getting it, will likely be less than pleased with her sex life. Another women with different sexual expectations could receive the same style of lovemaking that the first women is getting and be ecstatic. They just approach sex with different attitudes, desires, and expectations. Remember, too, that an important part of sex is communication. A less than satisfying lover, given a bit of judicious and tactful prompting, could well improve his style to meet a woman's desires. And a good lover could become a great one! In addition, our numbers may include women who at present do not have a sex partner but would like to find one or more.

**How many women think men are informed about female sexual desires and responses?**
*15 percent.*                              (Reference: 65)
Yet, the remaining 85 percent do not think all men necessarily are uninformed. True enough, 59 percent do think all men are uninformed (with 2 percent saying it is because men don't care enough to learn). But most of the rest take a somewhat more positive view. Eight percent say the extent of knowledge varies from man to man, and 6 percent take matters upon themselves and inform their lovers about female sexuality. The final 12 percent suspect that most men are ignorant, but their own lover, they say, is well informed.

**How many churchgoing women find sex pleasurable?**

*53 percent.* (Reference: 67)

**How many non-churchgoing women find sex pleasurable?**

*64 percent.* (Reference: 67)

As the figures above indicate, church-attending women generally find sex less pleasurable than do non-churchgoers. Nor is this the only instance where the churched–unchurched chasm comes into play. Throughout the range of issues covered in this section, the churched female responds with less enthusiasm to matters sexual. We must be careful not to conclude a cause–effect relationship based on this correlation. It should be realized that, although in some cases religious worship may be responsible for less pleasureful sex, unsatisfying sex is also often reponsible for female church attendance. Many of our women patients have admitted that they substitute church attendance and its comfort for the lack of comfort achieved in their sex lives. Nonetheless, many religious institutions do ardently condemn nonprocreative sex. Sex for enjoyment is a sin, they insist, and you would be surprised by the number of ex-nuns who come to us seeking to eliminate guilt feelings so they can learn to enjoy sex as it should be enjoyed.

**Do women let their partners know when they are ready for sex?**

*Yes.* (Reference: 139)

Cuddling, say more than half (54 percent) of all women, is a woman's most frequent invitation to the party. But there are more direct ways. About one third (38 percent) prod their lover to sex by touching his genitals. Some women let words do their work—32 percent flat out tell their lovers what is on their minds. The belles try a bit of flirting (14 percent). And, with 18 percent, "he just knows." (The responses add up to more than 100 because some women provided more than one response.) Relying upon a lover's clairvoyance, as 18 percent reported, is tricky business. You cannot expect to receive the gourmet dinner you want in a restaurant unless you order it. So, the best way to begin is by communicating your wants by words or actions.

**How many women think orgasms are important?**
*87 percent.*                                          (Reference: 65)
Women, by their own forceful testimony, attach a good deal of significance to having orgasms. Only 1 percent say orgasms are not important in sex. The remaining 12 percent think orgasms are not always necessary or not "really" important.

**Do women try to have orgasms quickly?**
*No.*                                                (Reference: 122)
In a survey of the nation's psychiatrists, only 18 percent judged that their women patients tried to rapidly have orgasm. Over three fourths (78 percent) thought women took their time about approaching orgasm. The rest, 4 percent, were uncertain or offered no opinion.

**How many women say their regular sex partner always knows when they have had an orgasm?**
*77 percent.*                                          (Reference: 65)

But this is an answer with many convolutions. First, some basic answers: 8 percent of women say their partners do *not* know if they have climaxed; another 5 percent just do not know what their partners know. About one third (30 percent) say all their sex partners, whether regular lovers or not, know. But 47 percent say only their regular partner knows; more incidental lovers do not. The final 9 percent say their partners usually know, but not always.

**How many women feel frustrated if they are on the verge of orgasm but then it doesn't come?**
*92 percent.* (Reference: 65)
A woman nearing an orgasm can fail to have one for hundreds of reasons. The sex play may cease. She may lose her concentration. Perhaps there is an urgent interruption. No matter how it happens, a woman denied an orgasm admits to frustration which, in some cases, includes anger and the feeling of being "ripped off." Only 3 percent say it is *not* a frustrating experience. And the lucky 5 percent say they have never had this experience.

**How many women fake orgasms during intercourse?**
*33 percent.* (Reference: 65)
An orgasm, as any good actress knows, is not terribly difficult to simulate, especially if one's lover is not fully tuned in to her feelings. Blend loud moans and some physical palpitations, and a fine performance can be accomplished. In this way one woman in three sometimes fakes it.

Should females ever simulate orgasms? Our advice

to women who ask this question is that they should. If a women attempts to act out an orgasm, she very often can get into the part and experience an authentic orgasm. We often recommend that non-orgasmic women try rehearsing orgasms. Our experience is that many non-orgasmic women refrain from orgasms for fear of displaying the sounds and frenetic motion that are often associated with orgasm. They are fearful of looking foolishly out of control and in addition they fear that their partners might laugh at them. Once they make the sounds and motions in a staged orgasm, they discover that no man will laugh. Their performance is usually appreciated, and their fears are thereby extinguished, a process that frees the women to enjoy sex and have a real orgasm.

**If offered a choice of only clitoral or vaginal stimulation, how many women would choose clitoral?**
*64 percent.*                          (Reference: 41)
This is a choice that generally does not confront a woman. In sex play they can easily have both. But the question does probe which area women most want stimulated. The clear-cut winner, with nearly two thirds of the ballots, is the clitoral region. The vagina received only 36 percent of the votes.

**Of all the aspects of sex, how many women most prefer the feeling of closeness?**
*40 percent.*

**How many most prefer orgasms?**
*23 percent.*

**How many most prefer satisfying a partner?**
*21 percent.*

**How many most prefer intercourse?**
*20 percent.*

**How many most prefer foreplay?**
*17 percent.*

**How many most prefer oral sex?**
*10 percent.*

**How many most prefer masturbation?**
*4 percent.*

**How many most prefer anal sex?**
*1 percent.* (Reference: 139)

On this list, women were permitted to check more than one response, but closeness emerged the decisive favorite. But the catch-all category "anything and everything" placed second, with 31 percent offering this response.

Sift through what we have already discovered about female sexual psychology and these numbers hold no surprises. What is evident is that women highly prize the communication aspect of sexuality, which is why many like best the feeling of closeness sex affords and many others enjoy the process of satisfying a partner. Nonetheless, women also are looking out for their own interests—thus the heavy support for orgasms and the blanket "anything and everything."

**Do women play an active role in intercourse?**
*Definitely yes.* (Reference: 139)

Purely passive sex, most women say, is no fun at all. That is why 37 percent always are active; 39 percent usually are; and 11 percent are half the time. A more bashful 12 percent say they are active only sometimes and a scant 1 percent never are active.

Is it desirable for women to be active? Certainly, at least in the eyes of most men. Males, as we saw earlier, join in castigating unresponsive partners. Besides, when sex is viewed as communication, mutual activity is naturally the best method for mutual communication. All listening and no talking tends to make for very dull conversation.

### How many women enjoy giving oral sex?
*62 percent.*             (Reference: 139)

Fellatio, while fun for most women, is not nearly so popular with women as its flip-side, cunnilingus. Nonetheless, 34 percent say fellatio is very enjoyable; and 38 percent say "somewhat" enjoyable. Thirteen percent can take it or leave it; they've no opinion on the topic. Twelve percent dismiss fellatio as unpleasant, and for the last 3 percent it is downright repulsive.

Different as these numbers are from the corresponding figures on cunnilingus (discussed below), they come as no surprise. Fellatio's primary end is male stimulation, which is not to suggest women don't find performing it to be stimulating, too; many do. Offer a choice, to put matters in perspective, between doing something that gives most of the pleasure to another or performing a different act that is calculated to please one's self, and most will opt for the latter. That is natural and it is precisely what women are saying here. Fellatio and cunnilingus are *not* mutually exclusive and maneuvering permits simultaneous performance of these oral gambits in a position commonly called "69."

**Why do women give oral sex?**
*To enhance their partners' pleasure.*

(Reference: 118)

That's the opinion of 69 percent of the nation's psychiatrists. But 20 percent think women do it because they enjoy it, and 4 percent say the act is performed to create an aura of sexual sophistication. The rest, 7 percent, offer no opinion.

**How many woman enjoy receiving oral sex?**
*90 percent.*                            (Reference: 139)

Few numbers more forcefully drive home the point that our culture has passed through a sexual revolution. Proof of the extent of the change is provided by the many state laws banning oral sex that remain on the law books, even though these statutes are very rarely enforced.

No wonder. Prohibition diminished the nation's thirst not an ounce. Antioral sex laws are roughly as effective. Completely ineffective, that is, considering 62 percent of women invariably find cunnilingus to be very enjoyable; and another 28 percent think it is "somewhat" enjoyable. Add up those numbers and only 10 percent remain to be accounted for, and 4 percent of them have zero reaction to receiving oral sex. Another 4 percent deem it unpleasant and for 2 percent, perhaps with antioral-sex preachings in mind, it is still a taboo and "repulsive" idea. As

262

always, there is no disputing taste. But, if the numbers have it, this is one sexual activity women heartily endorse.

### How many women like anal sex?
*41 percent.* (Reference: 139)

Ten percent of women say it is very enjoyable and another 31 percent receive "some" pleasure from it. As we pointed out earlier, because the anal area is an enormously sensitive region, orgasm via this route is thoroughly possible for both partners. Even so, many a woman remains less than keen on this pastime. Granted, besides the ones who like it, another 10 stand neutral on the issue. But 42 percent think anal sex is unpleasant and for 7 percent it is repulsive. Add the results, and what we have is a fairly even split. Not quite half the females like it; a shade over half do not.

### How many young women fantasize during lovemaking?
*59 percent.* (Reference: 133)

Although we suspect the results apply to older women too, this survey restricted itself to college students. Among them, 6 percent almost always fantasize during coitus; 53 percent sometimes do; and 41 percent never do.

### Why do women fantasize during lovemaking?
*To facilitate arousal, say 45 percent.*
(Reference: 133)

Forty-five percent of women report that fantasies both speed up and heighten their arousal level, and thereby help prepare the way for enjoyment of sex. Another 22 percent fantasize that their partner is more attractive; 13 percent imagine new sexual techniques that they and their partners do not explore; and 5 percent use imagination to relieve boredom. However, 15 percent of these women admit they do not know why they fantasize.

**What do women most frequently fantasize about during lovemaking?**
*Others finding them irresistible.* (Reference: 133)
Here, women who fantasized could check as many responses as correlated with specific fantasies they had experienced, and 53 percent indicated they imagined that they were irresistible to men. A very close second, with 51 percent of women marking it, is oral–genital sex. More infrequent fantasies include: former lovers (42 percent); imaginary lovers (24 percent); and men giving in after first resisting (24 percent).

**How many women have fantasized about raping men?**
*2.5 percent.* (Reference: 67)
Violently aggressive fantasies are extremely rare among women. Of those under 35, 3 percent have entertained such thoughts. With older women, ones 35 and above, only 2 percent have. Uncommon as such fantasies are, some women express an occasional desire to be a powerful sexual aggressor and sometimes the thoughts turn to rape fantasies. Quite obviously, the fantasy is one thing; action is another.

**How many women have fantasized about being raped?**

*18 percent.*                          (Reference: 67)

Younger women, on the whole, again, are more prone to having these fantasies. Twenty-four percent of women under 35 have had rape fantasies; just 12 percent of older women have.

If a woman fantasizes about being raped does that mean she would welcome this violent sex? Certainly not! Thinking about something neither makes it so nor means that we would enjoy the real thing. Indeed, the difference between a rape fantasy and rape itself is that in the former a woman does her own casting, set design, and direction. The imagined rapist often possesses moviestar good looks and his purpose is to afford her pleasure against her will—all done in a setting she finds comfortable and in a style of lovemaking she deems exciting. However, rape in fact is never a form of sex; it is physical and mental aggression. Fantasy, in short, is fun; but it is not reality and, in the case of rape, the reality is very far removed from fun.

**Are women less aggressive than men?**

*Yes.*              (References: 37, 38, 82, 93, 126)

But the reasons are unknown. What researchers do know is that at least three factors come into play here. For one, women tend to be smaller than men and relatively greater size ordinarily increases the chance of success for physical aggression and, in the process, makes it a more attractive option.

Women, too, are socialized, are brought up, differently from men. In the male culture, violence frequently is rewarded, and the little boy who fights to defend his "honor" is applauded as a hero. Not so for females. Even though recent changes in our culture are affording women greater plaudits for prowess in athletics and related activities, aggression is still an expression applauded only in little boys.

But the chief reason for males' greater aggressiveness, many researchers currently theorize, is hormonal activity. Men and women have a significantly different hormonal mix. It is very much that hormone difference that explains why men and women are physically different. It may also explain the attitudinal differences. In one experiment, when male hormones (testosterone in particular) were administered to pregnant animals, the female offspring not only were reported masculinized anatomically (some, for instance, were born with scrotums), but their behavior was reported to differ from typical female behavior, too. In particular, these females were reported to have exhibited proclivities to be highly aggressive (called the Phoenix-Goy-Young Effect, after the University of Kansas team that performed the breakthrough work in this area). Hormone research, however, remains in its infancy; much fundamental work still must be done before firm conclusions can be reached. Nonetheless, as it presently stands, most investigators are convinced both that there are significant differences in male and female behavior and in sex behavior, too, and that at least one of the major causes is hormones.

**How many women can have an orgasm through fantasy alone?**
*2 percent.* (Reference: 75)

Surprised that anyone can do this? Don't be. Our most powerful sex organ is the brain and many more women could experience a fantasy-induced orgasm if they wished. It is the scenic route to that goal and like most scenic routes, it takes a bit longer to travel than more direct avenues, which is perhaps why few women have given this sexual exercise a try.

**How many women have seen sexually explicit materials?**
*70 percent.* (Reference: 110)
The puzzlement is how 30 percent avoid them. Erotica is everywhere. Major movies—from *Coming Home* through *Straw Dogs*—are markedly explicit. So are dozens of magazines and not just men's titles. The number of women who have seen sexually explicit materials is rising, perhaps in response to the plentitude of erotica. A full 70 percent of women under 21 say they have already seen depictions or descriptions of intercourse; and more than half have by age 15.

**How many women are aroused by pornography or erotica?**
*72 percent.* (References: 2, 139)
Science derails prim protests. Only 51 percent *report* that erotica arouses them, but experiments show the numbers are far higher. About three women in four (72 percent) respond to a viewing of erotic films and slides with vaginal lubrication and related responses. True enough, 28 percent show no reaction, but that is a distinct minority.

267

**How many women have used erotica for sexual arousal or in foreplay?**
*56 percent.*                              (Reference: 139)

Many couples, especially since the advent of home videotape recorders, unspool a hard-core movie before or during sex. Others wander through the pages of magazines that frequently feature photographs of couples engaging in sex (like *Chic* and *Penthouse*). Three percent spice their sex with such doings often; 43 percent do it occasionally; and 10 percent tried it once.

**How many women enjoy being bitten during sex play?**
*41 percent.*                          (References: 47, 75)

Over one quarter, 31 percent, report that a nip sometimes produces an erotic response in them; and another 10 percent say it often is a turn-on. Again, with most women only gentle dental caresses produce pleasure. Ravenous bites, on the other hand, can be decided turn-offs, although there are a few women who like that, too.

**How many women like to dress in erotic clothing to add spice to sex?**
*66 percent.*                              (Reference: 139)

There definitely are women who like to ride bareback, but of the rest, 40 percent cast ballots for lingerie and other lacy garb as erotic accoutrements. Another 20 percent go for traditional low-cut and black bedtime wear and 6 percent opt for casual current clothing.

**How many women enjoy being undressed by their lovers during sex?**
*90 percent.* (Reference: 148)
The favorite in-bed activity of women by far is having their lover undress them. Many, many fewer ballots (10 percent in total) are cast for pinching, biting, slapping and the like.

**How many women like their natural fragrances?**
*53 percent.* (Reference: 65)
A majority of women (53 percent) believe their vagina smells good. Another 19 percent say it "sometimes" smells good. But 9 percent think it smells neither good nor bad. And 4 percent say "sometimes" bad. Just 15 percent say it definitely has an unpleasant scent.

**How many women sometimes switch settings to add flair to their sex?**
*76 percent.* (Reference: 139)
Eat the same dish night after night and, no matter how tasty and original it is, it will begin to bore. Much the same can be said about eating at the same place. In female eyes, all of this applies to sex, too. That is why over three fourths of women from time to time like to change the setting by having sex anywhere in the house but the bedroom (a change liked by 38 percent); in a hotel or motel (17 percent); or in the good old outdoors (14 percent). Another 7 percent also like spatial experimentation, but they are reluctant to be pinned down to just one preference—when the mood strikes, they prefer a variety of places for their lovemaking.

**Which part of sex do women least like?**

*Anal sex.*                              (Reference: 139)

The backdoor route is blocked by 27 percent
of women. Also disliked is routine, mechanical and
boring sex, which 23 percent criticize. Not reaching
orgasm is nixed by 19 percent; intercourse's natural
messiness is checked by 18 percent; and 6 percent
veto oral sex. But a final 16 percent find nothing at
all they dislike about sex.

Is there something amiss or strange, many women
wonder, with disliking a particular aspect of sex?
No! And especially not if you have tried it before
rejecting it. But to enjoy some sexual practices, a
taste for them must be acquired. Remember that
many of us greeted our first sip of wine with a stark
grimace, but we now view this refreshment as a
pleasant complement to an enjoyable evening. So it
goes with some sexual practices, and many people
learn as they mature to enjoy techniques they disliked when younger. But it is better if you and your
partner agree on what you both enjoy. He enjoys one
sex act and you dislike the thought of it? Thorny a
dilemma as this may pose, the solution is simple.
Compromise; seek out new, untried options; and
above all communicate. Those are the keys to solving
sexual dilemmas. Put more specifically, therapists
often resolve such sexual dilemmas by employing a
technique known as "pairing." This technique comes
particularly into play in instances where one partner
especially likes a given sex act and the other dislikes
it. The goal in pairing is to psychologically pair the
disputed act with another sex practice that both
partners very much like. In this way, the pleasure of

one act can become associated with the previously undesirable act and it too can become pleasurable.

**How many women say guilt feelings have inhibited their sexual expression?**
*33 percent.*

**How many women believe religious training interfered with their sex lives**
*22 percent.*

**How many women say fear of pregnancy has restrained their sexuality?**
*45 percent.*

**How many women believe social pressures interfered with their sex lives?**
*21 percent.*

**How many women's sex lives were affected by fear of VD?**
*7 percent.*                         (Reference: 139)

Women cite a multitude of barriers that have blocked their sexual expression (and many mention more than one). Even so, 26 percent still traveled freely; their sexual expression, they report, has never been restrained.

Put these numbers in another light and we see that 74 percent of women *have* had their sexual expression blocked. That high result is hardly surprising. Many of the fears women enumerate are rooted in sound *physiology*, such as worries about pregnancy or venereal diseases. Others, although social and not biological in origin, are just as understandable. It is a rare woman who has *never* felt even an ounce of guilt about sex or a morsel of antisex social pressures. Those pressures, notwithstanding our relatively permissive age, are still at work. But for women who feel and resent these inhibiting pressures, submission is not the only alternative: communication and discussion, perhaps with a trusted lover or a professional, often ease feelings of unwanted inhibitions.

**How many women are turned on by watching animals mate?**
*16 percent.*                                    (Reference: 75)

Those beastly alley and backyard rituals offer little attraction for 84 percent of women. But 16 percent, one woman in six, responds affirmatively to this question. Most of the rest report no reaction, and a handful are repulsed. Some of the "repulsed" ones may be like those who used to hurry to their windows with tubs of boiling water to scald away the passions of copulating animals. Although one may not enjoy the sight, burning the critters is cruelty. Intriguingly, dogs, once they commence coitus, are hard pressed to cease before the male ejaculates. Long ago these males forever solved the problem of impotence; they are equipped with a bone in their penis that, no matter what, always allows quick penetration of a bitch. Once an erection is achieved within a female, however, the dog's penis expands, and withdrawal poses a hard problem until ejaculation produces the necessary shrinkage.

**How many women are married?**
*65 percent.*                          (References: 136, 146)

We are a marrying nation. Nearly two out of three women over 18 are married and 90 percent will wed at least once in their lifetimes. Nor do women think the importance of the marital institution will decline. Only 27 percent believe that such factors as unmarried cohabitation and freer sexual attitudes will result in a diminishing stress on taking conjugal vows.

### How many college women definitely want to get married?

*60 percent.*                                    (Reference: 52)

Proof of sorts that marriage is not dimming in significance is that, in addition to the 60 percent who are certain they want to wed, 30 percent more report they probably will. Seven percent are uncertain and 2 percent say they probably will not put marriage on their agendas. Only 1 percent definitely rule it out.

### How many women approve of extramarital sex?

*73 percent.*                                    (Reference: 2)

But they attach many strings to this approval. Only 3 percent give this unsanctioned sex their unequivocal approval. For 30 percent, it is fine if "special" circumstances prevail such as a lengthy and unavoidable separation or a truly miserable home-life. Another group, 19 percent, give their approval if the married partners *agree* to give extramarital fun a fling. Seventeen percent think the idea is fine but warn against the possibility of dire consequences.

And 4 percent, a silent minority, approve it "if you don't talk about it." Just 3 percent give extramarital sex their unequivocal approval.

### How many women believe they will have an extramarital affair in the future?

*51 percent say maybe they will.* (Reference: 139)

Forty-nine percent say, come high water or low, they will *never* have an affair. Not so cocksure are 38 percent who concede almost anything can and does happen. For them, they report, it is safe to say an affair "might" happen. Nine percent are more certain; they will "probably" wander into illicit love at some point. The remaining 4 percent are married women who *know* they will have extramarital sex—it will "definitely happen," they say.

Interesting as it is to survey female responses to this hypothetical question, the truth is not nearly so easy to ascertain. These women are honest about their *present* feelings, but what the future holds for them is always a huge question mark. Adamant as a woman may now be that she will not have an affair, circumstances can alter her convictions. Troubles at home can erupt; she might meet an alluring man; her husband could embark on an extramarital fling of his own. All are factors that prompt a wed woman to explore new lands. It is *not* that what these women state about the probability of their having an affair is not interesting. It assuredly is. But, in many ways, it is more appropriate to view these reports as assessments of current lives and happiness than to see them as valid prognosticators of the future.

### How many women who have not had extramarital affairs want to have them?

*38 percent.* (Reference: 139)

Remember, only 29 percent of married women have had an extramarital romance. But ask the ones who have held back, and 38 percent admit to having had "fairly strong" desires to explore extramarital relationships. Nonetheless, the majority (62 percent) are happy with matters as they stand.

### What's the most common reason for infidelity in a marriage?

*Sexual frustration* (Reference: 57)

In a survey of married men and women who had practiced extramarital sex, 70 percent cited sexual frustration as a contributing cause. Free to mention as many causes as they liked, 50 percent more reported they were curious; revenge prompted 40 percent; boredom motivated 30 percent; and a need for recognition or acceptance played a role with 20 percent.

### How many women who have tried extramarital sex say it is enjoyable?

*74 percent.* (References: 67, 139)

Moral strictness may condemn the practice; religious figures may preach against it; but extramarital sex, say the women who have explored it, is plain fun. Thirty-seven percent report their extramarital adventures have been very pleasurable; and another slightly less enthusiastic 37 percent say they have been enjoyable. Fourteen percent are neutral. But 8 percent say the experience was unpleasurable, and 5 percent say it was bad news.

**How many women approve of unmarried couples living together?**
*52 percent.*                                     (Reference: 136)
This practice now is so commonplace it is a wonder that 48 percent do not accept it. College students by the thousands live together in co-ed dormitories. Older unmarried couples jointly rent apartments and open checking accounts, and banks that once dimly viewed the practice welcome the business. Most of these couples see their relationship as "trial marriage," yet many others openly admit to thinking marriage is an obsolete institution. In any case, many cohabitators have relationships that are indistinguishable from those of their legally wed peers. All that differentiates them, they argue, is their lack of a "piece of paper." Nonetheless, there is still that 48 percent who put great stock in that "paper." But their ranks are dwindling as increasing numbers of cohabitating couples gain in approval and acceptance of their status.

**How many women favor group marriages?**
*6 percent.*                                        (Reference: 2)
Marriages involving more than two lovers are firmly endorsed by a scant 2 percent; another 4 percent "mildly" like the notion. There is an uncommited tally of 37 percent. But the rest of the opinions

are negative: 18 percent "mildly" disapprove; 30 percent are passionately against the idea.

Can group marriages succeed? Definitely! The Mormons, for instance, long practiced polygamy (church leader Brigham Young claimed over 70 wives at his death) and their culture flourished. Hippie communes sprung up in the seventies, and a few still exist today and many successfully integrate group marriages into their lifestyle. Granted, the one man/one woman dyad is our society's norm, but it is far from the only way to express love, affection and devotion.

**How many women have tried mate swapping?**
*4 percent.*                    (References: 2, 139)
This much ballyhooed rage of the seventies, it seems, garnered much of the publicity's sizzle but delivered very, very few steaks. Not only have just 4 percent tried it, but half of them did it once and swore off further encounters.

**How many women want to try mate swapping?**
*2 percent.*                    (References: 2, 139)
Again, we see, this is not the proverbial idea whose time has come. Only 2 percent say sure; 5 percent indicate they might; and another 17 percent are not certain. But 76 percent say they are definitely not interested.

What's wrong with mate swapping in the eyes of these women? The practice, some who have tried it report, is a somewhat controlled way to venture into new sexual horizons. But women fear the aftermath. Many remember the swapping experiment of New York Yankee baseball players Mike Kekich and Fritz Peterson (and their wives)—a gambit that splashed across the tabloids when both marriages dissolved. That is a well-publicized lesson that is hard to ignore.

**How many college-age women want to have children?**
*50 percent.*                    (Reference: 52)
Those are the ones who are certain they want to hear little feet. Another 28 percent think they "probably" will want to become mothers. But 16 percent are uncertain, 4 percent think they "probably don't," and 2 percent are sure they do not want to be mothers.

**How many of those college-age women expect their first child will be born before they turn 31?**
*85 percent.*                    (Reference: 52)
Eleven percent expect the first child before they turn 26; 74 percent expect it when they are 26–30; and 15 percent say 31–35.

**How many children do most women want?**
2.                    (Reference: 39)
Big families are *déclassé*. A decade ago, most women yearned to hear the patter of eight little feet—on four children, of course. Now just 16 percent favor mothering that many babies. Most, 51 percent, want a tidy two, neither more nor less.

**How many women cite birth control pills as their preferred contraceptive?**
*22 percent.*

**How many say female sterilization?**
*12 percent.*

**Vasectomy?**
*10 percent.*

**Intrauterine devices?**
*7 percent.*

**Condoms?**
*7 percent.*

**Rhythm or withdrawal?**
*5 percent.*

**Diaphragms?**
*3 percent.*

**Foams?**
*3 percent.* (References: 136, 148)

Convenience and reliability, this order of preference suggests, is what most want from the contraceptive technique they choose, with the three most
effective approaches topping the list of preferences.
It is certain, however, that this list is fluid. The health
professions continually unearth new devices and
unearth, too, problems with older ones. Reports, for
instance, that birth control pills are sometimes correlated with blood clotting and other serious disorders
have reduced that method's popularity. IUDs (intrauterine devices) are in a tailspin as well, with new
evidence suggesting that some users suffer serious internal damages. Those developments, not unexpect-

edly, are precipitating a renaissance of interest in older methods such as condoms, diaphragms and cervical caps in particular.

**How many women approve of abortion?**
*71 percent.* (Reference: 146)
Abortion may be a hot political issue but the reasons for that baffle pollsters. A clear majority of American women and men are unwavering in their support of a woman's right to choose for herself whether to terminate a pregnancy or not. And the number of supporters, despite actively vocal anti-abortion lobbying, climbs annually. This current approval rate is up from 45 percent in 1976.

**How many mothers approve of a son's premarital sex?**
*47 percent.* (Reference: 139)
Certainly the odds are high that a son is partaking of his share of premarital adventures. However, do not be confused by the relative dearth of mothers who approve. Another 39 percent, perhaps aware that premarital sex abounds but not quite ready to embrace it, frankly say that they are not sure what to think. And 14 percent flatly object to the idea.

**How many mothers approve of a daughter's premarital sex?**
*33 percent.*

**How many mothers object to a daughter's premarital sex?**
*25 percent.* (Reference: 139)
Sons, it seems, are allowed more freedom than

daughters. Men traditionally have been seen as sexual explorers; women as protected territory. That stereotype is collapsing under the force of mounds of evidence that indicate women are every bit as fascinated by sex as men. But, in this instance there is a physiological basis for restraint: pregnancy, a condition few mothers wish on their young daughters. Nonetheless, in addition to the women who are sure what their positions are on premarital sex for their daughters, a full 42 percent admit to uncertainty about where they stand.

### How many women think homosexuality is always wrong?

*72 percent.*                                (Reference: 53)

That is the number who disapprove of homosexual relations. Women, the researchers note, are a bit more tolerant than men on this issue; but breakdown in the responses by sex was not provided.

In any event, besides the 72 percent who say "always wrong," 6 percent say homosexual relationships are "almost always" wrong and another 8 percent think they are "sometimes wrong." Just 14 percent say they are not wrong.

In light of this finding, you may be confused by the fact that women nonetheless would have homosexual friends (as the next question discusses). The explanation, we suspect, is that although women do think homosexuality is wrong, they just do not see it as an automatic barrier to friendship. Many of us might think group marriages are wrong. But would we instantly dismiss a friend who entered into one? Probably not. That is precisely the same reason women are in no hurry to lock homosexuals out of their lives.

How many women would accept a friend who happened to be a lesbian?

*55 percent.* (Reference: 47)

Women, it appears, are fairly tolerant of homosexuality. Lesbians would be excluded from friendships by just 22 percent and 23 percent are unsure how they would handle the situation. Gay men fare a shade worse. Again, 23 percent of women are uncertain but 26 percent say "no." Only 51 percent are certain they would accept a gay friend.

# CHAPTER 8

## Afterglow

It becomes apparent from our research that some people want sex more than others. How can we explain these differences in sexual desire?

The desire for sex may be compared to the desire for food. We recognize two distinct cravings for food: hunger and appetite. Hunger is somatogenic, caused by a physiological need for energy and tissue-building protein. In contrast, appetite is psychogenic, caused by a history of favorable experiences with eating. So it is with sex.

Two distinct desires for sex can be recognized: sexual hunger, caused by physiological need; and sexual appetite, caused by a desire to repeat favorable and emotionally rewarding sexual experiences. Many people refuse to try certain sexual practices merely because they believe that "normal" people do not practice or approve of such acts. Like under-weight or slender individuals, they are "finicky" consumers. By definition alone, nobody can be expected to develop an appetite for anything without having tried it and having found it pleasureful. Whereas the differences in sexual *need* can be explained by variations in physiology, the differences in sexual appetites can be explained by variations in the quantity, quality and diversity of one's sexual history. There is little doubt that most sexual desire is a result of developed appetite not innate need, so that sexual appetite is largely responsible for sexual desire, and enlightenment about the sexual acts and attitudes of others may lead to a willingness to try more exploration, which in turn leads to a more highly developed sexual appetite. As a result, strong sexual desires are not attributable to deprivation, but rather to a rich and varied sex life.

Sexual attitudes resulting from ignorance are more important than any anatomical or physiological quality in explaining most cases of sexual dissatisfaction. As we have seen in preceding chapters, the norms in sexual equipment and performance are far more modest than most of us have previously believed. This is reassuring, for it makes less secure people realize that their sexual equipment and practices are not seriously sub-par but are well within normal limits.

Furthermore, many people who have been disturbed by fantasies and acts that they considered bizarre or deviant can take comfort in the figures in this book. The figures indicate that significant numbers of people share almost all of the secret sexual desires that any person might consider unusual but find arousing in solitude. The knowledge that others, out there, share similar sexual thoughts and experiences reduces the loneliness that comes from believing that one is alone and "perverse" in his or her harmless sexual thoughts and behavior.

The figures in this book also indicate that the era of sexual attitudinal and behavioral differences between men and women is ending. It is clear that the sexual beliefs and practices of men and women are becoming more similar, and both women and men seem to approve of the convergence of sex roles.

Finally, far too many people believe that their sexual self-worth is dependent on the condition of their bodies. This is nonsense. In sex, your body is equipment; like your automobile, there is a driver inside. Good driving, like good sex, does not depend upon the size, shape, or color of the vehicle but on the attitudes and skills of the driver.

Long ago, in professional sex workshops we learned from partners of physically handicapped persons, such as disabled veterans, that their mates displayed sensitivity, consideration, imagination, innovation, and sexual prowess that made sex far more satisfying and inspired than when they were with partners with complete equipment and agility. When all is said and done, the former characteristics are all that count for all of us.

# CHAPTER 9

## References

(1) Alston, Pat, "Incest: Crime Against the Family," *Evening Outlook* (Santa Monica, CA.: May 12, 1980).

(2) Athansiou, Robert, et. al., "Sex," *Psychology Today* (July, 1970).

(3) Angrist, Shirley S., "The Study Of Sex Roles," *The Journal of Social Issues* (January, 1969).

(4) Bacheller, Martin (ed.), *The Hammond Almanac* (Maplewood, N.J.: Hammond Almanac Inc., 1979).

(5) Bell, Robert R. and Peltz, Dorothyann, "Extramarital Sex Among Women," *Medical Aspects of Human Sexuality* (March, 1974).

(6) The Boston Women's Health Collective, *Our*

*Bodies, Ourselves* (New York: Simon and Schuster, 1976).

(7) Brecher, Edward M., *The Sex Researchers* (Boston: Little, Brown and Company, 1969).

(8) Brecher, Ruth and Brecher, Edward M. (eds.), *An Analysis of Human Sexual Response* (New York: New American Library, 1966).

(9) Brown, Daniel G., "Female Orgasm and Sexual Inadequacy," in *An Analysis of Human Sexual Response* (op. cit.).

(10) Buchwald, Art, "Sex As Taught At Sam's," *Philadelphia Bulletin* (April 22, 1969).

(11) Bukstel, Lee. H., et. al., "Projected Extramarital Sexual Involvement In Unmarried College Students," *Journal of Marriage and the Family* (May, 1978).

(12) Burton, Richard (tr.), *The Perfumed Garden of the Shaykh Nefzawi* (New York: G. P. Putnam's Sons, 1964).

(13) Calderone, Mary Steichen, *Release From Sexual Tensions* (New York: Random House, 1960).

(14) Caprio, Frank S., *Female Homosexuality* (New York: Grove Press, 1954).

(15) Chernick, Avinoam and Chernick, Beryl A., The Role Of Ignorance In Sexual Dysfunction," *Medical Aspects of Human Sexuality* (September, 1971).

(16) Comfort, Alex, *The Joy of Sex* (New York: Crown Publishers, 1972).

(17) Comfort, Alex, *More Joy* (New York: Crown Publishers, 1973).

(18) Cronin, Denise M., "Coming Out Among Lesbians," in Goode, Erich and Troiden, Richard R. (eds.), *Sexual Deviance and Sexual Deviants* (New York: William Morrow & Corp., 1974).

(19) Cunningham, Earl L., "Weathervane," *Rutgers Alumni Magazine* (February, 1978).

(20) "Current Thinking On Sexual Dysfunction," *Medical Aspects of Human Sexuality* (August, 1977).

(21) Dank, Barry M., "The Homosexual," in Spiegel, Don and Spiegel, Patricia Keith (eds.), *Outsiders: U.S.A.* (New York: Rinehart Press, 1973).

(22) Department of Health, Education and Welfare, "Contraception: Comparing The Options," (Washington, D.C.: U.S. Government Printing Office, 1978).

(23) Diamond, Milton (ed.), *Perspectives in Reproduction and Sexual Behavior* (Bloomington, Ind.: Indiana University Press, 1968).

(24) Diamond, Milton, "Genetic-Endocrine Interactions And Human Psychosexuality" in Diamond (ed.), op. cit.

(25) Dickinson, R. L., *Atlas of Human Sex Anatomy* (Baltimore, Md.: Williams & Wilkins Co., 1949).

(26) Dickinson, Robert Latou and Beam, Lura, *The Single Woman* (New York: Reynal & Hitchcock, 1934).

(27) Dublin, Louis I., *Factbook on Man* (New York: Macmillan, 1965).

(28) Dullea, Georgia, "World Conference on Women Calls For End To Female Circumcision," *Evening Outlook* (July 22, 1980).

(29) Edwardes, Allen, *Erotica Judaica* (New York: Julian Press, 1963).

(30) Edwardes, Allen and Masters, R.E.L., *The Cradle of Erotica* (New York: Julian Press, 1967).

(31) Elias, James E., "Adolescents and Sex," *The Humanist* (March/April, 1978).

(32) Eliot, T. S., *The Family Reunion* (London: Faber and Faber, 1939).

(33) Ellis, Albert and Abarbanel, Albert (eds.), *The Encyclopedia of Sexual Behavior* (New York: Hawthorn Books, 1961).

(34) Ellis, H., *Studies in the Psychology of Sex* (New York: Random House, 1942).

(35) The Environmental Fund, "1979 World Population Estimates," (Washington, D.C., 1979).

(36) Evans, Ray B., "Biological Factors In Male Homosexuality," *Medical Aspects of Human Sexuality* (July, 1973).

(37) Fairbank, L.A., et al., "Sex And Aggression During Rhesus Monkey Group Formation," *Aggressive Behavior* (1977).

(38) Feshbach, Seymour and Singer, Robert D., *Television and Aggression* (San Francisco: Jossey-Bass, 1971).

(39) "Fewer In Poll Favor Large Families," *New York Times* (April 27, 1980).

(40) Finkelhor, David, *Sexually Victimized Children* (New York: The Free Press, 1979).

(41) Fisher, Seymour, *Understanding the Female Orgasm* (New York: Bantam Books, 1973).

(42) "Folio 400," *Folio* (January, 1980).

(43) Fryer, Christopher, "Fifty Things You Never Knew About Sex Until You Read This," *Oui* (July, 1980).

(44) Fury, Kathleen, "Sex And The American Teenager," *Ladies Home Journal* (March, 1980).

(45) Gagnon, John H., "Sexuality and Sexual Learning In The Child," in Gagnon, John H. and Simon, William (eds.), *Sexual Deviance* (New York: Harper & Row, 1967).

(46) Gebhard, Paul H., *Pregnancy, Birth And Abortion* (New York: Harper & Brothers, 1958).

(47) Gebhard, Paul H., "Human Sexual Behavior," in Marshall, Donald S. and Suggs, Robert C. (eds.), *Human Sexual Behavior* (New York: Basic Books, 1971).

(48) Gebhard, Paul H. and Johnson, Alan B., *The Kinsey Data* (Philadelphia: W.B. Saunders Company, 1979).

(49) Gebhard, Paul H., et. al., *Sex Offenders* (New York: Harper & Row, 1965).

(50) Gifford-Jones, W., *On Being a Woman* (New York: Macmillan, 1971).

(51) Gilmartin, Brian G., *The Gilmartin Report* (Secaucus, N.J.: The Citadel Press, 1978).

(52) "Glamour's Sex, Dating and Marriage Survey," *Glamour Magazine* (August, 1980).

(53) Glenn, Norval D. and Weaver, Charles N., "Attitudes Toward Premarital, Extramarital, And Homosexual Relations in the U.S. in The 1970s," *The Journal Of Sex Research* (May, 1979).

(54) Godpaille, N.J., "Innate Masculine–Feminine Differences," *Medical Aspects Of Human Sexuality* (February, 1973).

(55) Goode, Erich and Troiden, Richard R. (eds.), *Sexual Deviance And Sexual Deviants* (New York: William Morrow & Co., 1974).

(56) Greenbank, R. K., "On Medical Students Learning Psychiatry," *Pennsylvania Medical Journal* (1961).

(57) Greene, Bernard L., et. al., "Conscious and Unconscious Factors in Marital Fidelity," *Medical Aspects Of Human Sexuality* (September, 1974).

(58) Gregersen, Edgar, *Atlas Of The World And Its Sexual Anthropology* (London: Mitchell Beazley Publishers, Ltd., 1981).

(59) Guze, Henry, "Anatomy And Physiology Of Sex," in Ellis, Albert (ed.), op. cit.

(60) Hartman, William E. and Fithian, Marilyn A.,

*Treatment Of Sexual Dysfunction* (Long Beach, Ca.: Center For Marital and Sexual Studies, 1972).

(61) Hass, Aaron, *Teenage Sexuality* (New York: Macmillan Publishing Co., 1979).

(62) Headley, Gene, "Hollywood's Hottest: The Long Dong Club," *High Society* (February, 1980).

(63) Hemingway, Ernest, *A Moveable Feast* (New York: Bantam Books, 1967).

(64) Henry, George W., *All The Sexes* (New York: Octagon Books, 1978).

(65) Hite, Shere, *The Hite Report* (New York: Dell, 1976).

(66) Hume, Ellen, "Unwed Teen-Age Birthrate Soaring," *Los Angeles Times* (April 4, 1979).

(67) Hunt, Morton, *Sexual Behavior In The 1970s* (Chicago: Playboy Press, 1974).

(68) Hyams, Leonard L., "The Vagina; Abnormalities, Functional Aspects, And Size," *Medical Aspects Of Human Sexuality* (January, 1973).

(69) "Interferon From Foreskins Faces Test In Cancer Fight," *Los Angeles Times* (June 30, 1980).

(70) Jersild, Arthur T., et. al., *The Psychology Of Adolescence* (New York: Macmillan Publishing Co., 1978).

(71) Kaplan, Helen, *The New Sex Therapy* (New York: Brunner/Mazel—Quadrangle, 1974).

(72) Katchadourian, Herant and Lunde, Donald T.,

*Fundamentals of Human Sexuality* (New York: Holt, Rinehart and Winston, 1975).

(73) Kerckhoff, Alan C., "Social Class Differences In Sexual Attitudes And Behavior," *Medical Aspects Of Human Sexuality* (November, 1974).

(74) Kidder, Margot, "Margot," *Playboy* (March, 1975).

(75) Kinsey, Alfred C., et. al., *Sexual Behavior In The Human Female* (Philadelphia: W. B. Saunders, 1953).

(76) Kinsey, Alfred C., et. al., *Sexual Behavior In The Human Male* (Philadelphia: W. B. Saunders, 1948).

(77) Kolin, Irving S., et. al., "Psychosexual Aspects Of Mammary Augmentation," *Medical Aspects Of Human Sexuality* (December, 1974).

(78) Lerner, I. Michael, *Heredity, Evolution And Society* (San Francisco: W. H. Freeman and Company, 1968).

(79) Lief, Harold I., "Controversies Over Female Orgasm," *Medical Aspects Of Human Sexuality* (April, 1977).

(80) Lief, H. I., "Preparing The Physician To Become A Sex Counselor And Educator," *Pediatrics Clinician North America* (1969).

(81) Lief, H. I. and Reed, D.M., *Sex Knowledge And Attitude Test* (University of Pennsylvania School Of Medicine, 1980).

(82) Lorenz, Konrad, *On Aggression* (New York: Bantam Books, 1967).

(83) Luckey, E. and Nass, G. A., "A Comparison Of Sexual Attitudes And Behavior In An International Sample," *Journal Of Marriage And Family* (1969).

(84) Masters, William H. and Johnson, Virginia E., *Human Sexual Inadequacy* (Boston: Little, Brown and Company, 1970).

(85) Masters, William H. and Johnson, Virginia E., *Human Sexual Response* (Boston: Little Brown and Company, 1966).

(86) Masters, William H. and Johnson, Virginia E., *The Pleasure Bond* (New York: Bantam Books, 1967).

(87) McGarvey, Robert, "Stimulating Sales," *Oui* (March, 1980).

(88) McWhirter, Norris and McWhirter, Ross, *Guinness Book Of World Records* (New York: Bantam Books, 1977).

(89) Milton, Ronald, "Reflections Of A Tit Man," *Genesis* (May, 1980).

(90) Money, John, *Sex Errors Of The Body* (Baltimore, Md.: John Hopkins Press, 1968).

(91) Money, John and Ehrhardt, Anke, *Man & Woman, Boy & Girl* (Baltimore, Md.: The Johns Hopkins University Press, 1972).

(92) Morgan, Elizabeth, "Your Body," *Cosmopolitan* fl(*July, 1980*).

(93) *Morris, Desmond, The Naked Ape* (New York: Dell, 1967).

(94) Morris, Scott, *The Book Of Strange Facts and*

*Useless Information* (Garden City, N.Y.: Doubleday & Co., 1979).

(95) Murdoch, George P., *Social Structure* (New York: The Macmillan Company, 1949).

(96) Murphy, John Michael and Gilligan, Carol, "Moral Development In Late Adolescence And Adulthood," *Human Development* (1980).

(97) Murphy, Pat and Dazzo, Barbara, "Sex And The Single Rutgers Student," *Rutgers Alumni Magazine* (February, 1980).

(98) Neveris, N. and Roll, P., "Primary And Secondary Male Characteristics: The Hairiness And Large Penis Stereotypes," *Psychological Reports* (Volume 26: 123–126).

(99) "A New Big Push For Homosexuals' Rights," *U.S. News And World Reports* (April 14, 1980).

(100) Noyes, Robert W., "Perspectives In Human Fertility," in Diamond (ed.), op. cit.

(101) Peacock, Mary, "A Matter of Size," Ms. (June, 1980).

(102) Pietropinto, Anthony and Simenauer, Jacqueline, *Beyond The Male Myth* (New York: Times Books, 1977).

(103) "The Playboy Advisor," *Playboy* (June, 1980).

(104) "Playboy Interview: Masters And Johnson," *Playboy* (November, 1979).

(105) "The Playboy Report On American Men," *Playboy* (March, 1979).

(106) Pomeroy, W. B., *Dr. Kinsey And The Institute For Sex Research* (London: Nelson, 1972).

(107) Radell, David R., *How To Meet Interesting Men* (Malibu, Ca.: Inter-American Books, 1978).

(108) Raley, Patricia E., *Making Love* (New York: The Dial Press, 1976).

(109) Reed, Lou, "I Wanna Be Black," *Street Hassles* (Arista Records, 1978).

(110) *The Report Of The Commission On Obscenity And Pornography* (Washington, D.C.: U.S. Government Printing Office, 1970).

(111) Roemer, John, "The Normal Male," *Oui* (March, 1980).

(112) Runciman, Alexander, "Sexual Therapy Of Masters And Johnson," *The Counseling Psychologist* (1975).

(113) Schlesinger, Benjamin (ed.), *Sexual Behavior In Canada* (Toronto: University of Toronto Press, 1977).

(114) Schonfeld, William A., "The Body And The Body-Image In Adolescents" in Caplan, Gerald and Lebovici, Serge, (eds.), *Adolescence: Psychological Perspectives* (New York: Basic Books, 1969).

(115) Scott, Vicki, "Advise & Consent," *Hustler* (August, 1979).

(116) Seaman, Barbara and Seaman, Gideon, *Women And The Crisis In Sex Hormones* (New York: Rawson Associates, 1977).

(117) "Sex News: Female Orgasm, Where Are You
*Playboy* (July, 1980).

(118) "Sexual Survey #15: Current Thinking O
Oral-Genital Sex," *Medical Aspects Of Human Se:
uality* (October, 1978).

(119) "Sexual Survey #14: Current Thinking O
Recreational Drugs and Sex," *Medical Aspects (
Human Sexuality* (September, 1977).

(120) "Sexual Survey #3: Current Thinking On Se:
ual Fantasies And Extramarital Sex," *Medical Aspec.
Of Human Sexuality* (October, 1977).

(121) "Sexual Survey #2: Current Thinking On Fr
quency Of Sexual Relations," *Medical Aspects (
Human Sexuality* (September, 1977).

(122) "Sexual Survey #16: Current Thinking O
Female Sexuality," *Medical Aspects Of Human Se:
uality* (November, 1978).

(123) Shapera, Isaac, *Married Life In An Africa
Tribe* (Evanston: Northwestern University Pres:
1966).

(124) Sheehy, Gail, *Hustling* (New York: Delacort
Press, 1973).

(125) Sherfey, Mary Jane, *The Nature And Evolutio
of Female Sexuality* (New York: Random House
1972).

(126) Simons, G. L., *Book Of World Sexual Recor.
(Bell Publishing, 1975).

(127) Slater, Mariam K., *African Odyssey* (New Yor
Doubleday, 1976).

(128) Smith, Howard, "Scenes: Male Orgasm," *Village Voice* (June 23, 1980).

(129) Snider, Arthur J., "Turning To Best Friends," *Los Angeles Times* (May 23, 1980).

(130) Snider, Arthur J., "Wives Find Boon In Being Hugged," *Los Angeles Times* (July 18, 1980).

(131) Sorenson, Robert C., *Adolescent Sexuality In Contemporary America* (New York: World Publishing, 1973).

(132) Stephen, Beverly, "Women Are Losing Their Shirts," *Los Angeles Times* (May 15, 1980).

(133) Sue, David, "Erotic Fantasies Of College Students During Coitus," *The Journal Of Sex Research* (November, 1979).

(134) Suggs, R.C. and Marshall, D.S., "Anthropological Perspectives On Human Sexual Behavior" in Marshall and Suggs, op. cit.

(135) Suiland, Mary Ann P., "Helping Elderly Couples Become Sexually Liberated: Psycho-Social Issues," *The Counseling Psychologist* (1975).

(136) Talese, Gay, *Thy Neighbor's Wife* (Garden City, N.Y.: Doubleday & Company, Inc., 1980).

(137) Tarshis, Barry, *The "Average American" Book* (New York: Atheneum/SMI, 1979).

(138) Tavris, Carol, "Forty-Thousand Men Tell About Their Sexual Behavior, Their Fantasies, Their Ideal Women, And Their Wives," *Redbook* (February-March, 1980).

(139) Tavris, Carol and Sadd, Susan, *The Redbook Report On Female Sexuality* (New York: Dell Publishing Co., 1977).

(140) Vatsayana, *Kama Sutra* (New York: Castle Books, 1963).

(141) Velde, Van De, *Ideal Marriage* (New York: Random House, 1965).

(142) Wallechinsky, David, et. al., *The Book Of Lists* (New York: Bantam, 1978).

(143) Wallechinsky, David, et. al., *The People's Almanac* (Garden City, N.Y.: Doubleday & Company, 1975).

(144) Wanderer, Zev and Cabot, Tracy, *Letting go* (New York: G. P. Putnam's Sons, 1978).

(145) Weygandt, Chris, "The *Oui* Sex Survey: Fellatio," *Oui* (June, 1980).

(146) "What America Is Thinking," *Family Weekly* (July 6, 1980).

(147) Wilson, Robert Anton, *The Book Of The Breast* (Chicago: Playboy Press, 1974).

(148) Wolfe, Linda, "The Sexual Profile Of The Cosmopolitan Girl," *Cosmopolitan* (September 1980).

# References Addendum: As We Went To Press

(149) Barker, William J. and Daniel Perlman, "Volunteer Bias and Personality Traits in Sexual Stan-

dards Research," *Archives Of Sexual Behavior* (Vol 4, No 2, 1975).

(150) Comfort, Alex, "Behavior Therapy For Sex Problems," *The Lancet* (June 1973).

(151) Downey, Lois, "Intergeneration Change In Sex Behavior: A Belated Look At Kinsey's Males," *Archives Of Sexual Behavior* (Vol 9, No 4, 1980).

(152) Ford and Beach, *Patterns Of Sexual Behavior* (Harper and Row: New York, 1951).

(153) Giarrusso, Roseann, Johnson, Paula, et. al., "Adolescent's Cues and Signals: Sex and Assault," Paper presented as contribution to symposium at the Western Psychological Association meeting, (San Diego, April 1979).

(154) Glenn, Norval D. and Weaver, Charles N., "Attitudes Toward Premarital, Extramarital and Homosexual Relations in the U.S. in the 1970s, *The Journal Of Sex Research* (Vol 15, No 2, May, 1979).

(155) Goodchilds, Jacqueline, Zellmar, Gail, et. al., "Adolescent Perceptions of Responsibility for Dating Outcomes," Paper Presented at Eastern Psychological Association, (Philadelphia, April 1979).

(156) Hite, Shere, *The Hite Report On Male Sexuality* (Alfred A. Knopf: New York, 1981).

(157) Jacobs, Marion, Thompson, Linda, Truxaw, Patsy. "The Use of Sexual Surrogates in Counseling," *The Counseling Psychologist* (Vol 5, No 1, 1975).

(158) Johnson, Weldon, Kupperstein, Lenore et. al., "The Impact of Erotica," *The Report Of The Com-*

mission *On Obscenity And Pornography* (U.S. Gov
Printing Office, Washington, D.C. 1970).

(159) Malamuth, Neil, Pfeiffer, Ken., *Sights And
Insights In Psychology* (Hwong Publishing Company, Los Alamitos, Calif, 1976).

(160) Malamuth, Neil; Wanderer, Zev, Sayner,
Richard B., Durrell, Doris, "Utilization Of Surrogate
Partners; A Survey Of Health Professionals," *Behavior Research And Therapy* (1975).

(161) Perry, J., Whipple, B., "Pelvic Muscle Strength
Of Female Ejaculators: Evidence In Support Of A
New Theory Of Orgasm," *Journal Of Sex Research*
(17:1, 22–39).

(162) Taylor, Barbie., "A Comparative Study Of
Sexual Attitudes, Behavior and Personality Characteristics Between Swingers And Non-swingers,"
(Thesis, University of Calif, Riverside, 1973).

(163) Wolf, Linda, *The Cosmo Report* (Arbor
House, New York, 1981).

(164) Zellman, Gail L., Johnson, Paula B., et. al.
"Adolescent Expectations For Dating Relationships
Consensus and Conflict Between The Sexes," Paper
Presented at the Meetings of the American Psychological Association, (New York, Sept 1979).

(165) Zelnik, Melvin, Kantner, John F., "Sexual
Activity, Contraceptive Use And Pregnancy Among
Metropolitan Area Teenagers: 1971-1979," *Papers
On Population* (Johns Hopkins, Baltimore, 1980).

# THE BEST HUMOR
# FROM WARNER BOOKS

**PUNISHMENT: THE ART OF PUNNING or HOW TO LOSE FRIENDS AND AGONIZE PEOPLE**
*by Harvey C. Gordon* (V97263, $2.95)
In this hilarious book, Harvey Gordon emphasizes that "what makes punning an art is the ability to blend puns smoothly into normal conversation and the ability to create clever puns spontaneously in appropriate situations." Whether used as a training manual by aspiring punsters or enjoyed exclusively as a book of humor, PUNISHMENT has unlimited potential for making you and your friends laugh.

**GRIME AND PUNISHMENT: A COLLECTION OF SEXCITING PUNS**
*by Harvey C. Gordon* (V97026, $3.95)
This off-color, off-beat, off-the-wall, offly funny book contains over 350 of the most sexciting puns ever put into print, along with 31 illustrations and some proven techniques for working puns smoothly into everyday conversation. This will go a long way toward expanding the highly creative art of punning by tapping one of the greatest of all creative resources—the dirty mind.

**THE 2000 YEAR OLD MAN**
*by Mel Brooks and Carl Reiner* (V51238, $9.95)
Share the timeless wisdom of two millennia! Now, for the first time, Carl Reiner (Interviewer) and Mel Brooks (The 2000 Year Old Man) bring you the complete text of their smash comedy albums, the fruits of a perfectly meshed partnership that began at a Hollywood party when both were recent alumni of Sid Caesar's Your Show of Shows